Sensations

by Kevin Byrne

NEVER STOP NEVER QUIT
Portland, Oregon
NeverStopNeverQuit.com

Dedication

I wrote this tale for no other reason than to record the constant storylines running through my mind.

I published this novel for no other reason than to raise awareness in our efforts to fight the devastating effects of multiple sclerosis (MS).

- Nothing on the market today will cure my MS or send it into remission.
- It is debatable whether my current medications slow the progression of my MS or even give me an extra year when, before, I only had a month.
- There is no known way to recover the function I have lost, and will lose, due to the damaging effects of my MS.
- There is no way to predict, identify, or isolate early-onset MS, to eradicate the disease before it affects the next generation.
- Not yet....

Please consider a donation in support of our fight to create a world free of MS:

NeverStopNeverQuit.com/Donate

Contents

Chapter 01

She was coming for him. Searing afternoon rays burned into a windowless office, bleaching his view as she emerged from the water. It was an obstacle that only provoked his yearning for more, until crisp images of her form came into focus. She sauntered closer to join another in massaging sharp-scented oils into his neck and torso. Slow-tempo music from the last century hung in an air laced with savory notes that poured from barbecue-lathered shrimp grilling nearby.

He lost the need for another swig of beer when she stepped between him and the blinding sun. Every mood hinted at seduction as she untied her white triangle bikini top before dropping to her knees. He felt her drying skin pull tight as her salty breasts stiffened when they glided across his fingers, teasing their excitement. She reassured him they were only there for his pleasure. Tastes of the other beauty left lingering reminders on her lips. Whatever he wanted, even before his desire became a command, they placed it in his senses.

A sharp knock on the flimsy balsa-wood door interrupted the moment.

"We're on in twenty minutes, Michael."

⁎⁎⁎

"Don't worry, tomorrow will be your day to judge me," she reassured the figure scurrying across 14th Street as a red upraised hand flashed its warning in vain. When a grocery bag that the man carried tore open, tragedy sent apples scattering as a bottle of something shattered against the asphalt. There was nothing she could do but press her finger against the glass-panel window while watching from twenty-one stories above his misfortune.

As he raced for safety, crosswalk signals stopped flashing. Delivery trucks and monster SUVs destroyed the former contents of his tattered paper sack, all except one apple he had rescued. Before taking a bite, he rubbed the fruit on his shirt while cursing the worthless tote tasked with one purpose.

"I can soothe your anxiety and guide you to a path to ease your suffering." But she questioned if her efforts mattered to a world set in motion long before that day arrived.

"Okay, Ellie. They are ready for you." A voice from behind pulled her back from the window. A once-open floor plan disappeared as over twenty workers put their finishing touches on a "studio presentation." In the northwest corner, a harbor-gray interview couch muted signs of life. Oversized planters blotted out yet another once-grand view of New York City. The producer hollered that he wanted viewers to know they were filming live from Nickerson Towers, but with no urban distractions. He only succeeded if his aim was to imitate the dullness of every other Global News studio. They could broadcast from Anytown, USA, for all it mattered. No one would know the difference.

"This place looks ridiculous, Sandy," Ellie vented.

"It looks fine," Sandy said. "Let's just get you ready for the interview. The quicker we get this charade over with, Ellie, the faster we can get back to work here."

"Back to...." Ellie paused and took a deep breath, nodding her head while the conversation continued in her mind. "Okay, where do you want me?"

When she recognized her boss's surrender, the assistant guided Ellie into a chair. An army of stylists went to work on her hair and final makeup touches.

"So, here's the plan," Sandy said while Ellie sat still. "Michael is getting prepped in his little studio room there. We go live in ten minutes. He will start out sitting at one end of the sectional. When the stage manager motions, you walk over and join him on the other. Are you sure you don't want to start out seated?"

Ellie reacted with a minuscule shake of her head. "I'm not going to do this interview propped up like a fucking rag doll."

Sandy smiled anyway. "Great. The director will cue you when to enter and move to your seat. Do you have any questions?"

"No." Ellie kept her eyes closed as they dusted her chiseled features with powder and assaulted her with eyeliner brushes.

"Did you have a chance to review the interview outline?"

"No."

"But you are ready, though?"

"Yes."

"Of course you are," Sandy said. She closed her portfolio containing the event outline and a list of questions. "Piece of cake!"

Ellie reached out for her assistant's arm. "Thank you, Sandy. You and Danette pulled me through this."

Sandy smiled again and repeated, "Piece of cake. Now, let's see what their creation looks like." She walked behind her boss and unsnapped the makeup cape, keeping its flaked residue off her clothes. When Ellie stood, every eye on the floor turned toward her.

Eleanor Nickerson was a commanding presence. Already tall, at five-eleven, she opted for simple leather, block-heel pumps. Without her suit jacket, the pink-veal blouse draped uncomfortably over her petite upper frame, confirming that neither the garment nor its host was used to their current arrangement. A light-gray wool skirt emphasized her powerful legs. She had a cross-country body molded by thousands of hours running Central Park trails, around Manhattan, and into the other four boroughs. Running was the perfect counter to prolonged periods caged behind a desk. Coal-black hair framed her body to the waistline, though it spent more time coiled in a bun on most days. Round facial symmetry and high cheekbones contrasted with her dark skin. Uncomfortable with her fame, critics warned their followers that "Americans are being marched to their demise by a Black Russian." Their outcries only strengthened her reputation.

"Five minutes!" someone yelled.

"I feel absolutely fucking ridiculous," Ellie said. "Why do I let you talk me into these things, Danette?"

"Because, Ms. Nickerson," she answered, "you are about to sit for an interview that every nation in the world will watch—every believer in your product, every opponent, and every politician, businessperson, philanthropist, lawyer, priest, and drug lord. It would be nice if you didn't show up in sweatpants covered with coffee stains."

With no plan to concede, Ellie waved off Danette's response.

"And, if you remember, E, you're the one who set this up."

"Two minutes!" someone yelled.

As Ellie watched, Michael made his way over to his end of the makeshift studio's sectional. He seemed harmless, with that look of an older man sitting to share stories with his grandkids. Instead, he was waiting to confront one of the most influential people in modern history. But she knew her reputation did not intimidate him. "Michael will be direct, he will be fair, but he won't hold back," was her remark when they first scheduled the interview.

"We're live!" someone yelled.

"Good morning," Michael proclaimed, "and good day around the world. It's Saturday, April 27, 2024. I'm Michael Yao, and this is Global News." His lead-in hit the post, even though crooning melodies from The Temptations replaced the network's classic opening of prerecorded orchestral horns. Sandy never explained to the network why they had insisted on the change.

"That's for you, Oleg," Ellie whispered as Michael switched to address viewers behind camera two.

"Today, we are speaking with Eleanor Nickerson...."

Ellie watched the host present a rundown of Nickerson Enterprises and their product line, commonly called Sensations. He described it as technology that would capture mental impressions in real time, creating an exact replication. "As a result," he said, "the recipient experiences the recorded emotion with no associated physical response."

"Close enough," Ellie whispered. "I'll clean that up later."

As Michael reviewed how the world had once heralded Sensations as their salvation when social isolation threatened our existence, Ellie waited for her cue. An image of three people appeared on the screens. Most prominent was a well-presented White man with a fresh, tight haircut, cuffed slacks that matched his blue suit jacket with thin salmon piping, and a leather briefcase. Next to him sat an emaciated Black teenager wearing ragged jeans and a dirty hoodie, and an Asian woman whose appearance hinted she was about seven months pregnant. They were sitting on cheap foldout lawn furniture. Captioning placed them in the projects of South Harlem. Huddled around a thin black disc, they shared the same catatonic expression. Ellie had seen that staged video several times. Under her breath, she murmured surprise that Global News, with its infinite resources, could not find a better clip.

"Besides," her conversation turned audible, "that's not even how it works." Her lawyer always said there was no value in debating the accuracy of one publicity shot.

"Instead," Michael continued, "Sensations have now risen to opioid crisis levels." She did not appreciate his dramatic pause, walking on camera before he completed the introduction.

"Ms. Nickerson, thank you for joining us today."

"Please, just call me Ellie," was her quick reply. She chose not to smile under the image of strung-out addicts.

A hulking man with whispers of gray in his tousled hair sat on concrete flooring next to a worn mattress. There was no other furniture in the dingy one-bedroom apartment. He smiled when Ellie appeared on his smartphone. An overweight older man glared at the same image somewhere else as it beamed through the oversized flatscreen mounted to the wall in a lavish office space.

"Ellie. Perfect." Michael was too professional to respond any other way. "Tomorrow, you will address a joint session of Congress at the invitation of Senator Troy Hargraves, Chairperson of the Joint Congressional Committee on Sensations." The US Capitol, the symbolic *Savior of the Weak and Oppressed*, replaced the *Face of Addiction* image. "There must be quite a few things you would rather spend your time on today."

Ellie smiled. "Not at all. I dedicated my day to you, Michael."

When he pressed, "But what about everything else that needs to happen?" Eleanor's response was simple.

"Tomorrow, the world will judge what I should have achieved long before our time here."

Ellie folded her right hand over the left, rubbing the faded band of her gold solitaire before she pulled back to avoid revealing her tell. Without looking, she knew the exact spot her thumb always found itself. Every morning, when she opened the simple wooden jewelry box on her bureau, memories of that day flooded her mind.

She could hear his voice as she remembered the warnings he had shared: "At some point, every desire will come into play: promote, aid, mediate, leave be, oversee, regulate, intervene, restrict." Ellie needed to know what that meant. But the answer did not come. It never came. "Time will tell," was the only clue he had left her. Every morning, she sighed over the imperfection her habit had caused. The years had not been kind to her ring.

In the office, now studio, a video monitor continued to share the same images television viewers saw. As Michael discussed her childhood, a picture showed six-year-old Ellie with her parents. She was lighting a menorah. Ellie smiled.

"That was the eighth day of Hanukkah in 1998. My dad had just come home on leave that morning."

"What a beautiful moment," Michael said.

Ellie remembered her daddy lifting her over the table, his thick Angolan hands wrapped around her waist as she extended a burning match. That was the last picture they took together as a family. Robert and Anya divorced early the following year.

As she turned her attention back to the host, Ellie commented, "Pictures lie, Michael. The camera only records the façade we create. A photograph can't recall my father's pain from two shattered ribs, the result of bullet wounds received during the supposed *missiles and bombs only* campaign ten days before his visit. It doesn't know about his exhaustion from nearly two days of Space-A travel from the Middle East."

Ellie turned and addressed her jury behind camera two.

"A picture cannot smell that pungent reek of the whiskey he needed to calm them both. The smile captured on my mother's face masked her anxiety. She knew Robert was leaving the next day, but beyond that truth, she had nothing. If you just look at that image, you will never understand my reluctance to touch the match to the wick. Even though my fingers stung when the flame brushed my skin, that pain was an easy trade if he would have held me in that position indefinitely."

"Make it personal." She remembered the guidance. "For the first time, they need to know all about you."

Turning back to her host, Ellie said, "He wasn't around a lot when I was growing up."

"Your father was in the Army," Michael added to the picture of Master Sergeant Robert Nickerson on the monitor.

"He was. Third Group." Robert's image remained frozen on the screen. Four rows of colorful ribbons decorated his midnight-blue uniform jacket's left breast, recognizing twenty-nine years of service and achievements. Just below them, shiny badges read "Special Forces" and "Ranger," while others were the traditional markers of an Airborne, Halo, and Expert Marksman. Above everything, his Combat Infantryman Badge failed to acknowledge how often his country called on him to use his service skills, achievements, and qualifications.

"When my parents married, Anya lived with him on what's now Fort Liberty. She got pregnant with me, so Robert moved her up here to have friends and family close."

Their dance lasted another thirty minutes. Michael expanded on Global News's research into the formative years of their guest. Ellie's responses were to either confirm his suspicions with a simple, "That's correct, Michael," or refute any conclusions with a detailed correction of the storyline. Beyond those replies, she remained silent and unresponsive as Michael picked at the scabs of her family tree. They discussed her parents' individual lives, their marriage, and their divorce. Anya was a descendant of Russian Jews who escaped before the October Revolution. She died of lung cancer in 2021, after battling the disease for nearly four years. Robert, with his proud family history of military service from the few post-slavery generations recognized as human, was killed in action in Afghanistan in 2004. She knew why it mattered, why Global News needed to set the stage. It still hurt.

Ellie avoided shifting her weight on the unpleasant interrogation chair. Displays of weakness were not part of her agreement. Danette and Sandy were the only two who recognized her anxiety. Her movements were deliberate, sharing her attention between Michael, the camera, and the imagery on the monitor. Her legs remained crossed at the ankles, that half-carat engagement ring on proud display as her left hand sat atop the right. None of it was Ellie. Danette tried to use a commercial break as an opportunity for distraction by discussing corporate legal matters, but her boss declined the invitation.

"Ellie," Michael said after shifting his approach, "nobody wants to listen as I fire questions off one at a time." He raised a white stack of papers, showing the title "Yao-Nickerson Interview 4/27" printed along the top. Ellie recognized the outline.

Eleanor agreed, "Especially if you ask the same questions I've already answered a thousand times over."

"Correct."

"You want to know details that don't exist in the public eye, but you're lost and looking for direction since you can't find the right questions to ask." Ellie understood why Global News had selected Michael Yao to conduct this interview. He had a knack for probing with questions that proved it was never his story to relate.

"I don't know what to ask next," Michael admitted, "besides *What happened?*"

A smile bordering on arrogance splashed onto Eleanor's face as she shifted her torso and settled into the couch in an uncultured but comfortable position. As she rested on her left forearm, she slid her right hand up and across her blouse, tapping one finger along with the vascular rhythm underneath her skin. No longer a participant in this discussion, Eleanor Nickerson commanded focus as the novelist of her favorite anecdote.

"I tell you, Michael," Eleanor recounted, "if I could do it all again, I wouldn't change a thing. Given a chance, I would not hesitate one bit to go back and repeat every event of the last four years, enjoying every success and suffering every heartbreak once more, if it meant I could relive that moment from May 11, 2020."

Unaware of where she was going, Michael nodded in agreement, perhaps thinking of a treasured snapshot from his past. No words followed, though. He knew it was not his time to speak.

Eleanor continued, "But I don't have to wish upon a star, nor do I ever regret the loss of days gone by. I know exactly what I experienced on May 11, 2020, because I recorded attempt number 432."

Chapter 02

Not much fit into Ellie's four-hundred-square-foot, one-bedroom walkup in the Bowery District. Fortunately, it was more than enough room for everything she possessed. After she moved out of the rented home she had known her entire life, her mother downsized. For her treatments, Anya needed to be closer to JJ Peters, up in the Bronx.

There was never any need for Ellie to hold sentimental items from her youth. The memories were in her heart and mind. At Anya's insistence, she took a few boxes the day she left Brooklyn Heights. They remained stacked under her raised bed: a few photo albums, Freddie and the rest of her favorite stuffed animal collection, and a box labeled "Dad things."

SEQUENCE 432–202005111945L

Ellie stood at the workstation, her heart pounding as she typed the test protocol header information and parameters. That was going to be her final evaluation for the evening. Two weeks before the end of the term and her capstone project was still unsuccessful. After 431 failures, she figured it was her last run-through, regardless of the outcome.

EVENT CAPTURE SYSTEM CHECK

With a quick scan, Ellie confirmed her preparation. She had cleared a fifteen-by-fifteen-foot space in the middle of her apartment, the only room besides that cubbyhole where she slept. Insignificant devices placed at four corners fed data back to her processor, recording her movements by reading the seventeen sensors sewn into her desert-sand bodysuit and headband.

CAPTURE SYSTEM CHECKS CONFIRMED

Ellie opened her computer's music folder and highlighted a title, the only piece ever chosen. Then, with a nod of her head, silent agreement with whatever conversations flooded her mind before those thoughts faded, Ellie started her capture protocol.

"Capture system sequence will begin in two minutes."

The soothing digital voice originated from and over to every corner of the room. Barefooted, Ellie scampered across the empty hardwood floor. She had cleared the collection of black wires snaking their lazy way back to the computer. Once in the middle of the square, she slipped on a worn pair of Juliet leather split-sole ballet shoes.

"Capture system sequence will begin in one minute."

Fear and doubt will cripple a person if no one is there to reach out and offer hope. But, without a way to rationalize her uncertainty, Ellie had no use for that instance of distraction.

"Capture sequence will begin in thirty seconds. Eleanor, take position."

Ellie rose and took several deep breaths to slow her racing heart. She stepped into the center of an area that resembled a VFX movie set missing its green screen, stood tall, and assumed her preparatory stance. With her heels kept together, both feet turned outward in a straight line while her arms hung down the bodysuit's sides and pitched forward. Her hands trembled as she bent her wrists inward, touching the tips of her fingers together. Anxiety mounted, but that was no reason to break first position. Ellie's back and upper body must remain straight; her chin could not move from that lifted position until she received her cue.

"Capture sequence will begin in five... four... three...."

Ellie remained still. Fragrances of seasoning garlic and vinegar from the restaurant below brushed across her nose, but she dismissed the distraction. With the piccolo's first melodic sequence, her head leaned back as her arms took position. "Dance of the Hours" echoed as her graceful slide mimicked orchestral rises and falls. Soft, sustained motion across the stage pulled her frame while the symphony pieces rained in harmony. They brought Ellie a sense of serenity and calm only possible under intense conditions. When she recognized that her toe position was a half-note behind the ensemble, an added strain elevated her heart rate past the masterpiece's rhythm until her movements reunited and remained in sync for the duration of her performance. Even when their pieces clashed, the orchestra never pulled Ellie from her trance. She refused to submit even after the last note of music faded, once again leaving her apartment in silence. Her arms remained extended. Both feet were turned outward, resting with her heels spaced twelve inches apart. Perfect second position.

"Capture sequence completed."

In a graceful surrender to her flesh, Ellie crumbled to the floor and sat cross-legged, coaching her heart rate back to normal as her mind withdrew from its performance. She wondered if May 11 would be the day she captured the digital markings of her form, the rhythmic surge and rest of every muscle fiber her body commanded when it lost itself in the rapture of Amilcare Ponchielli's score.

Her only fear was that her efforts would continue to fail.

"If it doesn't work this time," she said, "I'm done. I'll just see if George needs a full-time IT girl to automate our coffee and donuts."

Ellie chuckled, but there was truth in her resolution. That incessant pattern of trial and failure needed to end. Months separated her from her last peaceful day; Ellie's body welcomed that brash decision, even if she knew quitting would never be an option.

Ellie stored her high-tech wizardry. She cleaned, indexed, and packed everything in custom foam inserts, securing them in plastic clamshell cases. After changing into her favorite sweatpants, she shuffled to the kitchen corner for a snack. That was her preferred way to dine. Nutritious creations enjoyed seven or eight times a day were more satisfying than dealing with a hefty meal that left her stuffed and lethargic. Ellie was an athlete. Every aspect of her life required proper conditioning.

To keep her body strong and her mind sharp during tedious sessions at her computer, fitness consumed every other part of her day. Runs strengthened her long, thick legs. Years of ballet dancing honed the grace and agility she expressed with every movement. Of course, nothing groomed endurance like those ten-hour shifts at George's Diner. Her dad had sparked that idea when she was a child.

Home on leave, Robert first took his daughter to George's when she was four. As they made their way through the packed diner, heading for his favorite table in the back, he yelled loud enough for both his audience members to hear.

"I tell you what, darling," he said, "if you ever want to get an idea of what I do in the Army, try schlepping tables here for a few years. A full breakfast tray carried to a table of six while keeping track of ten open tabs in your mind will build everything you need in life. You have to be willing to break your back in service of others. There's no time to stop and write anything down. Isn't that right, George? Are you gonna teach my girl the tricks of the trade?"

George laughed and told Ellie that any time she wanted a job, it was the least he could do for Sergeant Bobby's daughter.

"Is that what you do, Daddy? Break your back for others?"

His answer, "Self-sacrifice in the service of those in need will always be a noble profession," left an enduring mark on Ellie.

That was a lifetime ago. Before 9/11, before the virus.

Meals were no exception to her regimen. Ellie portioned a generous wedge of her homemade blueberry protein bread on the plate, then popped it into the microwave to remove its chill. After smearing a robust serving of crunchy peanut butter over the warm loaf, she stopped and looked at her workstation. Ellie pressed her right hand across her chest to confirm her breathing had slowed and her heart rate had returned to normal. It was time.

Ellie knew she was frittering away the minutes, delaying the inevitable. For her, it was the last patch of time where there was no cause for anxiety. Ten minutes prior, her fears had given way to the first note of Ponchielli's score. Her mind drifted into a grueling routine she had performed hundreds of times before, savoring an experience that held no consequence. The next action path was academic success or defeat. The computer already knew if her programming had generated an enhanced, three-dimensional rendition of a body in motion. It was Ellie's time to face the server's judgment.

With a few mouse clicks, Ellie navigated to the playback algorithm. She took a quick bite of her crunchy-peanut-butter-smeared protein bread before rolling the chair across the well-worn surface. As the plate rested in her lap, she waited.

"Playback sequence will begin in five... four... three...."

Nothing was on the file, just a random sequence of buzzes and hums.

Her body remained motionless when that first sharp tone stroked every nerve fiber in Ellie's brain.

The disregarded plate slipped from her grasp and crashed onto the floor. Unwilling to remove her focus from that noise, she reeled from a familiar panic over what would happen next. While nothing moved in her apartment, Ellie's emotions searched for an impulse to feel, something to fear. While fighting to suppress the pain of a thousand needles piercing deep into her tissue, her mind pushed on without regard for its safety. All the while, she was counting and searching.

There was no time to learn if her suffering was real—only to use its location as a marker for her body's position. While she sat in her chair, Ellie executed movements she was not performing and experienced the harsh tearing of flesh that sat at rest. Still, her thoughts continued to count a rhythm in sync with sounds that no longer existed.

"Bungee jumping" was how Eleanor Nickerson came to describe the next episode—an experience when the ground is fast approaching, yet it never closes that distance as your body continues its uncontrolled plummet. It is moment after moment perched at the instantaneous intersection of helpless abandonment, accepting your inevitable suffering and realizing that your body is in absolute control of every move you make. Through no effort of your own, something interrupts your demise. Only then do you realize nothing threatens your safety anymore. Nothing ever did.

Ellie's body remained in that inescapable state. She felt as if her heart rate elevated and her nerves strained to drive more from their host, yet she never gave a command that time.

This is where I want to be. This is where you want to go.

Ellie reveled in her emotions, but the thoughts were not her own. Her lungs recognized the acceleration of each phantom breath. Her joints cursed every action they did not take. She accepted the tension in her arms and legs, yet none of that was her. As her body continued exhausting every bit of energy it had ever stored, her mind relished the comforting ebb of her daredevil leap. Her physical form remained subdued in the rolling chair at her workstation when, without warning, that familiar surrender overcame every conflicting emotion.

"Playback sequence completed."

Ellie regained the composure and awareness stripped from her by digital noise. She stared at the lifeless hardware, the pores in her skin pulled tight into a dumbfounded expression. Nothing disturbed the room; no intruder had ransacked her studio. The computer, ignorant of any blunder, remained docile while awaiting further instructions. Her mind settled into its automatic ritual of a well-orchestrated cooldown until she realized it was unnecessary. Everything was tranquil, just the way it was before the playback sequence.

"What the fuck was that?" she whispered.

The results were the same every time Ellie executed that digital clip. When she selected *Replay*, coded signals struck her body with a perfect imitation of pain and emotion. She concentrated on a prescribed routine and the satisfaction of each step applied to perfection. As the third replay began, the pungent sazón wafting into her apartment—Jorge always over-seasoned his empanadas—disappeared as earlier meals once again filled Ellie's nose with garlic and vinegar. Each time she played the file, anxiety burst into her consciousness before settling into a monotonous routine of agony and ecstasy.

Whenever she stepped into that captured moment, Ellie was dancing. She recognized the secrets her body always tried to conceal when performing her favorite score. She confirmed the perfect match by overlapping the original music file with her recorded sequence. She believed it was true.

With no proof, Ellie convinced herself she had stumbled into the roots of human perception. Somehow, she could capture what people crave, sense, love, and fear.

Unfortunately, that wasn't enough—the audacity of what she had considered snapped Ellie back to reality.

"There's got to be an explanation for what happened." She dug through her thesis documentation. "Static analysis, passed," she confirmed. "Unit testing, yep. Integration testing, yep. System testing, perfect."

Ellie laid her documentation binder on the floor and walked back toward the desk. Careful not to step on any shattered remnants of her dish, she ran her fingers along the sleek metal casing, hoping to seduce an explanation.

"Acceptance testing. What the fuck went wrong?" She traced each wire on the back of the computer, but the lifeless system refused her advances. "We tested you every step of the way without a hiccup. What did you do?" Ellie tried to coax the answer from her hardware as if there would be repercussions if it did not provide the information she wanted.

"I need more data," was her conclusion. "I can't move forward with one Mickey Mouse recording as my reference." Mocking the only consistent passion she had ever known offered little solace. In a world of suffering and loss, Ponchielli had shown Ellie compassion by creating an escape from her reality. Maybe now, in another moment of crisis, the composer reached from beyond the grave to trust Ellie with his greatest creation. Ellie sat at her station and clicked open the file folder labeled *Software Testing–Fail*. In it, 432 files stared back at her, proof that she had the persistence needed to realize her objectives. All 432 files proved her original goal was meaningless. She opened a new root folder and moved *SEQUENCE 432–202005111945L* over to her new project, labeled *Sensations*.

A review of the changes made after testing failure 431 left her unsatisfied. So, she took the next logical step for a seasoned software engineer and searched the Internet for "How do you test something you can't prove?" Ellie had taken a blind step into the world of metaphysics, hoping to capture her favorite emotions and passions. Six hours later, Ellie had a small collection of cause-and-effect sequences:

Laughing

Eating
Exercising
Masturbating
Standing Still

But every attempt was an imperfect imitation of her activity. She struggled to find familiarity with each playback. Anxiety and frustration clouded each of them.

"I can't get this fucking project out of my mind," she realized before running the next test sequence. Ellie looked around, disgusted by the mess in her otherwise spotless apartment. A line of sugar ants scampered from across the room, soldiers charged with gathering every morsel of spilled bread and peanut butter for their colony buried somewhere deep into the wall. The nighttime breeze shoved biting cold in through windows left open long after any stale air had departed, leaving a thin layer of moisture on the equipment cases left out in her rush to set everything up again.

Disorder produces chaos.

Ellie found a new reason to feel like the world was crumbling apart. Her uncomfortably small living space was no longer the antiseptic layout she demanded, a mistake corrected in less than ten minutes, but it led to another discovery. Focused on her lapse in organizational skills, she had set the program to *Record* by mistake before her sudden urge to clean and sanitize. Like Ponchielli's dance, her obsession did not cloud the sequence with project failure. Instead, it started as blank, empty feedback. Each time she passed through the capture area, her original focus replaced any other distractions. When her mind pushed away any distraction, she recorded a perfect rendition of moments when she laughed, ate, exercised, masturbated, then stood still.

Ellie grabbed her phone and texted Danette.

We need to talk. Let me know when you are free

It was 4:23 in the morning.

Text me when you wake up

Better yet, call

Important

As her mind scrambled to make sense of what had happened, energy, creativity, and logic gave way to exhaustion. Ellie changed clothes, grabbed a mask, and gave one last look around her studio before heading out for a sunrise run up along the East River.

Chapter 03

An odd assortment of machinery napped on the deserted factory floor. Fluorescent lighting whitewashed the entire ceiling, matching its complexion to the walls and floor. Lingering scents of almonds hung in the air.

A polished steel tank sat in one corner. It was larger than any other piece. Dozens of simple, black clamping knobs secured its massive lid, and three metallic supply lines ran from the vat and pierced the clouds on their way somewhere beyond the ceiling. The scene resembled a 1950s comic book depiction of our futuristic world ruled by machinery. An out-of-place industrial display system hung from that fossilized stockpot, monitoring the condition of something cooking inside its belly. Three ear-piercing tones kicked off a ritual when a timer on the digital screen reached zero. A person entered and snuck up on the tank, silencing its cries with the press of a button. Mummified in a white cleanroom uniform, complete with a respirator and a pair of goggles, they placed a stainless-steel bucket underneath the drain valve and turned its stopcock, collecting a thick, milky goo. After taking the sample, the disguised handler switched a status placard on the rounded side from IN-PROCESS to COMPLETE, then pressed a second button. A conveyor whisked the completed batch through a sliding door. Moments later, a placard marked PASSED was in place. A third button triggered a symphony of flashing lights and gentle hums across the complex line of machinery occupying the rest of the space. In the next six hours, 6.5 million counterfeit pharmaceutical tablets were pressed, packaged, and ready for worldwide distribution.

That was the inaugural run for one of at least nine manufacturing facilities in Russia's West Siberian economic region. In an upper-level observation room, seven men wearing white lab coats waited for the eighth to respond.

"Very good," said the man dressed in a light-charcoal-gray business suit. "How long before the first shipment leaves my factory?" His unrefined manner showed itself with the harsh Russian words scraped from his throat.

One individual stepped forward. He looked like the oldest of the lab coats, perhaps their leader, but it was difficult to know for sure. Those who called the Khanty region home endured a bitter life. The man was likely no more than thirty-five years old, despite his balding gray hair and worn, sagging facial features.

"Dema Zlovich Sokolov," he said in his most formal presentation voice, "our first four trucks will depart for the rail yard before noon today." He paused, waiting to see if his answer was acceptable. None of the other lab coats offered their opinion on the matter.

Sokolov approached the man and rewarded him with two sharp pats on the back. As he raised his arm, traces of tattooed skin appeared above his wrist. They bore no resemblance to the serpent markings that peered out from his white dress shirt, which was unbuttoned at the top. He did not wear a tie.

Ashes from the cigarette in his hand scattered across the man's lab coat. Neither tried to brush them to the floor.

"Very good, Mikael Petrovych Medvedev," he said in his abrasive Russian tone.

Sokolov continued, "This is a momentous day. You should be immensely proud," then nudged a smiling Medvedev to rejoin the others. The other lab coats greeted him with smiles and congratulations.

"Comrades." Sokolov's snap called the men to focus on him. "Today is a holiday." They shouted a raucous cheer to support those words. "Today, we are no longer *vory v zakone*. No, we have moved out from beneath the underworld. We are an enterprise that will grow as fast as modern technology will take us." More cheers erupted.

In a softer tone, Sokolov made two promises. "Continue your excellent progress," he said, "and you will become the wealthiest families in Surgut." The promise of such an opportunity created a fevered reaction. Medvedev smiled as he shook hands with the short one, then jubilantly hugged the fat one while the others waited for their turn to recognize their facility director.

Sokolov then finished his speech inaugurating the Surgut facility. "Fail to live up to my expectations, and I will peel the skin from your flesh and feed it to my dogs." He landed a stare at the muscular one but did not wait for a reaction before returning to

Medvedev. "Now, let us go look at the warehouse operation."

The two men left the other lab coats in the observation room.

Chapter 04

Danette Reddy sat in silence. Distrustful eyes evaluated her friend's shifting and squirming on the park bench. Ellie's hands were in constant motion, emphasizing every syllable of the bizarre story she told.

"So, I figured you were the best person to talk to," Ellie said. "You can tell me if I'm crazy."

"E, I'm a lawyer, not a psychotherapist. My clients might be a bit crazy, but we prefer to call them eccentric in IP law. It's a distinction without a difference."

Ellie assured Danette that she was past the point of concern for her sanity. By her third validation test the night before, *overworked* or *exhausted* were words that could no longer explain the results—a perfect reproduction every time.

"My home test was negative," she said. "It's not some Covid hallucination."

As she ran through the list of alternate possibilities she considered, Ellie rekindled her spark—that level of arrogance only possible when you are always right because you have looked at every conceivable way you might be wrong.

The early morning sun was creeping somewhere above the low layer of drab clouds that blanketed the city. "Listen, I'm in the office today, but why don't I swing by your place later?"

"You're back in?" Ellie jumped on that strange description of normal life.

"Just once every two weeks," Danette said. She flipped her hands through the air like a toddler trying to shoo away a pesky fly. The sign language was New Yorker for "Listen to this crock of bullshit."

"It's stupid. I have to get dressed up to file electronic motions and sit in teleconferences with remote clients."

But Danette always wore a suit to work, even when it was the six-foot commute to her ad hoc office in the living room. It was not the outfit that bothered her. She told Ellie it was the forced crowding with so many others. Infected people following her down the street. Commuters on those dingy, packed subway cars sharing the same sour air. Her coworkers were the worst—a mob of arrogant lawyers threatening liability suits like they were *Go Directly to Jail* cards, aimed at anyone who took their mask off or toward others if they demanded that anyone close put one on. The city was at odds over clashing versions of basic human decency because they knew any of them might carry the virus that was trying to kill the world.

"I just miss being around people," Ellie said. "George is only doing orders to-go or delivery. The tips are good, but nothing beats that chaos of a jam-packed diner." It was a new world where morbid reminiscences over everything lost always kicked off a ripple of one dreary topic after another.

"How is your mom doing?" Danette's question was the next domino to fall.

A frosty gust rushed in off the river, carrying the conflicting smells of an urban seaport. Ellie shrugged her shoulders. "She's back in the hospital. Visitors aren't allowed, but we talk and text all the time."

"When's her next treatment?"

Ellie was not ready to discuss if, not when, Anya would go through another round of chemotherapy. Tightening muscles and a growling stomach offered the perfect distraction.

"We don't know yet," Ellie said as she stood and began a clumsy demonstration of stretching exercises. "Let me get these last four miles in so I can grab breakfast before work." She looked at her watch while pressing two fingers up against her neck. "I have to hurry," she said. "I have the lunch shift. What time do you get off?"

At around 7:00 p.m., Danette's cynical look returned. This time, it was in Ellie's apartment. She listened to the sound of that 1980s Internet dial-up she remembered from old movies while staring at Ellie, who acted as if she was under demonic possession. She considered calling 911, but her friend warned her it would happen "to both of us." Not feeling any effects, Danette pulled out her cell phone and recorded the scene.

"I don't know what you're expecting, E," she said while pacing the hardwood floor during the sequence playback, "but here is what it sounds like in your apartment right now." More clicks, pops, and static. She turned the camera toward her face.

"This is what I look like." She blew a blonde bombshell kiss and shared a seductive pose with her followers on the other side of the lens.

Then she recorded Ellie's corpse sitting in the chair.

"This is you."

Danette put her phone away but continued to pace. While waiting for the charade to finish, she tried to map out her approach.

"How do you tell someone there was never really a Santa Claus, Tooth Fairy, or Hanukkah Harry, and, by the way, she didn't record squat?"

No one listened as the lawyer practiced her argument, pacing before the jury box.

"I mean, who could blame the poor soul if she lost it a bit? Her dad's dead, mom's dying, and she has no other family left. The girl is a twenty-eight-year-old student working part time as a server in a diner that can't seat customers. She has no other friends besides her old freshman roommate, that damn computer, and her running shoes. No, Ms. Nickerson was a shut-in long before the world shut down."

Danette walked past the studio's kitchenette. She picked up a dirty dish left on the counter.

"Should I pretend, just for a little while, that the contraption worked?"

She dropped a dollop of soap onto a sponge and cleaned the dish, placing any evidence of confusion and disorder onto the drying rack. "Nah, E would see right through my bullshit. Mocking her might be the proverbial straw."

Of the many potential reactions her friend could have had, Danette was unprepared for what she heard when Ellie finally returned.

"Something must code the output to my sensory nervous system."

It was a well-constructed, hasty reaction that impressed the attorney just as much as it concerned the friend.

"I need to measure you doing something."

Danette played along, put on the ridiculous spacesuit, and stood in the middle of the apartment and watched Ellie banging away on her keyboard like some comical rendition of a mad scientist.

"Give me some time to work it out," was the last thing she said before brushing her friend out the door. On the way to the stairwell, Danette offered her closing comments to the imaginary jury.

"All I can do is wonder if I should be scared."

**

Three days later, she should have been terrified when her torso swung back and slipped under her legs. Blood drained from her feet, pooling in her palms and fingers. Vision clouded until her sight became so distracting that her body turned off the function.

Danette should have feared the slow march toward death. She was supposed to have an obligation to fight for survival. Instead, as her heart rate slowed, the only message her brain shared was someone, possibly her, saying, "This is normal. This is perfect."

It took a moment to realize her awareness had returned. She was back in Ellie's apartment, safe and sound. She had never left.

Ellie told her friend, "When I was a kid, my dad taught me how to meditate, calming my body and mind." She pointed to an inversion table in the corner of her studio. "His old commander, Colonel Drew, gave me one when I graduated high school. He's the one who hooked me up with the JSOA scholarship so I could go to Columbia." The colonel had often looked out for Ellie over the years.

"So, I was here the whole time?"

Ellie was merciful and gave Danette time alone to explore her own senses. Her friend's journey was a mirror image of that first night of discovery. The following morning, as thermometers finally agreed to begin their springtime climb past seventy degrees, she nudged the weary voyager.

"Good morning," she said, tossing an olive-green pair of sweatpants and a T-shirt on top of Danette, still lying on the floor where she had surrendered to exhaustion the night before.

Angry growls roughly translated to, "Why the fuck are you up already?" She sniffed but could not tell whether Ellie had handed her dirty laundry to wear. Instead, her nose pursued more pleasant aromas—fresh-brewed coffee filled the air.

"Please tell me that's real, not just a hangover from last night's hallucinations."

"I got a quick five miles in," Ellie said between steaming sips of French-press coffee, no milk or sweetener.

"You are still a crazy wench," Danette said.

Ellie filled a black coffee mug stamped with the words *De Oppresso Liber* in a plain yellow font. "Besides, I needed to figure out the best way to get your input."

While swapping yesterday's wrinkled business suit for possible fresh sweats, Danette muttered, "Input about what?" She pulled the T-shirt over her head.

"About what I should do next."

Danette took the extra coffee her friend held and stared at her with that *Are-You-Out-Of-Your-Freakin-Mind* look she had learned before grammar school. "E, you need a scientist, a therapist, or a priest. Not me."

Ellie reassured her. "I need a lawyer. I know companies that would kill or die for this tech. Kill or die might be a bit dramatic, but you get my point."

Danette stood in front of the mirror and enjoyed the way she filled out her friend's T-shirt. Her blonde hair, pale blue eyes, and 36DD breasts used to eclipse Ellie's presence in public. A T-shirt that ran far too small was perfect back when social lives existed. "What a waste," she exhaled. Her attention turned back to the conversation.

"Hey, all I can tell you is: get copyrights and patents on that puppy."

"And then what?" Ellie refused to let her off that easy. She'd had enough trust in her friend to introduce her to that asynchronous world, but now she expected something in return. Answers. Guidance. If you planned to be friends with Eleanor Nickerson, you had to be direct, be truthful, tell her what you wanted, and answer the question.

Danette reached over, grabbed Ellie's sweaty ball cap off her head, and covered her own before saying, "Then, we fight like hell. Will George let us eat in the diner?"

"Of course," Ellie replied.

Danette looked around for her sneakers before shaking her client's hand. "Perfect," she said. "That'll be my retainer."

Danette instructed her client on what to do while she prepared the legal documentation for her discovery.

First, she told Ellie to keep working. "Figure out what this thing can really do," Danette said. "Then, make me a set of all equipment. Do not turn in any of the source code for your school project." Ellie nodded her head.

"Most important," her lawyer demanded, "don't tell anyone about this. Not your teacher, your mother, not even George. No one."

Ellie always wondered why a coffee shop owner would care about her silly computer program.

*
**

By the end of a fevered weekend, Danette Reddy had submitted the paperwork and documentation for Eleanor Nickerson, LLC. She filed all source and object code copyrights and device patents for SCARS, the Sensation Capture-and-Release System. After Danette uploaded the final document, Ellie looked on in anticipation, like she expected the computer to blare digital horns in a fanfare of congratulations while splashing digital confetti across the monitor with a message that read, "Congratulations! You've got patents!" None of that happened.

Danette closed her laptop and looked back to see her friend waiting for directions.

"Well?" Ellie said. The spastic gestures of her hands had a much longer interrogation.

Danette chuckled and said, "Well, what? That's it." She glanced at her watch and then out to catch the sun rising over buildings that masked the city skyline. "I'm going to drop off one set of your equipment with their New York City office today." She packed her computer into the rolling briefcase while talking to whoever wanted to know the boring details. Ellie just wanted an answer. "That tweak should speed the filing process."

Frustration spewed out in one long, exasperated appeal. "Just tell me how long it'll take."

"Four months" was an answer she did not want to hear. Danette called in late for her 9:00 a.m. meeting with a prospective client so she could introduce her current one to the maze of intellectual property law roadblocks.

"There's nothing we can do," she said. "This shit moves slow."

It took thirty-five days.

Chapter 05

The frail woman nodded, her pillowcase creasing a heartbroken smile beneath weak movement. Ghastly shadows sank deep into the orbits of her eyes. The cracked folds of skin that spread out under her chin were an eerie reminder of her youth. She was once a plump girl who enjoyed cooking lavish meals for her loved ones. Arms that lay limp by her sides had been architects of the most savory fish and vegetable stews anyone had ever tasted. Her mixed-race family dined on thick servings of *calulu* one week and *ukha*'s meaty portions the next, each meal served with imaginary stories of the Nickerson and Filatiev ancestors.

But that was ages ago. Except for one daughter, her family and friends were dead. Now, it was her turn. She spent her remaining time thankful for a long, blessed life instead of fighting with poisons that condemned her to another cursed day. She used to cherish every moment of her long life, longer than her parents' or their parents', but it was finally time to let go.

Anya was only fifty-one when she chose long-term care over one more round of chemotherapy. Her doctor offered reassurance that moves to the other facility were quick. Ellie wondered what number her mother was in line for a bed. How many patients had to die to make room for those waiting? Was it callous disregard to hope for an end to a stranger's suffering, for the Lord to take their pain away, so her mother could finally rest in comfort until their bedframe was once again added to the queue? Ellie fought her urge to cry. Anya had more important things to occupy her focus. Too much time had passed since she had seen her daughter. Sadness was an unwelcome distraction she did not have time to entertain.

The doctor stepped aside to give them time alone. Ellie whispered, "I'm here now, Mama." She gently stroked the arm that had soothed her back to health countless times, that once made her meals, mended her clothes, and held her tight when the news of Robert's death reached their door. "The hospital said I can come anytime when you're in the new wing." A single tear escaped Anya's eye, tracking through wrinkles until it faded into the corner of her broad smile.

"I missed you so much, Eleanor." Her faint words pulled Ellie closer. "This is all I want." In that sanitized, white hospital room, a symbolic place meant to ease the suffering of a woman beginning her journey toward death, Anya's only wish was to be with her daughter.

But what if she could have more?

Ellie turned her head to see if the doctor had left the room, then opened the box she had brought with her. She placed a small object, what looked like a refurbished soda can, on the hospital tray. It was spray-painted black with a single white dot in the middle. Anya watched her daughter without curiosity or confusion. She was happy to have her there—it did not matter what she was doing. Ellie rotated the can to point the dot toward Anya before pressing a small button on the top.

Ellie finally asked her to describe the unimaginable.

"What if you could have more?"

She caressed her mother's hand and arm again while she pressed for details. "What if I could bring you something, take you somewhere, do something with you? What would you want it to be?"

As Anya's lungs struggled to pull the air her body needed to fight and feed her cancer, she drifted off into one last longing for unrestrained indulgences. Coney Island Beach was where she first wished to be, standing right on the edge where warm sand begins to cool and dampen as the afternoon tide creeps closer toward the boardwalk. She yearned for more time with her daughter, away from the incessant buzz of doctors, attendees, monitors, cell phones, and machinery crowding that cold, silent hospital room. What did she want to remember? The gentle sway when she held Ellie's hand through her first ballet steps, or one of the countless times when they snuck sweet dabs of cinnamon and sugar while rolling fresh rugelach together, just as she'd done with her mother. Anya told these wishes to her daughter, then vowed to never again long for days gone forever.

With one hand still reassuring her mother, Ellie reached for the homemade device. She pushed its button again and promised, "Soon, Mama. How about I take you there next week for Shavuot?"

"Take me where? What do you mean?"

"Never mind, Mama," Ellie said. She tapped her leg before standing up to leave.

A voice from behind her interrupted. "Excuse me."
When Ellie turned, she saw a slender Black man
standing in the doorway. He had groomed his hair in
finger coils that rested just above his brows. Beyond
the mask, he was clean-shaven. Ellie first imagined a
pencil-thin mustache, though she preferred nothing.
Intimate curiosity followed the veins running from
his fingers, across his hands and arms, and
underneath his pale-blue scrubs.

"I need to give Ms. Anya her medication and take
vitals." The thick words took her by surprise.

Ellie sized him up, then said, "You look like you
should sound more Creole than you do." She followed
up with a pleasant smile.

"I am French," he said, "but you have a good ear.
My parents were from Haiti."

Anya remained silent, careful not to interrupt as
she watched her daughter flirt with her favorite
nurse on the floor.

He pointed at the black soda can on the food tray
and asked, "What's that?" His hands were dark, but
not as much as her own. This made sense to her.

Ellie remembered the instructions Danette had
given her less than three days earlier: "Do not tell
anyone about this."

When she investigated his hazel-green eyes, any
reservations faded.

"It records human emotion and perception," she
said in a matter-of-fact manner. "I needed a baseline
for my mother."

"Ah, you must be Eleanor, the computer genius."
He was friendly and not taken aback by her short,

abrupt responses. Ellie figured he had been in New York for a while.

"I'm trying to sync this SCARS device to my mother's sensory input, but I don't know if this prototype works." Psychological operations. It was a trick her dad taught her when she was twelve, the summer she spent with him down at the old Fort Bragg. Honesty is sometimes the best distraction. How a target responds when blindsided by the truth tells you everything you need to know.

"Did you test it on someone already?" Hesitation delayed his thought, but just for a moment. "Yourself, perhaps?" The nurse paused once again. "I hope you did not. You built it," he said, mocking himself for being hasty. "That would taint an unbiased test."

Ellie found relief in talking with someone who understood her predicament. "Exactly, um…" her voice hung on the last sound.

"Owen," he said. "Owen DeVault." Ellie watched his cheeks rise in response to a smile that no mask could hide. She wondered if he noticed her grin.

"It's a pleasure to meet you, Owen DeVault."

"The pleasure is all mine, Ms. Eleanor," Owen replied with a politeness that charmed her usually unflappable demeanor.

"Just Eleanor," she said. "Or Ellie," she added. "Or just plain E," she added again. "Or," she jumped in one more time, "whatever. People call me a lot of different things." Fumbling words showed an insecurity she had not felt since Bobby Dack asked her to their high school prom. He was also Haitian. Ellie thought maybe she had a type.

"It is your name," Owen said, his accent stressing the importance of every word. "You tell me what you want it to be."

"Ellie." Her definitive answer introduced a fresh surge of confidence. She stepped aside so Owen could take her mother's blood pressure and temperature. Ellie kept track of his hands—a firm hold that applied the gentlest touches to his patient. They reached behind her back to lift her weakened torso with tender care, making it easier to swallow the pills, before resting her back and straightening the now-wrinkled blanket. Ellie stepped between him and the door when he finished caring for Anya.

"So," she began, extending that first word longer than usual, "Owen, how would you like to be that unbiased test of my SCARS algorithm?" Only when she heard herself did she imagine the ghastly vision her solicitation must have created. She tried to explain, but that only made things worse. "It's not, like, hospital scars. It's just a computer program that captures biometric data to...."

Five words cut her rambling. "I am happy to help."

"Really?" was her surprised reaction.

"Ellie," he said, "in my years as a nurse, I have spent quite a bit of time around doctors and specialists who go on and on about tests, and procedures, and analyses." He reached out and held her hand. "I just listen for the important things."

In a world where social contact had turned taboo, touch came easy for Owen. His role in a hospital filled with doctors, patients, and family members quickly reintroduced him to human connections. Or, perhaps he had never severed those ties with society when the virus struck. Besides her mother and Danette, Ellie had not had physical contact with another person in over three months. She welcomed the press of his hand, an echo of life before the virus, even if she fought the nagging fear that it was still too early.

"How about tonight?" she said while handing Owen her cell phone. "Seven, my place. Give me your number, and I'll text my address."

They set the course in a matter of minutes. Owen DeVault returned to his rounds, unaware he was stepping into an unimaginable world once reserved for fantasies and nightmares. Eleanor Nickerson had four hours to prepare her SCARS device for an unexpected test subject, explain to Danette that she had to cancel that night's work meeting because their secret was out, and find something in the back of her closet suitable for a date. As they performed their elaborate courtship ritual, Anya Nickerson sat in her hospital bed without interrupting, grateful she had another moment to see the look of pure joy on her daughter's face. In the same breath, the morbid surroundings forced their reminder of why she would never get to meet the precious grandchildren they were going to give her.

Chapter 06

Ellie scampered to prepare for Owen after she ended her call with Danette. Offering guarantees to your lawyer that "he promised not to say anything" had no credibility in the legal community.

When she opened the door and saw him, any concern for a verbal lashing faded. Owen's dress was casual—faded jeans and loafers. His unbuttoned cinnamon-brown pea coat exposed a well-worn New York Yankees T-shirt. Thick rawhide gloves hid the veins on his strong caramel hands that carried a stockpot pouring savory aromas of meat, vegetables, cabbage, garlic, peppercorns, and cloves into Ellie's apartment. She struggled to remember the last time so many distinct fragrances had blended under her nose.

"My Haitian pork recipe was slow cooking all day," Owen said. "I thought I would bring it over for us."

Ellie shot back, "You do realize I am half Jewish?" But those details were insignificant when Owen had an ally in his corner. Anya had told him that pork had been a favorite of Ellie's ever since her dad used to bring ribs, tender meat slathered with tangy North Carolina barbecue sauce, when he came home on leave.

Owen continued, "It still needs another hour or so. I figured we could get started with your computer thing. I just took a test. But if you prefer, I have a mask in my pocket." He lulled Ellie into a sense of security she forgot existed, one that she was powerless to reject.

By the time dinner was ready, Ellie had pulled Owen into a world where thoughts and feelings were no longer private, even if only for a moment. She showed how she could replace his perceptions with someone else's. He experienced the serenity and surrender of a transcendental meditation session Ellie planned to share with her mother. He felt as if his heart raced when she danced the gopak.

"Anya defied my grandparents when she dressed her little girl in the baggy trousers and red hussar boots of a male Cossack to perform in front of members of our Russian community." Ellie told Owen how friends praised them for "introducing the world to a new Russia."

After explaining her discovery, Ellie took over meal preparation, broiling the pork until it was a uniform golden brown. That gave Owen time to reflect on what he had experienced. She set up the collapsible kitchen table, further choking her cramped space, and placed settings at either end. When he agreed with her wine choice, saying, "A German Riesling pairs well with the pork," Ellie melted with the way his accent highlighted the sexuality of every over-pronounced word.

They sat and ate in silence.

With her first bite of the succulent pork that had been cooking, simmering, then broiling for the better part of twelve hours, Ellie's mind lost count of how many unique flavors she enjoyed.

"Wow," was the only reaction she could speak. She devoured a second bite, then a third, before refilling her plate. Owen looked on with the satisfaction of a painter revealing their greatest masterpiece before a captivated crowd of art enthusiasts. "This is absolutely amazing."

"With your device," he asked, "would I feel the same way every single time?"

Ellie scarfed one more piece of pork, ensuring her fork snagged spice-drenched chunks of vegetables, before she forced herself to put the utensil on the table. "Do you remember what it was like when I was dancing? When you were dancing?"

"I do."

"Before I played the sequence, you didn't think it would work."

"I knew it was not going to be real."

"And now? Do you believe it was real?"

"No."

"But how was it during the playback?"

"It was me," Owen confessed. "I was there, but something else. I was...."

"You were me."

"I was you."

Ellie pulled back the curtain of her creation to reveal an unimaginable world where yesterday's reality could become ghosts of the present again and again. Then, they brushed aside the curiosity that had first set their date in motion.

Ellie suggested they discuss anything but the SCARS device.

Owen countered, "Anything but the pandemic."

They stared through each other, unsure what to do and hesitant to say the wrong thing.

"I'm glad you don't have a mustache," Ellie admitted. "I was trying to picture what you looked like underneath your clothes." Owen never again saw Ellie blush. "I mean, your mask!"

Psychological operations.

Owen passed with flying colors. When blindsided by the truth, he offered a dismissive chuckle and moved his folding chair to Ellie's side. He pulled his phone out of his pocket to show pictures of when he wore a mustache, goatee, and even that one full, scrappy beard. Every image had a story, and every story filled in a piece of his life before that day. With each bit, Ellie shared a scrap of hers. By the time Owen's untouched plate had become as cool to the touch as the windowpane holding back the brisk Manhattan night, they found connections that were so much more than shapeless memories formed in a soda can.

**⁎
⁎⁎**

Danette's knocking on the apartment door grew feverish. "Come on, E, it's freezing this morning," she moaned. "Let me in."

The deadbolt latch gave way.

"Sorry, I had to run to the bathroom after buzzing you in."

"Did you get all of your upgrades completed?" Danette asked. It was her responsibility to keep the client on task and on time. "I don't want you losing focus like you do every time you get lost in your programming and design."

But there was no answer.

Danette pulled a thick manila envelope from her backpack on her way to the table. Two settings of half-eaten food from the night before were still out. She looked at her friend, who emerged from her bedroom wearing her favorite Columbia sweatpants and an oversized Yankees T-shirt. The makeshift door remained closed. Danette raised her nose in a prominent gesture. Scents of garlic pork lingered in the air, blending with subtle hints of perfume and sex. Ellie's ear-to-ear grin was a dead giveaway, even if she were to deny any accusation.

"He's not hiding," Ellie boasted. "He's just getting dressed."

Owen called from her bedroom, "Can I get my T-shirt back?"

"No," she said. "I think I've earned this one." A wink rubbed the conquest in her friend's nose. "There's a box that belonged to my dad underneath the bed. His stuff should fit you."

Ellie assured Danette that she had completed the modifications and even made a few tweaks. "We were up late," she said, while clearing her throat, "testing my new algorithms." Thousands of lines of computer code scrolled down the screen as Ellie pointed to changes she had made.

While she detailed the new ability to filter a single individual's sensations in a crowded space up to twenty-five feet away, Danette interrupted. "Do you care about the details of my applications, filings, copyrights, and patents?"

Ellie did not.

She handed her client copies and receipts from the filings while demanding, "Then, just tell me if the fucking thing works." Her attitude shifted when Owen emerged from the bedroom. He exchanged quick pleasantries during the few steps needed to hold and caress Ellie's body again. His now-scruffy face and tousled hair told the same story as her disheveled look.

"Better than before" were the only words Ellie returned before Danette stepped in with her agenda.

"You must be Owen," she said. "I can tell by that same just-fucked look." In most instances, Danette Reddy was the polar opposite of Eleanor Nickerson. The unfiltered conversation was one trait they shared. When Owen's smile subdued, she extended her hand. "I'm Danette Reddy, Ms. Nickerson's attorney." He responded with a firm grasp.

"I'm Owen DeVault, Ms. Nickerson's friend." The quiet showdown continued for an extended moment until the lawyer and the lover chuckled at their game. "It is nice to meet you, Danette. Ellie has told me quite a bit already."

At a disadvantage, Danette admitted, "She hasn't told me much yet, but I hope to get the juicy details after you leave."

Ellie cleared her throat and told Danette that she had asked Owen to stay for their meeting.

"Before you say anything," she said, "hear me out. I have two chips to barter with."

Danette chuckled as soon as Ellie's hands started flying.

"Owen's a nurse. His experience is exactly what I need if I'm going to model this thing for palliative care." Both women looked over at Owen, gauging his reaction. That was the first time he heard Ellie had recruited him, but he shrugged his shoulders and nodded his head in that "sure, what the hell" way.

"I am in for all of it," he said. Ellie reacted with her broad grin and subtle wink.

The lawyer shook her head and conceded. "Fine, whatever," she said, adding, "What's the second?"

"You don't need to hear my juicy details from last night. You can experience them yourself."

Danette released a gasp of air as her eyes remained locked on Owen. His slim figure was a consequence of his fitness rather than any lack of muscle tone. Without visible tattoos, piercings, or jewelry, his physique filled imaginations with stories of what it could do instead of where it was flawed. She, too, tracked the protruding veins that formed underneath the T-shirt, solid green with the same *De Oppresso Liber* quote printed across his chest, then ran down his arm wrapped around Ellie's waistline.

Ellie held a small red flash drive in front of her lawyer, waving the distraction back and forth to break her stare.

"I assume you're just talking about a SCARS experience," Danette said with the slightest tone of disappointment.

They made informal agreements for their partnership before Ellie and Owen left to bring Anya the gift of peaceful meditation.

Chapter 07

Anya Filatiev Nickerson died early in the morning on June 14, 2020. For the last four weeks of her life, Ellie delivered salvation. As her mother's cancer mushroomed, unleashing an endless stream of suffering, she was faithful to her promise and took Anya anywhere her mind wanted to go. She experienced the satisfaction of that first candied bite of a fresh apricot sliding into her daughter's empty belly. Anya treasured it the way she held the memory of when her father returned home carrying food purchased with his bimonthly food stamp allotment. She fed Ellie stories of her joy in being young and lighthearted before responsibilities, divorce, and cancer imprisoned her silliness. Ellie spent a day with Owen racing from one subway car to the next when they paused at a station, having water pistol fights with random people in Central Park, and imitating every movement of a monkey up in the Bronx Zoo. Ellie savored meals that violated every rule of her nutrition and fitness program. She watched in fear as soldiers marched off to war. She looked into the eyes of the man she was falling in love with and told him they were going to have a baby, entertained by his shocked reaction but confident he would make a wonderful daddy. Ellie watched her dying mother and thanked the Lord that she got to hold her granddaughter, even if it was that one time. Intimate experiences created and recorded for Anya made dying bearable. She filled her library

with sensations and emotions, sharing them in six-
to-nine-minute bites.

Ellie sat shiva until June 21. Owen visited every
day. When her mourning was over, she deleted those
experiences—they were never hers to own—and
returned to work at the diner the following morning.

George was relieved to have Ellie back. In-person
dining had finally reopened, even if it was just
outdoor seating. The staff laughed when they
watched patrons spaced apart across sidewalks and
parking spaces, nothing resembling a typical pre-
pandemic Saturday breakfast crowd. Ellie used to
wrestle her food tray through a battlefield of
transients waiting for an open table or fresh donuts,
doling out piping hot omelets and pancakes to her
customers as a reward for their patience. But, in
their new world, lines formed outside.

The least organized of the three queues had no
respect for the queue, celebrating when their pickup
was ready ahead of those fools who had arrived early.

Occupants of the donut line surveyed the scene
with jittery anticipation. They were eager to get in
and get out with no one breathing on them as they
protested, "How long does it take to go in and buy a
fucking donut?" while praying they had not wasted
their risks of exposure, and fearing that their favorite
selections were sold out. But once they were the sole
customer inside, their mood softened while others
behind them waited and griped over how long it took
to go in and buy a fucking donut.

The third category was devotees of the George's Diner experience. They waited in silence for their turn. They reminisced over the once-grand, twenty-by-fourteen-inch laminated menu, with tempting pictures of savory offerings, demoted to a webpage studied on tiny smartphone displays. When Ellie deemed them worthy to walk past the ropes and sit, they marveled at the rediscovery of a lost treasure. They peered through the plate-glass window and told stories of when they sat in "that booth" or what happened one time at the lunch counter. They wondered what George did when he was closed (he never was). On the way to their outdoor table, they pulled sanitary wipes from a container like gunslingers walking into a saloon, prepared to ambush anything or anyone threatening their survival. They snapped staged presentations of their food when it arrived, eager to share their bravery on social media. They took deep breaths of city sidewalk air before unhooking their masks to shovel a hearty helping of freedom into their mouths and cover up again as fast as they could move. An orgasmic sigh of relief accompanied each chew until they realized nothing was quite how it used to be.

Ellie watched the carnival play out countless times. Her exhaustion and emotions had run far beyond their typical course by the time she got home that night. She drifted to her favorite playlist, mixing songs from every genre of her and her parents' generations, raising the volume enough to feel pulsing rhythms while still able to carry a conversation if one presented itself. But her distracted thoughts paid little attention to Owen or other surroundings. They had sex only because her out-of-practice diner feet canceled any plans she might have had for running. Lying in the aftermath, she shared with Owen her study of their city through its new lens, one where aimless social behavior seemed to be the only human trait weathering the virus.

"I could help them," she said with little emotion.

Owen probed her claim. "I don't understand." It was not a language barrier.

Despite the wealth of problems with Ellie's apartment, her cubbyhole bedroom was remarkably cool in the summer. Still, there was no need for modesty. Ellie rolled on top of Owen and sat up, resting on her knees. Thick, textured hair that draped over her shoulders shrouded her firm silhouette, outlined by a single beam of light from somewhere in the studio. She smiled while running the back of her hand across his abdomen.

"This," she said while continuing to caress his naked body. "This is what we're losing. The simple ability to connect."

Owen asked a question he said had been on his mind for some time. "Ellie, what is your motivation with the device?"

As she felt the results of her seduction again take effect, Ellie considered delaying that answer in favor of immediate satisfaction. But she figured that if they had not screwed away those burning images earlier, why would it work this time?

"If I can give people what they need, shouldn't I get something in return?" She raised one finger in the air. "Money," was her first answer. "It sure would be nice to make money someday. SCARS may be the best shot I have." She added a second digit. "Power. With money comes power," prompted the third, "and with power comes opportunity." Owen looked up at her with a half-crooked smile. No one in the tiny den was buying her bullshit.

Ellie fell back to her side of the bed while screaming a low, raspy howl. "Fuck, Owen. I just want it out there," she admitted. "People need this. They are hurting, and I can help."

Wrestling himself free, Owen straddled Ellie just above her hips—his uncircumcised penis lay across her belly button. That time, nothing covered his form as she watched him graze a hand across her cheek and snake his fingers down her neckline, across her torso, breasts, then stomach.

"Thank you for sharing that with me," Owen said. He commanded the speakers to lower their volume to a hush, then leaned down and rewarded Ellie with a quick kiss on her closed lips. "But there must be more to it."

"Everyone needs to feel." Ellie's voice had grown soft; her lust continued to influence him. But, like the heartless computer, she could not pull her thoughts from the script running in her mind's background. "My mother desired nothing more than reminders of her life. Every customer today," she said, "was desperate for connections to what used to be normal, to make that seem real again."

Harsh West Coast hip-hop beats from the 80s melted into smooth jazz riffs on the eclectic playlist just as Ellie reassured Owen, "I can give them a safe version of what they want."

Owen warned her, "Be careful, *mon amoureuse*. At some point, every desire will come into play: promote, aid, mediate, leave be, oversee, regulate, intervene, restrict," accenting each point with a firm press to her chest and torso. He continued his subtle attack on her body. "It will be a terrible burden if you become the one who must decide whose craving will be fulfilled."

Her thoughts stopped racing when she reassured Owen, "I am not a god. It's their right to make that choice."

"Time will tell," he said as passion outmatched every other emotion the two had formed, lasting through the early morning. Owen was the first to leave. His Sunday shift began at five thirty. Ellie did not have to be at the diner until noon. She remained in bed, again enjoying the Sensations of their first night together, that time indulging in Owen's perspective as the stimuli of her nails raking across his back matched the pace of his hips, thrusting himself inward and upward inside her walls until muscles quivered in his legs, his face, and his groin. His standpoint left her amazed by the affection of his brutal beauty.

Chapter 08

That Tuesday morning, the desire to regulate knocked on Ellie's door. It took the form of an enormous fellow who went by the unfortunate name of Arthur Clarke. Clarke never saw the irony in working for a government agency designated as Group 220, an organization that reviewed patents for their scientific or mathematical value to the United States, making the determinations to withhold secrecy for the sake of national security. Ellie stood in her studio, holding the paperwork Danette handed her as Examiner Clarke reviewed the broad swath of software code and devices his office expected her to turn over the following day.

"Is this a fucking joke?" she barked, directing the question toward whichever of the two wanted to answer first.

"Ms. Nickerson, the Invention Secrecy Act of 1951 grants...." Danette cut Examiner Clarke off before going down that rabbit hole with Ellie, warning him the fight would not be a pleasant experience. Clarke backed off without a fight. "As long as I make it home by dinnertime," he said, "I don't care what explanation you need."

Danette handed a second paper to Ellie. "Here's the kicker." She explained how the prototype devices they submitted with the application had kicked off a shitstorm at the Patent and Trademark Office. For a week, the examiners created and experienced Sensations. One of them injured herself when she drifted off into an induced state with a piping-hot cup of coffee in her hand. Ellie chuckled.

"It went offline, though, E."

Ellie's insignificant, graduate-school computer project had made its way to the secretary of commerce, tenth in line to succeed the president of the United States. They shared it with members of the president's cabinet. After generating a stir, it stopped working.

"The vice president was wearing that ridiculous jumpsuit you made, and all she got in return was a test of the emergency broadcast system!"

Ellie snorted while mimicking her impression of government officials making baboon sounds while doing jumping jacks before rushing to see if it had recorded their idiocy, like children who played with one of those toy karaoke microphones at a birthday party.

"Did you try it out?" she asked Examiner Clarke.

"I did, Ms. Nickerson."

"Please, call me Eleanor." She was curious. "Did it work?"

"The prototype was still functional when we were evaluating it," Clarke said.

"What did you record?"

"I don't remember," he said. Ellie could tell he was lying. His face grew flush, probably over the embarrassment of having to explain the sensual pleasure that rushed through his mind as he savored a grotesque wedge of chicken-Parmesan hoagie. How much would he be willing to pay for the ability to recreate that experience without adding more fat around his belly?

"But now, they want to take away my creation so they can indulge in perversion at their own will," she thought.

The twenty minutes Ellie spent bargaining with Examiner Clarke, a man who knew nothing about his namesake's passion for science, invention, and the future, proved useless. By the end, she cursed every government agency that arbitrarily defined what was acceptable, restricting individual autonomy.

She closed the gap with Clarke until her body pressed into his fat flash, inching him backward, closer toward a window of the outer wall. Ellie recognized he was uncomfortable with conflict. At least four inches taller, she left him with two options: fight back or wait until the moment passed.

"Tell your bosses that none of you are gods," she screamed. "They have no idea what real power is."

As her legal counsel, Danette stepped in to coordinate the next steps. Clarke provided detailed instructions on where to meet the following day, to surrender her original source code plus any concept development and prototypes created since the application. Before he left, Clarke tried to offer praise for Ellie's achievement and regret for the steps he had to take. Ellie told him he could go fuck himself.

"Give me the night to figure out our legal options," Danette said after locking the door behind Examiner Clarke. "This isn't over."

At Ellie's request, she left to give her friend time alone, texting an update to Owen on her way out.

Ellie looked over toward the silent hum of her child, sleeping yet never fully at rest. "We could break it again," she debated with either the hardware or herself, "but that only creates something stronger." She sat in her chair and remembered that first time, that shocking moment an uninvited event took root and became the only seedling worthy of nourishment. She leaned on the armrest and pinched her index and middle fingers to the side of her neck, just below her jaw. Ellie stared at her reflections on the two idle monitors while she counted the plunging beats of her heart.

"On the first day," she said to the images, "I created a gateway into my awareness." She gathered her colorful binders with complex coding sequences and loose sheets of white printer paper marked with random scraps of inspiration, collecting them into a cardboard banker's box. She labeled it *6* and placed the box on the floor, a temporary location before it would join *1* through *5*.

"On the second day, I opened that access to anyone." Ellie moved back toward her computer and jerked the mouse across its pad, waking those two monitors with an instant splash of commotion. They awaited her first command as she smiled. It was the same expression of blessing her dad had worn every time he came home to see his little girl. She clicked through digital folders until her dive found its target. Hundreds of thousands of lines scrolled down one screen, cryptic nonsense without the six boxes of translations and rationale in her mind.

With another matter-of-fact declaration, "On the third day, I made you portable," she began typing. The usual weekday hustle and bustle of the Bowery District never made its way up to her apartment, silent except for the feverish clickety-clack of keys as Ellie typed over existing lines of code. Without notes, she scrolled across the pages, changing wording, adjusting formulas, and adding profound declarations. For several hours, the only times she spoke were quips of easing suffering on day four and rediscovering rapture on five.

Each of her final eight keystrokes accented her achievement when she said, "On the sixth day, I gave you purpose."

Satisfied with what she had accomplished, Ellie leaned back in her chair.

"Finally, on the seventh day, I rested. And when I did, they came to take you away from me."

When Owen came home that night, Ellie could not tell him how long she had been sitting there. It was enough time for the kaleidoscopic screensaver to pop up and present its mystic dance of preservation. But even that jester had long since retired into a lifeless void. The screens were once again sleeping. He walked through the door and saw her slumped in the chair, her hands cupped and resting on legs that seemed to go on forever until they disappeared under her workstation. She was idle, not working or screaming, crying, cursing, or any other emotion Owen expected.

"El?" he inquired. His tone was soft as he approached. "How are you doing?"

"I'm fine," she said, scraping the mouse across its pad. And she was, asking if Danette had filled him in on their meeting with Examiner Clarke. Owen repeated the details she had provided, which was everything Danette knew. Ellie smiled and stood up to wrap her arms around his waist. She called up their favorite soft R&B music to play throughout the studio. "I have a gift for you."

"*Un cadeau?*"

Ellie smiled. "Didn't see that coming, huh?" She kissed him on his soft lips before rubbing her cheek along the scruff of his face. The shadows reminded her that his days at the hospital were long and tiring. Plus, the commotion at home. Her lips murmured a conversation not meant for his ears. It was not fair to levy so much pressure at once, but that was her only chance. She knew tomorrow would be different, an irreversible course toward an unguarded future.

"No," she thought. "It's today or never."

"I'll give you my gift if you agree to marry me," she said. Ellie's awkward proposal was a promise that someday everything would somehow come together, either as a reward for how they lived their lives or retribution for what she was about to do.

With a polite stiffness he never outgrew, Owen asked if he could decline her offer, get the engagement ring he had purchased three weeks before, and "offer a proper proposal."

"I wanted to ask your mother for permission." He held the ring in front of her hand, "but I will just have to move forward, believing she said yes."

When Ellie told Michael Yao that story, it was the first time she had shared their harebrained engagement with anyone. She even included Owen's question after Ellie accepted his official proposal.

"Do I still get my present?"

Ellie chuckled when she agreed, "Yes, my love. Before I tell anyone else, I want you to know that I found my motivation."

Another inviting smile spread across Owen's face, assurance that he knew what she was trying to say. "Tell me," he pleaded as while sliding the half-carat solitaire over her finger.

She looked at the modest stone, its brilliance reflecting natural light onto the walls, across her computer, and straight into her chest. She whispered a prayer of thanks to Anya for guiding her toward that man.

"The examiner said they are taking my Sensations away from me." She cocked her head to the side. "But I realized it was never mine to possess." She walked to her workstation and typed two letters.

"So, on the eighth day, I give my creation to the world."

Eleanor clicked one button on her screen before manually setting her computer station to sleep for the night. Then she turned back to Owen.

"So, what wine pairs with a diamond?"

*
**

At 10:45 that evening, Danette was wrapping up unsuccessful research at the office law library. Her despair paled compared to the fear of what she had to tell her friend.

"The government would shut down any legal action and probably put the both of us in jail for revealing national security secrets." Danette continued her one-sided grumbling as she picked up her cell phone. "Maybe Jennifer is up for a little distraction tonight."

But when she looked at her phone, she noticed 642 notifications across social media apps. Her thoughts ranged from "What the hell?" to "Who died?" to "Where are we going to war now?" the instant before she clicked on the first unread icon.

@ENickerson92: Here's the Secret to Unlocking Your Sensations

She scrolled to the next link, then the next, before howling with laughter.

"That fucking girl is gonna need a lawyer."

Chapter 09

Bobby "Prohibition" Rodgers had just hurled his stock racer into the speedway's 120th and final lap, its candy-apple frame speckled with asphalt and rubber, when the driver heard a familiar voice piping through his headset.

"Keep it low and tight through the hairpin turns, left-right-left, then open her up when you hit the straightaway."

But Prohibition didn't listen. He never did. The track record was his objective. He lost everything else in the engine's scream as it ripped him through the first curve, slamming his body into the harness as all four tires fought to keep traction. Although focus was almost impossible to maintain through the dizzying turn, he caught sight of the track barrier fast approaching on the right side. Thick clouds of melting rubber kicked when Prohibition created distance from the wall while guiding the beast back toward the center of the track. He set in position just in time to lean into the next turn.

"Goddamnit, slow down," the voice screamed. "You're gonna get yourself killed!"

Prohibition took the second curve with even more confidence. On his approach to the third, he looked at the dash panel and wondered what would give out first: the overheating engine, the near-zero fuel tank, or the tires ready to explode. Fear was not an option, even as the final turn threatened to rip the helmet clean off his head. Prohibition could see the finish line in the distance. Then, when he hit the straightaway, a violent shudder struck with the force of an atomic blast.

The pit boss shared a defeated tone. "You bent the chassis on that last turn. She'll never make it in with that."

A blue racer pulled alongside the damaged stock car. Prohibition watched the driver taunt with a feigned look of pity, an act that flushed his face with rage. He dropped the transmission a gear and slammed his foot on the accelerator. "Not today," he thought as the tach blew past its redline. Warning lights flashed across his dashboard as sirens drowned out the screams from his pit boss. For the last half-mile, nothing else mattered but the fast-approaching sight of a checkered flag flapping in the wind.

Only when he crossed the finish line and lifted his foot from the gas did Prohibition think of anything else. One by one, the moments came back into focus. The roar of the crowd. The blue racer finally catching up with him. And, best of all, the howling on the radio from his pit.

"You son of a bitch! You did it. I don't know how, but you did it."

Everything went black as fanfare lowered to a hush. It fed through speakers mounted in every corner of a ten-by-fifteen-foot room painted floor-to-ceiling in rich acrylic black. One long wall curved outward. Soft lighting came up as the recorded noise faded, revealing a room that was empty except for one occupant seated in the middle.

Prohibition.

Ellie was the first to enter and congratulate the stock car champion.

"Great job, Bobby," she said. "It looks like you are the winner. That was awesome!"

Bobby moaned a distorted noise as he smiled and thrashed his head from side to side, rocking the wheelchair that restrained him with a five-point harness. A crowd of supporters piled into the room behind Ellie. They wore bright-red T-shirts with star-splatter images, like the ones that say "Pow!" or "Wham!" in vibrant yellow comic-book font. These read "Team Bobby." Overjoyed spectators celebrated with noisemakers while others raised big foam fingers in the air. One woman rushed to Bobby's side, squeezing his shoulders as tears streamed down her face.

"Oh, my little Bobby!" She tried to say more, but her emotions hampered any chance. She pulled back and held Bobby's face still with her hands, staring at his overstretched smile while sharing an equal grin of her own. The woman kissed him on the forehead before stepping back to give Bobby's fans their chance to congratulate the champion.

No one realized Ellie had long since left the room. As the celebration continued, she joined a group watching Bobby's escapades on closed-captioned TV from a lecture hall with a capacity of seventy-five people. There were twelve, plus Ellie, each wearing a mask. Ten sat spaced apart across the first two rows. Three in the seats wore business suits while the others dressed in casual outfits ranging from khakis and a button-down to cargo shorts with a T-shirt from Tech Expo '19. Ellie wore faded jeans and a royal-blue polo shirt with *Nickerson, Enterprises* stitched in white above the left breast.

She started the conversation with, "I hope everyone enjoyed the demonstration of our latest technology, integrating Sensations with real-time audio and visual input."

Unlike their varied fashion choices, the audience shared the same appreciation of Bobby's performance with a roar of applause. The guy in cargo shorts leaned over to a woman beside him and said, "That was so cool!"

"Now," Ellie continued, "please give us your attention as Leonard Powell, our chief operating officer, takes over the presentation."

Dressed in a red version of the Nickerson polo, Leonard stepped forward and stood next to his boss. "Sandy, please dim the lights," he said. Ellie's assistant prepped the room for a short video presentation as ten of the occupants fidgeted, scrolled through their smartphones, or just waited to see what they had in store next. Ellie grabbed an apple pastry from a half-emptied dessert tray and moved to the back of the meeting room.

The lights dimmed as words scrolled through the image of flat desert sand projected onto a bare wall of the conference room.

"What is it like to...." A soft female voice narrated the question. The thunderous roar of a sonic boom that jolted the seated observers cut her off mid-sentence. A single military jet tore from the left side of the desert floor. In an instant, it disappeared past the right edge of the projection, leaving nothing but four miles of sand kicked up across the twenty-foot projection. Image after image challenged viewers' imaginations for five minutes while the narrator kept pace.

"What if you could think what they thought?" the voice questioned as two boxers squared off in the middle of a ring, exchanging crushing blows into the other's head, shoulders, and kidneys.

"What if you could feel what they felt?" she asked as a muted production showed a baby's head crowning from their mother. Noiseless gasps and struggles gave way to the explosive sounds of rapture when her son took his first breath of air.

"What would you want?" was the last question posed as a camera circled above a man, his eyes closed, his face turned toward the sky. He modeled the definition of peace as he sat alone on the mountaintop...

on a tropical beach...

in the lush rainforest...

and, finally, in the comfort of his own home.

The narrator promised, "Experience Sensations today and enjoy the moment for the rest of your life."

After the projector darkened, Sandy brought the room's lights up as Leonard addressed the crowd. "Before I go into details on investment opportunities, I want to start by fielding questions you have." Ten hands shot into the air in unison.

Ellie leaned in and whispered to Sandy, "I hate these fucking investor pitch meetings." They both nodded. Tech Expo '19 had either very sharp hearing or a bug planted somewhere. Rather than waiting for Leonard to call his name, he stood up and faced Ellie.

"Ms. Nickerson," he said. "I'm sure you hate these investor pitch meetings as much as I do, so can I just ask one question?"

Ellie nodded her head in agreement. "Great idea." She took one more bite from the pastry before placing the dish onto an empty corner of the food tray, buckling her knees a bit as her eyes rolled toward the heavens. "My permanent cheat treats! Perfect, as ever, George." She licked bits of frosting off her fingers before rubbing them dry on her jeans and re-masking as she walked up to the front of the room.

"Please, Mr. Barnett, call me Ellie," she said. Andy returned the gesture. "Andy, this is our third investment meeting in five days. Our goal is to raise $500 million by the end of the month." As she paced, her hands showed how that sum of money was "just about this high," and they were still "this far" from that goal.

"You want to know why you should invest in a technology that anyone can download off the Internet for free." It was hard to tell if Andy was embarrassed or if his freckled face was always flushed, matching the frizzled strands of curly red hair that hung in no obvious pattern. Ellie looked toward Leonard. "I told you we should have led with the why." Random chuckles broke the tension and brought another smile to Ellie's covered face.

Leonard stepped back as Ellie paced back and forth across the front of the room and up and down the center aisle that split the rows as her hands expanded on the answer to Andy.

"The truth is because I know exactly what SCARS technology can do." She held up the latest version of her device, an object the size of a ballpoint pen. "I wrote every line of its code."

She reached into her pocket and pulled out a similar pen-shaped device.

"I totally understand that my software and products are copied by thousands of individuals and organizations because I released my coding and designs to the public domain five months ago." She held both pens in one hand. They appeared indistinguishable. "Every software and design update I make is immediately uploaded as freeware."

Andy stirred, as did several other investors. Ellie gave them time to consider her remarks. "The truth is," Ellie admitted, "Nickerson technology uses the same source code and the same design specs as our competitors."

She turned toward the blank wall used for the opening presentation. With a quick snap of her wrist, she launched one of the pen-like devices toward the wall. With a subtle smack, it dropped to the low-pile nylon carpet. "You can use the same oil, chalks, and charcoal as Picasso," she said. "You can use the canvases and wood frames he favored. Hell, make it with a Picasso paint-by-number overlay." She threw the second pen against the wall, shattering its casing and spilling pieces of cheap electronics across the low-pile carpet. "But, if you are not Picasso, it ain't the same. The art world will decide which one is a masterpiece."

She returned to the front of the room where Sandy had brought in ten presentation binders. Together, they distributed them among the investors.

"Leonard will take you the rest of the way, detailing how Nickerson technology is vastly superior to anything you will see out in the Sensations market space." Standing in front of Andy, Ellie handed him the final binder, adding, "The quality captured by our devices and the output calculated and transmitted is unparalleled." She paused, offering a grateful nod for his predictable participation.

"Does that answer your question, Andy?"

Andy's eyes widened as he leafed through the binder. "Yes, indeed," he said. "Thanks."

"Great," she said as her hidden smile, which had never wholly faded, grew wider than ever. As Leonard began his corporate pitch, Ellie exited the windowless auditorium. She dropped her smile and leaned back against the closed door, pulling her mask off as her eyes grew too heavy to keep open. Her breathing turned into one extended exhale as trembling built in her hands.

A familiar voice mocked Ellie's effort to compose herself.

"Five hundred million dollars and that's what you got? 'If you're not Picasso, it ain't the same'?"

"A bug," she sighed, as the sarcastic question brought another smile to her face, but her eyes stayed shut.

"You're late, Colonel," she replied. "I expected your visit when I woke up 151 days ago."

"I was waiting for the right time," he said. "Besides, we needed to do our homework before making contact. Congratulations on getting your master's."

When the voice was close, Ellie peeked to see a short man in cargo shorts wearing a faded Tech Expo '19 T-shirt. The shaved wisps of hair on the sides and back of his head were graying. His middle-aged frame was a few pounds thicker than she remembered, but it still chiseled the silhouette of a soldier. He was wearing a mask, so she reached into a pocket to put hers back over her nose and mouth.

"I got a C+ for that failed design on motion-sensor capture. My professor told me it was a consolation grade for an otherwise excellent student." She extended her hand and said, "Thank you again, Colonel Drew."

"Please," he said, "Zach." He clasped her right hand with his, then covered both with his left. "You earned that scholarship." Ellie released her grip so she could wrap both arms around Drew with the embrace of a daughter clinging to her father when too much time had passed since the last time they were close. The day Master Sergeant Nickerson exchanged his life for that of his detachment commander, Zachary Drew accepted the role, not out of obligation but honor.

With one robust teardrop resisting the urge to fall, Ellie pulled back and wiped the unwelcome visitor from her eye. "Is this a personal visit?" she asked, knowing the answer.

In that stripped-down hallway of the office space rented on the campus of Ellie's alma mater, Drew's eyes broke her heart the way her first father did so many times throughout her childhood. Words like, "I have to go, but I'll be back soon," and, "I won't make that recital, but I'll be there for the next," taught her why reliance on someone else was weakness that always led to pain. Long before that day, she vowed never to need someone so much again. As she stood there waiting for him to speak, her thoughts cursed that man for teaching her to trust again. She cursed Owen for forcing her to love again.

Maybe Drew recognized the pending disappointment on her face. He reached in silence, stroking her cheek with his thumb as he gathered a few stray hairs, escapees from her loose fishtail braid, and tucked them behind her ear. "Not quite yet, Ellatony," he said. "We have some work to do first. Your computer game needs an upgrade."

That five-year-old child, the one who could still count how many times her heart had been broken, faded back into a place where she felt protected. It kept her innocence safe behind cynical walls, built and hardened by disappointment. Before Ellie's heartless stance returned, Drew offered a compromise.

"How about you and that fiancé join my team down at Bragg when you're done here?" Drew shrugged his shoulders like it was some great idea that had popped into his head. He backed away, ready to walk out of the building and let Ellie get back to work once she answered his question. "I'm sure Nickerson Enterprises would have no problem with you courting your new private investor."

Somewhere between shaking her head in disbelief and nodding in agreement, Ellie giggled as she mocked the colonel's blindsiding tactics.

"Yes, sir. Sounds great, sir. Sir, we look forward to it, sir."

Drew let out one loud "Ha" as he turned and headed toward the exit. Watching him walk away, she focused on his limp. Most people never noticed the slight imperfection. The first time she saw him after that firefight was at her father's funeral. Confined to a hospital bed for two weeks, he had been upgraded to a wheelchair days before by his doctors. Shrapnel from the enemy RPG had shredded most of his lower left leg. It was the only part Master Sergeant Nickerson's body failed to cover when he threw it over his commander, bearing the explosion's full force. It took Drew more than a year to walk again, but the price was one he never complained about having to pay.

"Great," he said. "We have a plane waiting up in Westchester."

"Okay, then." Ellie tossed her hands in the air as she responded. "I'll just track down Owen and meet you there sometime later, I guess."

She knew there was no need to ask for details.

"My guy gave Sandy all the details." Drew limped his way through the insignificant side-exit door.

Chapter 10

Any sighting of two young White men pulled over on one of the most dangerous streets in North Division at that late hour would be cause for alarm. Aimless search patterns failed to spot the countless threats staged everywhere. Still, they continued scanning to the front and sides, on occasion looking behind their sleek full-size pickup. Behind the driver, a disheveled Black woman with wavy curls in her thick hair climbed into the back seat. A red bodycon dress barely shrouded her crotch. Bruises and needle marks dotted exposed skin that flowed to her patent-leather ankle boots and peeked beyond the white cuffs of a cropped faux-fur jacket, which was too small to cover her enormous breasts. Red polish, slathered and chipped, failed to hide the dirt collected under her fingernails. At least two dozen costume bracelets dangled from her bony wrists, but no jewelry filled the seven pierced holes she had on her ears and nose. Experienced eyes sunken deep into her gaunt face made her look somewhere between eighteen and fifty.

She should not have been there. Not too many lessons from her childhood still held. "Never get into a stranger's car" was one that had survived—until that day. Tempting promises of candy were all it took to lure her into that trap. Plus, it was warm, a lot warmer than the bitter streets of Milwaukee.

"Try not to get your stink all over my cab," the passenger commanded. "She cost more than you've probably ever made in your life."

Lifting her arm off the center console was all she could do.

"Close the door."

He then told the driver, "Hit it, Mikey."

Mikey fist-bumped his copilot as both started giggling like two preppy adolescents heading to score some beer on a Friday night joyride in their father's sedan. But they were not petty juvenile delinquents. They were in their own vehicle, with a cold, filthy, strung-out prostitute in the back that they'd picked up for a bit of fun.

Mikey began the interrogation as he raced out of the neighborhood.

"What's your name, hun?"

"Lucy," she mumbled while trying to keep herself from flying around the back seat every time Mikey took a sharp turn escaping the ghetto. She never grabbed the center console.

Mikey glanced at her reflection in the rearview mirror. "Lucy, huh?" He smirked when she lost her balance as he threw a few more hard zigzags while racing down Teutonia Avenue. "You doing okay back there, Lucy?"

Lucy said she was good. She peered through a tinted window into darkness where the streets grew less familiar. She had never worked this far north before.

"You hold on just a bit more, darling," Mikey said. He pointed ahead toward an overpass. "We're going into the park, just past that road up there." He looked over at his friend, who just nodded in agreement. "Then, my buddy Joseph here is going to give it to you first." Mikey reached across and slapped his friend across the chest. "Isn't that right, Joe?"

Joe muttered something about "more than she can handle" as he reached down and turned the radio on, blasting a heavy metal riff that compelled him to jerk his head in rhythm with the pulsating drumbeats. But those blaring distractions meant nothing to Lucy as she continued to gaze out the window, picking a storefront far in the distance and counting the streetlights that zipped past before they passed her target. She spotted two gas stations, a discount outlet, and one local burger joint before they finally turned in to the wetlands that hugged a meandering Milwaukee River.

Mikey cut the headlights. Rumbles from the quad cab's 450-horsepower engine were the only sound when they pulled up to a wooded oasis framed by the urban boundary, an empty parking lot, and a hiking trail meandering along the river's bends and twists. He jumped his truck over the curb to sneak around the closed park entrance through a well-worn bypass for the flimsy wooden parking-barrier arm.

Joe's squinted eyes peered into the darkness. "Do you think we'll be alone here?"

"Dude, we're fine," Mikey said. "Besides, if someone comes along, maybe they'll want to take a run at Lucy when we're done."

Lucy stuck her head up between the front seats and said, "Whatever," with a sudden burst of energy. "We doin' this?" She chuckled at Mikey's attempt to turn the truck around on the off-road track as Joe popped open the glove compartment and fumbled like it was daring him to turn on an interior light.

"Ah," Joe finally exclaimed. "We're in business." He popped open a black case the same way a child does with their plastic lunchbox, then pulled out a pen-shaped device and placed it on the center armrest before pressing one end. A small red dot on the other side came to life. "All right, Lucy," he said. "When was the last time you got high?"

Toxic demons snatched Lucy's energy surge. She folded both arms across her chest and rocked forwards and back. "This morning." Her eyes darted between Joe's face and the black case. "My daddy gave it to me."

"Was it good?"

"Nah, man. Was some watered-down gunpowder shit." Spastic tapping on her arm sent specks of dirt and grime flaking off her coat's polyester fur as Lucy tipped her head back. Her eyes fell shut. "But it was H."

Joe pressed that moment. "And what did you have to do for it?"

"Just gave a few 'o his boys some uncovered," Lucy said as her eyes gazed through Joe.

Mikey jumped into the X-rated trip down memory lane. "Come on, dude! Don't waste our time."

"I'm just building up her need for a fix. You know exactly what I mean, Lucy," Joe hissed. He lifted the hinge of the case. "Do you see this?" In the moon's dim light, she caught the contours of a filled hypodermic needle. Its plunger waited just past a thin black line. Her shaking stopped. If possible, her eyes grew even wider. Wheezing gasps of air pulled the last traces of saliva from her cracked lips.

"Right here, Lucy, is the best Colombian-sourced PH you're ever gonna see. It's a clean needle, and there're three more bags in this case."

"What'cha want me to do for it?" Every other syllable hung in the air while Lucy fought to pull the next sound from her body. Desperation replaced the stench left behind by that morning's tricks. Manic urges amplified the longer she stared at a needle that looked like it could have been sitting on the tray in a doctor's office, waiting to treat a darling little White girl who caught the sniffles. But this one was a dangling carrot set out to tease a junkie whore. Any thoughts of stabbing the two with the pick she kept in the liner of her jacket and grabbing the case crumbled under her ability to do nothing more than beg, "Please. Please. What'cha want?"

"Nothing, Lucy. It's yours."

Instinct kicked in when Joe handed her the case. In seconds, Lucy had the needle inserted deep into the inside of her right thigh. A slight pull on the plunger drew blood, confirmation that her experienced touch hit the femoral vein on her first try. Her body stopped rocking as the slow, steady surge of heroin sidestepped her nervous throes of withdrawal with euphoria. Ecstasy flowed from her crotch as she took one extended gasp before she released her grip on the needle and leaned across the center console. Her unresponsive eyes rolled back as her wheezing breaths shallowed and slowed. A thin line of drool spilled from dry, purple-painted lips.

Neither Joe nor Mikey made any efforts to intervene, even when a foul channel of urine collected in the seams of Joe's black-and-red-striped leather interior upholstery. Instead, they exchanged wide-eyed glances in between their fascination over Lucy's trip and the occasional search for any danger approaching that truck. When the red light turned off, Mikey put on a pair of surgical gloves and motioned for Joe to do the same.

Joe picked the device up off the console and placed it in the shirt pocket of his blue button-down Oxford.

"Come on, man," Mikey yelled from outside the car. His frightened squeal echoed throughout the park after he opened the passenger door and tugged on Lucy's arm, trying to coax her out of the truck. It did not work.

"Help me dump her out."

Together, they yanked the overdosing prostitute from Joe's truck. Mikey had just pulled the needle from her thigh and placed it back into the case when he looked up to see his partner wiping down the back seat with shop towels.

"What the fuck are you doing?" he demanded to know.

Joe sounded distraught as he tried to describe how much piss and blood were all over the back seat of his truck.

"Get in, fucking dumbass," Mikey said. He snuck one last look at the passenger seat. It was a foul-smelling, putrid mess. "I'm glad we didn't take my Beemer," he said before grabbing the black case and closing the door. Lucy lay on the ground, curled up in a half-fetal position. He couldn't tell if she was moaning or snoring. With his gloves still on, he opened her jacket and stuck the case in the liner's pocket next to the chiseled pick.

"Here you go, Lucy darling," he whispered. "Keep it. You earned it."

Mikey jumped in the truck. A quick sniff turned his face sour, so he started the truck and rolled down all four windows.

"I tell you what, Joe," he said while cranking up the air conditioner.

"What's that?"

"If this shit works, I'll pay to have your hooker-mobile detailed."

Engine exhaust stirred a layer of ground fog around the truck that cleared the instant Mikey started moving. When they reached the park entrance and dropped from the curb, he turned the headlights back on and restarted the thrash metal tunes.

As two model citizens, shining examples of the next generation's success and prosperity, drove down the interstate, head-banging and howling out the windows, Lucy's half-naked, overdosed body slowly froze to death in the grass, staring up on that starless November night in Milwaukee, Wisconsin.

"I tell you, bro, this better fucking work."

Joe took another swig from his beer bottle as he paced behind Mikey. The preppy shirt from earlier that night was already in the trash, along with his double-pleated trousers and suede penny loafers. Fresh from a shower, he wore plain black knee-length shorts and a Packers sweatshirt. Three fingers ran through his short blond hair, inspecting the moisture to ensure he had no lingering hooker residue after cleaning up.

Mikey tried to concentrate on what he was doing at the computer, but every time Joe passed behind him, he cringed at the sound of wet flip-flops slapping onto the hardwood floor and then flapping up against his heel. He ground his teeth until the steps faded but knew that once his friend got far enough, the room would fill with that bloodcurdling screech as he pivoted on those cheap beach shoes he had bought in Cabo last year.

"Relax," he said, trying to reassure Joe. "It's gonna work. I did a test run on it with myself this morning." He looked back and smiled. "It's fucking sweet!" Mikey turned back to the computer and continued clicking through screen menus. "How about you make yourself useful and grab me another IPA."

"How about you make yourself useful and suck my dick," Joe snapped back as he walked into the kitchen of their two-story condo.

"You should've asked Lucy to do that."

Joe came back into the room with two fresh bottles.

"Yeah, I would have, but I didn't want my nads to rot off before I had that weekend with your mother." He knocked one bottle against the back of Mikey's head. "I'm serious. Do you realize how much I'm into this already?"

With his head still facing the computer, Mikey rolled his eyes and mouthed the words *over fifty thousand dollars.*

"Over fifty thousand dollars already."

Mikey smiled.

Tastefully decorated, the living room shared by the two was most certainly another person's style. Sleek, modern approaches defined the living area. Off-gray chaise sectional pieces matched the drapery. A cubed glass coffee table sat staged under the soft glow of halogen track lighting. Their fifty-five-inch flatscreen hung on the wall opposite the sectional. None of it screamed Mikey and Joe. Instead, someone had used modern bohemian artwork to add subtle accents. The boys had contributed their identity to the decor by scattering bright-yellow throw pillows across the sectional and floor and collecting their mostly empty beer bottles on the coffee table. Their newest addition was a cheap wooden fiberboard writing desk put together in the middle of the room. On its top sat a desktop computer. Their boxes and packing materials were left scattered on either side. While he sat on a carved wooden chair brought in from the dining room, Mikey continued clicking his mouse as Joe ranted behind him.

Flip-flop. Flip-flop.

"Fifteen thousand dollars for that computer," he started the cost breakdown. "Fifteen grand because we need all that," he highlighted in air quotes, "processing power."

The flip-flopping stopped.

Joe reached across the desk and grabbed the pen-like device. Before Mikey could protest, Joe barked at him. "Another fifteen for this capture crap that may or may not have recorded anything tonight." He placed it down in front of his friend.

Squeak.

Flip-flop.

"Ten more for a SCARS replay system that you can't seem to set up."

Mikey pressed his lips together as his body compressed forward.

"I'm trying, bro. I'm trying. I did it before, and I can do it again."

He continued clicking through the on-screen instructions.

Joe's volume grew over the sound of his flip-flops. His pitch rose higher. "Let's not forget the premium smack we had to buy." When the flip-flopping stopped, Joe changed his tone to a desperate observation. "And you just fucking gave the rest of it to some random junkie."

Mikey whipped his chair around, scraping its legs across the hardwood.

"Dude, if this works, we will never have to buy that shit again. You know what that means?" He raised a hand and counted out the points on his fingers. "No more drug deals. No more withdrawal pains. No more testing—we're gonna fucking get caught at work someday and lose our licenses." His ring finger and pinky counted points four and five while he said nothing. "Do you understand what I'm saying?" He didn't wait for a response before continuing. "We can get high whenever we want, as often as we want, without consequences."

Joe countered the argument with his middle finger.

"If that fucking stench doesn't come out, you're buying me a new truck."

"Fine," was Mikey's one-word response as he continued clicking his mouse through setup screens.

Chapter 11

Trips like Ellie and Owen's flight to Fort Bragg would soon become ordinary business travel. Still, that day had not yet arrived when a car service shuttled them to the private airport, where the two flew in luxury on a super-light jet boasted to "accommodate seven or eight passengers in guaranteed comfort." Every amenity possible was available for their indulgence, including a fresh selection of North Carolina-sourced pecans, figs, and pears. No, such travel was far from commonplace at that point in their careers. Funding for their prototype facility had left Nickerson Enterprises $3 million in debt. The seed money Ellie's startup sought from investors would augment the $3,500 they had in the bank, what remained of a $30,000 investment George made in Eleanor.

"You pay me back whenever you can," George cooed the day he stuffed a blank check in her hand.

Plush leather seating extended into its reclined position as Ellie tossed pecans into the air one by one but failed to catch any of them, while Owen looked on and smiled.

"I still think you should come work with the company," she said between pecan flips. "You could head up our palliative care initiative."

Owen clicked his tongue and smiled. "Congratulations, my dear. You have gone three hours without bringing up that topic. That must be a new record."

His sarcasm failed to distract Ellie from her game. "I think you are more comfortable with me as a silent partner, not an employee of Nickerson Enterprises."

"Meh."

After catching her first pecan, she shared another idea. "I think when we get our money, we should write the very first check to George." Forging for nuts lost in the seat cushion, she found three, then resumed her game.

Owen agreed, but added, "You probably need to wait until we complete something with our investors. We do not even have a single proposal." His lips created a childish slurping sound as he bit into a juicy peach.

With a fresh round of pecans ready to serve up, Ellie never turned her head.

"That doesn't matter," she said. "I won't take it, but Drew is going to offer the whole five hundred. He'll funnel it through whoever his partner on the inside is. I bet it's that Barnett kid, the one he shared a T-shirt with."

"All five hundred? Why?"

"Because the government still wants my technology." She stated a fact, not her opinion.

Startled by the silence, Ellie looked over in search of an audience. Instead, a pecan bounced off her chin and fell somewhere in the folds of her seat. Owen sat with his brow furrowed like he was thinking of the best way to respond.

"It's like this, babe." She pressed a button that pulled her seat upright. "Our government wants SCARS. They wanted it before anyone else even knew it existed." She lifted her shoulders and forced a grimacing scowl. "That's the only reason they sent Clarke the Examiner to our apartment."

"That did not go well for them."

"No, no, my love," Ellie said. "That didn't go well for them at all."

"So, they sent your colonel?"

The plane's sharp bank to the left was a not-so-subtle reminder to Ellie that she and Owen were thirty-five thousand feet in the air. Cabin insulation all but muted the high-pitched scream of the turbofans. After deviating from the original flight plan filed for Silicon Valley, the pilot announced their new heading was to Pope. Light cloud wisps broke the glow of random lights scattered along the earth. Everything remained surreal in that new world. Everything continued to be more than she ever imagined. But, most important to Ellie, everything was possible. One mistake sparked salvation in a world that seemed to go to hell overnight. Her greatest fear was that a careless blink of her eyes could make it disappear, leaving her once again alone as a new world passed by thirty-five thousand feet above her single light beaming somewhere in a blank void. Before she considered his question, Ellie shared her realization.

"You're just like him, you know."

Owen smiled in confusion. "Like who? The colonel?"

"Yeah."

"Because I am a short, balding, middle-aged White man?"

Ellie threw a pecan at him. "No, silly," she chuckled. "Because you care for the helpless, the ones who are wounded and ailing. You don't just want to figure out ways others can care for them. That's why you keep working at the hospital. Colonel Drew is the same. He would never do something that puts me in danger. He's putting himself in the middle to protect me from Clarke or any of his bloated government henchmen."

Owen smiled.

"That's why he's here. That's why you stay with me."

Heartache glistened through his frown when Ellie exposed a truth he would never admit.

"But mostly because you both love me."

Owen smiled again, nodding that he preferred her answer.

Like a child reassuring herself she would stay forever protected by her father's watchful eye, Ellie renewed her anticipation of their adventure. She reclined back and resumed her futile tosses. But the abrupt end didn't sit well with Owen. He jumped from his chair, snatching Ellie's latest throw in midair and popping it into his mouth before crashing over her body with gentle contact. She could feel his warm breath on her skin.

"I love you for your curiosity," he said before applying a single kiss to the nape of her neck.

"I love you for your compassion," he said before the next kiss.

Words became unnecessary. Ellie needed to explore his desire rather than debate objectives.

Owen decided there was no need for words, instead trailing more kisses down her plunging neckline. Unfortunately, one person on the plane was interested in more than their simmering passions.

"Ms. Nickerson, we began our descent and will be landing at Pope in fifteen minutes. Please make preparations for landing."

The pilot's warning to "quit whatever you two kids are doing back there" was effective in icing the couple. Owen returned to his chair across the aisle while Ellie brushed pecan dust off her clothes, but neither had any idea what other preparations they needed to make.

With nothing else to do, Owen continued his conversation.

"But, what you say does not make sense, *mon chérie.*" He let that comment hang in the air for a moment, watching Ellie's puzzled face struggle to understand the confusion.

"Why," he asked, "would they send a Special Forces officer to come do some bureaucrat's job?"

"Because he requested...." Ellie corrected herself. "No, he probably demanded the assignment." She stared out the tiny window like she was reminiscing over each of the memories that returned to her when she recognized several of the more notable landmarks near Fort Bragg. "Because he needs his daughter's help with something."

Owen cocked his head to the side. "With what?"

Without fanfare, the jet glided to a flawless touchdown on the runway of Pope Army Airfield.

Ellie never answered his question.

Chapter 12

"As the nation prepares for Thanksgiving weekend under continuing Covid lockdown, many Americans are left wondering what there is to be thankful for."

Michael Yao spoke to his audience from the corner of a deserted intersection in New York City's once-bustling Lower East Side. Rustic brick apartments, five, six, and nine stories tall, sat on top of pizza shops, laundromats, and storefronts that promised "Fashion and Style – $9.99." The bright red and teal of their signs were sun-bleached and subdued to match the lifeless copper and almond tones of the building faces. Iron fire-escape stairwells hung in symmetrical patterns from each apartment. While driving through the intersection, passengers in an orange sports sedan hung out the windows and waved their hands to capture Michael's attention as they drove through the camera frame. He turned to watch them pass underneath the dull silver arm holding up a traffic light and a green sign that read *Division St.*, once again alone in an empty city that still held nearly 8.5 million people.

Michael stared back into the lens and continued.

"But," he promised, "one woman is trying to make a difference."

*
**

"Poppa! Poppa, where are you?" A child's high-pierced Russian plea rattled three crystal chandeliers hanging from the twenty-foot ceiling in the private study. The boy managed to pull Dema Sokolov's attention away from the flatscreen TV, where a reporter announced, "Good morning, and good day around the world. It's Tuesday, November 24, 2020. I'm Michael Yao, and this is Global News."

"I'm in here, my *shchenok*," Sokolov sang as he crouched below his massive mahogany work desk. He challenged his little cub with, "Come and find me if you can."

The boy grunted, forcing open the olive-and-gilt-metal double doors that reached almost as high as the ceiling until he burst into the room with fanfare. His eyes scanned the massive space but did not see his father, so he used so much caution as he crept across the parquet wood flooring that the only disturbance was Michael Yao's report on "Eleanor Nickerson's bombshell technology that is turning the expectations for every industry upside down."

"Mama said it will be time to eat soon." The boy's Russian was quite good, but the trap failed. He reached behind the eighteenth-century tapestry hanging from a polished-gray stacked stone wall in case his father was hiding among the peasant workers stitched into the setting.

The curious child giggled as he approached the far side of the desk just as Michael Yao was interviewing a hospital director, discussing their successes using Sensations as an alternative to hallucinatory narcotics in long-term psychotherapy.

"I can smell you, Poppa," the boy declared, then nearly jumped out of his skin when his father popped out from behind the desk to wrap him in his arms while growling like a hungry black bear. Sokolov began rolling both of their bodies across the open floor. By the time he stopped, the room flooded with the bellyaching cackles of a boy amused by the game and the howling laughter from his loving parent. Underneath it all was the investigative reporting of Michael Yao, who declared, "But, Sensations have also become a dangerous playground for the wealthy and depraved." Sokolov turned his head to the television when he heard the description of a world "where the rich have nearly unlimited access to virtual sex, drugs, and the outer limits of moral corruption." He sat up and reached into his pocket. With one hand wiping a thin line of sweat from his son's short, brown, bowl-cut hairline, he scrolled through contacts with the other before pressing the phone to his ear. As it dialed, Michael Yao asked his viewers, "What will our nation become when this phenom called Sensations is in everyone's hands?"

"Mikael Petrovych, my friend," Sokolov said. "I have a new project for you."

Chapter 13

Overdue reconnections with cherished memory fragments replaced the surge that had threatened to drown Ellie for months. Silence was their companion on the ten-minute drive from the airfield, yet Owen fought his natural urge to fill the car's back seat with idle chitchat. Instead, he waited for when her words would come. Just after midnight, the silver SUV pulled up to an L-shaped brick office building, one of several insignificant structures that offered little insight into their purpose for coming to the Army base. Even at that late hour, its parking lot remained half full with a sampling of every two- and four-wheeled vehicle manufactured over the last fifty years. Floodlights perched high above that stockyard layered everything under their care with harsh brilliance. Softer yellow glows from lampposts marked two cobblestone lanes. One continued toward the building entryway while the other veered to the right. The second was the direction Ellie headed the moment their car stopped.

"Where...?"

Owen's question dropped off as he scampered around the back seat, gathering the few belongings they hadn't stuffed into the back.

"Leave them, sir," said the driver, who had introduced himself as Staff Sergeant Brooks. Dressed in a long-sleeved camouflage blouse and pants, the soldier offered reassuring words. "I'll take care of these things. Go ahead and follow Ms. Nickerson."

Brooks reached across the front seat into a brown paper bag. He said, "Take this with you," before handing Owen a long-stemmed red rose.

It was easy to catch up since she had stopped near the end of a marble-lined plaza, doing nothing but staring at the face of a long, black granite wall. It ran thirty feet along one edge. He could almost peek over most of the polished monument, but the middle blocked Owen's view of the building with a raised platform from which an eagle spread its wings like it was preparing to take flight from the red-and-bronze spearhead emblem where it rested. On the far side stood a larger-than-life soldier, a rifle rested against his sculpted hip as he turned back to rally everyone who dared follow his lead.

Ellie remained motionless, staring at one of the ten panels spaced across the wall. *IN MEMORY OF OUR FALLEN SPECIAL OPERATIONS SOLDIERS* was an etched tribute spanning their width.

Eight sparkled with a bronzed roll call of fallen warriors.

Two panels were empty, hungry for more names to honor.

Without a sound, Owen handed Ellie the rose.

"There are over eleven hundred operators on this wall."

Ellie knelt and placed the long-stemmed tribute at the foot of panel seven before turning toward the building's entrance, where Sergeant Brooks waited. A soft puff of wind pulled Owen's eyes from the center inscription, laid out for *Kinsman, Comrade, Friend* to the right. Without Owen searching, *MSG Robert F.*

Nickerson struck the reminder that Ellie's dad was more than old T-shirts and keepsakes that she kept in a box under her bed.

"*De Oppresso Liber*...." he whispered.

There would be a need to talk when they stepped into the US Army Special Operations Command headquarters. But when Owen rejoined the others, he wrapped a protective arm around Ellie as they walked in silence under the watchful eye of 1,226 special operators.

He strolled the halls with the wonderment of a six-year-old visiting the secret lair of his favorite superhero, twisting and spinning his head in futile attempts to appreciate all the memorabilia. Owen noted photographs of soldiers hiding under the thick canopy of a Vietnamese jungle or dangling their feet from helicopters as those hungry ants swarmed the sky. Other times, they posed with Afghan rebel fighters in remote mountain villages. His mouth gaped as he studied each piece of history hanging on dusty blue walls in their dollar-store frames and read the placard on every dated keepsake perched on a pedestal, wishing he knew their stories. Finally, when Owen realized he had fallen behind, he scurried to Ellie and tapped her on the shoulder.

"Do you think it's okay for me to be here? They know I am not an American citizen, correct?"

Ellie broke away from her trance long enough to look back and smile, remembering the day she had first walked those halls with her father.

"We're fine." She wrapped her fingers around his. "If Drew invited us here, I'm sure he's made every arrangement."

Owen finally smiled cautious relief. "Do you think it is okay for me to take pictures?"

"No," Staff Sergeant Brooks asserted, but Owen showed no concern for the censure. Instead, he returned his focus to the pictures and memorabilia until they reached their destination.

Doppelgangers filled a room secured behind the beep from Brooks' swipe card and his four-digit PIN that activated a sliding bolt inside the sturdy doorframe. Redheaded Andy Barnett's look-alike came in the form of a soldier dressed in sandy camouflage fatigues with a Special Forces tab on his shoulder, captain rank on his collar, and a nametag across his chest that read *HOFER*. Colonel Zachary Drew returned to the military role Ellie remembered, but the bird image once stitched onto his uniform was now a star.

"I see congratulations are in order, General," Ellie said as she shook his extended hand. Their greeting was professional, very static.

"Thanks," he said as Brooks closed the door on his way out, four beeps and the sliding bolt re-engaging security measures. "I think you might know a few people joining us today." Ellie inspected the seven individuals seated around a white rectangular conference table. A mess of wires and Internet cables emerged from the table's hub, connecting to nothing except for the two that fed a laptop computer and the control console. Around it sat four more tabbed soldiers, each blending into faceless insignificance the way they trained. Boring would be the best way to describe the three civilians. Two men wore cheap, discount-rack suits purchased sometime late last century, while one middle-aged woman was wearing a powder-blue smocked midi dress she most likely inherited when her grandmother died. Ellie scowled at the sight of two of them.

"I guess we are still waiting for your buddy Clarke to join us," she jabbed at no one in particular.

The unknown suit pulled the left side of his bearded face up in a crooked half-smile as he shot Ellie a sly look from the corner of his eye. "He's dead, so, no."

"Dead?" was her only response.

Owen spoke up from behind Ellie. "What happened?" He shook the general's hand, adding a slight bow of his head as he mouthed the word, "Hi." His awkwardness added to the stale air hanging in the meeting room. "We just had a videoconference with him last Tuesday."

Ellie added to his recollection. "He was still trying to force me to hand over intellectual property for future development."

"Covid, Ms. Nickerson," the suit said. "He was dead two days after that call."

General Drew spoke louder than the others.

"Mr. Clarke," he bellowed, "rapidly developed respiratory issues after contracting the virus." Drew walked toward the head of the conference table. "Ellie and Owen, the FDA is getting ready to authorize a vaccine for this thing. Everyone in this room and all my ODAs have already received the first dose." He stuck his pistol-pointed finger into his arm and dropped the thumb hammer. "We will get you two after this meeting, but for now, the test Staff Sergeant Brooks administered when you arrived will have to do."

Waving his hand toward the bearded suit, Drew continued, "This gentleman is Ned Fuerst with Health and Human Services. Of course, you know Olivia Beacon with the FDA and Mitchell Tao from the FCC."

Just as Ellie replayed her most recent tirade, Drew cut her off. "Relax, Ellie, you won." Confusion splashed across Ellie's and Owen's faces. "The government is not pursuing any more trademark bullshit. As far as they're concerned, it's a regulatory and tax matter now."

Ellie flopped into the chair at the foot of the table. "Does that make me your new cigarette?" She left the question for anyone to answer.

Loud hacking sounds cleared the phlegm from Ned Fuerst's throat when he took the lead. "Ms. Nickerson, we are not here as part of any governing agency. We are here to integrate your product with General Drew's mission requirements."

Sitting next to Ellie, Owen rested his elbow on the chair's arm and buried his head in his hand.

"Are you fucking kidding me?" Ellie shot back. She reached out to grab a set of phantom motorcycle handlebars, bucking them back and forth. "You've been riding my ass since the day you found out about my technology." With a poof, her open palms flew up into the air. "Now, suddenly, you tell me that someone else is going to fuck me with a checkbook while I come and play nice with you? Why do you think I want to play at all?"

Captain Hofer leaned over and whispered to the soldier sitting next to him. "I told you, Master Sergeant, she's not gonna go for this. Watch. You are in for a treat."

Freckle-faced Hofer whispered but still caught Ellie's attention the same way he did when he was freckle-faced Andy Barnett. It was never unintentional. As the two soldiers giggled over what might happen, she saw a young Captain Drew bonding with Master Sergeant Nickerson sixteen years earlier.

"Oh, I can picture it already, sir," Master Sergeant Sampson said, his smile telling the rest of the story. Probably ten years older, Sampson had more time in the Army and more combat experience. He was senior in nearly every way except rank. Ellie remembered her father's relationship with the young Captain Drew. The operations sergeant's role was to support his ODA commander in any way needed to complete missions assigned to their twelve-man team. Sampson would salute the kid, follow his every order, and make sure every enlisted soldier on the team did the same. If necessary, Sampson would use his large, Black frame as a shield to protect Hofer from the brutal force and razor-sharp fragments of a rocket bursting through the mud-brick wall in some random Afghan dwelling.

"General," Ellie shifted her focus, "before Mr. Fuerst says something else to piss me off, can we move on with a more productive agenda?" She glanced toward the master sergeant, who nodded his head in approval.

"We want controlling shares of Nickerson Enterprises" was the direct answer Ellie needed, even if it was still incomplete. For the next fifteen minutes, the one-star Army general and a twenty-eight-year-old computer whiz negotiated one of the most significant modern business transactions. Other attendees played the role of spectators as the two jockeyed for position.

Drew wanted controlling interest of the company.

"BravoTech can be the majority holder of issued shares. I still retain fifty-seven percent of Nickerson Enterprises."

The general wanted to develop programs for the unique requirements of his Special Operations community.

"We don't decide who does and does not get access to Sensations technology. How they use it is between them and their god, not us."

Drew offered to silence any actions the FCC or the FDA might take against Nickerson Enterprises in the future.

"General, their bureaucracy will in no way hamper my ability to move forward."

Drew wanted to identify and track "targets" who operated SCARS devices.

"My technology will not be used to isolate and infringe on the privacy of others, no matter what their actions may be."

"Come on, Ellie," said Drew as he slammed his fist on the table. "You got to give me something to work with here."

"How about I give you what you've been poking around for this entire time?" She held up a white thumb drive. The drive flew with a flick of her wrist until the general's outstretched hand snatched it.

"Muscle memory," she said while spinning the chair to free her legs from underneath the table. She uncrossed her calves and stood, approaching Drew with little-girl charm and a polite, "May I?" Ellie laid her palm out to reclaim the flash drive, sticking it back into her pocket. "I was just fucking around with that, sir."

Among the nervous chuckles, one sound stood out. A deep, baritone, gut-splitting laugh poured from Master Sergeant Sampson. Ellie paused for a moment, glowing in the aftermath of successful sarcasm.

"Sorry about that, sir," she said. "It was getting a little stuffy in here." Ellie began pacing behind an audience of confused spectators as she detailed her intent. "Is it safe to assume that Captain Hofer has been using SCARS technology to mimic real-world scenarios?"

With a "tell her whatever she wants to know" look from Drew, Hofer replied, "We are trying to replicate high-stress environments where our operators perform without hesitation, without freezing."

From behind Ned Fuerst, Ellie tapped him on the shoulder and made scribbling gestures in the air with her hand. Fuerst sat in disbelief for a moment. When Ellie gave the universal sign to "hurry the fuck up," he pulled a pad from his briefcase and took notes.

"High-stress environments," Ellie continued. "Can you give me examples, Captain?"

"Definitely. Let's see." He raised a fist, counting each answer with an extended digit. He marked "A failed parachute deployment" with his index finger. "Extreme interrogation" was his middle.

Ellie interrupted. "Go back to the parachute," she said. "What are you trying to accomplish?"

"We want to use Sensations so that an operator knows how to react when a 'chute fails."

"Because they've experienced it before?"

"Exactly."

"In training?"

"Yes."

Their conversation never paused when Ellie turned to Drew. "General, let's go skydiving tomorrow."

"Captain Hofer," the general snapped.

"Sir."

"Prepare your team," he continued. "0800 assembly at the airfield. Combat configuration Delta, live rounds. We are going to conduct a daytime HALO into Normandy drop zone."

With a short "On it," Captain Hofer, Master Sergeant Sampson, and the faceless team members rose from their seats and bolted out of the room.

General Drew paused, staring at Ellie before turning to follow their exit. A yellow legal-sized piece of paper was taped to the otherwise empty off-white wall. It was a child's drawing of the November 2020 calendar, with a handprint turkey outline and the days boxed by roller-guided edges that didn't quite line up. There were twenty-three crossed-out squares, some by a thick magic-marker X, others with just a hurried pen stroke. Before he exited, Drew pulled a ballpoint pen from his fatigues and crossed out the twenty-fourth.

"You're cutting it awful close to turkey time there, Nickerson."

⁂

Silence hung in the empty conference room for days or weeks, perhaps only minutes. Acoustic insulation muted any activity outside the door. There was a simple analog clock somewhere along the far wall, but no ambient light for anyone to read it, had anyone been in the space. Without warning, the distinct beep of a card swipe and four digital pulses from the keypad changed everything. As the deadbolt slid from its locked position, fluorescent lights overhead flickered and came to life. The analog clock read either 1:32 or 1332.

Captain Hofer led the spill of his twelve-man team into the room, their faces and hands still streaked with black camouflage makeup that blended their skin into the pattern of their fatigues. No one attempted to console their leader as he made his way to the far side of the conference table, jamming his boot into the first chair that got in his way. Master

Sergeant Sampson caught up to the young captain. With his hand on Hofer's shoulder, Sampson leaned forward and whispered into his ear. Hofer nodded in agreement and sat with no other disturbance. The other ten soldiers quietly filled the chairs behind them. After the team, General Drew, Ellie, and Owen made their way in and closed the door. They wore olive-green one-piece jumpsuits and tan boots. The three civilians were no longer part of the group.

"Listen up." Drew's command hushed any possibility of distraction. "I want you to give Ms. Nickerson your full attention." With a slight gesture of his hand, Ellie moved forward to take his place. Drew sat across from Hofer, then directed Ellie, "I want my men out of here by 1430, so make it quick."

"Yes, sir," Ellie replied, adding, "Owen, if you could please...."

Owen apologized no less than fifteen times as he wove his way around the soldiers gathered at the table. Without asking them to move or make space, he connected his laptop computer to a cable for the overhead projector. Ellie moved to the side before it could burn its light into her eyes. She slid two flash drives across to Owen.

"Right now," Ellie began, "my fiancé is syncing Captain Hofer's captured experience to the video from his helmet camera."

Drew nodded his head, having seen a video of the demonstration with the young Prohibition boy.

"With modifications to my SCARS device, I can now simultaneously transmit Sensations to multiple people. Everyone will experience exactly what

Captain Hofer did as they watch his video stream." She turned to Hofer. "Captain, as you relive that event, you will also be able to talk and explain what is going on."

"I can't fucking wait," Hofer replied, careful to stay within the guidelines Sampson had whispered to him.

Owen controlled everything from his laptop, dimming the room lights as the projected image came into focus. Every soldier had that unique twitch as their body responded when first connecting to the SCARS playback device. Neither Ellie nor Owen was part of the experience.

"Tell me what's going on, Captain Hofer," Ellie said.

"I had just received word from the cockpit that we were at altitude." Hofer's attitude calmed. His focus and emotions remained in the playback sequence.

"What was your mission?"

"My team was to insert a civilian asset to the rally point on Normandy drop zone." Hofer tracked images projected against the wall in the same pattern recorded by the camera mounted to his helmet. The cargo plane's stripped interior gave his team room to conduct a choreographed inspection of their equipment and the soldier to their front. Finally, Captain Hofer stood face-to-face with Ellie.

"What are you doing now, Captain?"

"I'm checking that your gear is secure." His gloved hands came into view, grabbing Ellie's camouflage helmet and shaking it violently. He did the same to the oxygen mask strapped across her face and the goggles over her eyes.

"What are you thinking?"

"I'm running through my checklist. Standard configuration. The asset is tandem strapped to Chief Warrant Officer Sasaki. There are twenty-seven points to confirm in this final check."

Sasaki was the assistant detachment commander, a subject-matter expert vital to the ODA.

"What are you feeling?"

"Nothing."

Cold blasts of wind forced their way into the plane when the back floor section dropped, marking the exit point with a bright splash of North Carolina sky. As team members filed out, none of the soldiers in the conference room showed any sign of stress. Instead, they were reliving Captain Hofer's experience of a textbook operation. As Hofer prepared to exit the plane, his camera scanned the cabin one last time. Two team members were behind him, the last to exit. Ellie, strapped to Sasaki, was to his front. Once they jumped, the only remaining bodies would be the pilots flying the plane, one Air Force crew chief overseeing the jump, and Owen, buckled into a flimsy metal cargo seat bolted to the front of the cabin.

"At what altitude did you jump?"

"Twenty-three thousand feet."

When he dove off the open ramp, everyone felt Hofer's muscles strain, fighting to stabilize his body as he plummeted to Ellie, tethered in front of Sasaki, and stared at her face.

"What is going through your mind?"

"Position. Equipment. Target."

"Where are you going?"

"Tracking with Staff Sergeant Davis."

"Are you thinking anything else?"

"No," Hofer said. When the three connected bodies passed through a thermal layer at eleven thousand feet, the room strained while the captain fought to stay in formation, twisting his limbs and flexing the muscles needed to hold his position.

"What is going wrong?"

"Nothing."

"What is the problem?"

"The target is not keeping her body in the correct position, but that is normal. Expected."

"What are you waiting for?"

"The signal to deploy our main 'chute."

"What else?"

"The target to fuck something else up."

When Hofer's camera picked up the soldiers beneath him separating, he looked at Sasaki before letting go of the harness. As their distance increased, he could feel himself counting and preparing his body to move back if Ellie's parachute did not deploy. Without warning, Ellie appeared to shoot up into the sky when olive-green material poured from its pack and unfurled into an open canopy. Captain Hofer pulled the ring on his harness to deploy his parachute.

A spike of adrenaline surged through every team member as Hofer's camera jerked upward.

"What is going on?"

"Parachute failure. Cigarette roll."

"Are you thinking about why it happened?"

"Doesn't matter. I'm deploying my reserve and bracing to hit the ground hard."

No one grew anxious, even as the camera twisted and jerked toward the sky, the ground, sky, then back to the ground as grass and dirt slammed into Hofer. At once, he stood and scanned the drop zone.

"What are you thinking?"

"Equipment. Position. Target. Team."

With confirmation that they had accounted for every person, Hofer gathered his parachute.

"Fuck," the Captain Hofer of the video yelled as his helmet and camera flew across the drop zone, cutting the video feed when it landed hard on the drop zone's dirty combination of scattered sienna-brown grass and sand. With a nod from Ellie, Owen closed his laptop and cut the Sensations feed to General Drew and the twelve members of ODA-3412. Silence hung in the air.

"That, gentlemen," Ellie said as she walked across the front of the conference room, the bright projector beam painting a sinister silhouette on the wall, "is muscle memory." She placed her hand on Hofer's shoulder, offering a compassionate squeeze as she caressed his wounded ego boiling through his dirt-and-grime-stained fatigues.

She reassured him, "It only works if you believe it's real," then looked up at Drew and offered, "I can train your team to extract the Sensations for flawless execution of a failed parachute deployment, from exiting the plane all the way through successfully hitting the ground." Owen hurried to collect his computer and everything else he had dumped from the bag.

"One recommendation, sir," she continued.

"What's that, Ellie?" Drew said.

"I would cut out the part where Captain Hofer realized I was the one who fucked with his parachute."

Chapter 14

October 11, 2022
He was a shining example of leadership.

Medvedev visited every studio—sectioned-off divisions of the old pill manufacturing plant—at least twice daily. The director needed a flawless operation that day for his twenty-four-hour Surgut Sensations Capture Facility. Sokolov would visit before the second shift's end.

From outside the room marked with a sign written in Russian that read *Capture Room 1*, he watched a steady stream of men, and the occasional woman, as they waited in the cold hallway until the red light perched above the door extinguished and its occupant exited. They handed their SCARS capture device to the technician wearing a white lab coat. The coat noted the time on her transaction log, then turned off the device before laying it onto a metal tray. When she called for the next subject, her orientation brief was simple. "Do not touch the device until you give it to me when you leave. Do not at any time touch the woman. Tell her what you want, then do not speak. When you finish, or when the buzzer rings, exit immediately." With those instructions, she picked up a clean capture device, pressed the button, and placed it in the participant's shirt pocket. Each person usually returned in five to eight minutes, but never more than ten.

Dressed in coffee-stained denim jeans and an oversized purple T-shirt with holes in the armpits,

Ellie battled insufferable boredom while sitting at a sleek black workstation. She commanded a magnificent view high above lower Manhattan, but not even the setting could brighten her mood. So instead, she tracked three jointed arms bracketed to the desktop. Monitors floated from the ends of their extensions. Across the Spartan floor plan of Nickerson Enterprises' office space, six other desks had similar designs, though they looked much more lived-in than hers. Some had jackets over their chairs or colorful notes and reminders stuck to the computer screens, while others were packed with file folders, highlighted computer printouts, and half-filled coffee mugs that proved the occupants were hard at work. Ellie's had none of those telltale marks. Instead, a keyboard, mouse, four unique SCARS devices, and a closed binder that read *2023 Roadmap* were the only inhabitants of an otherwise isolated terrain.

"I really wish you would wear something better," Sandy said while making final adjustments on where each of the seven items should sit.

Ellie huffed. "I'm not going to act like I sit at my desk and code wearing that hideous blazer you showed me." She had pulled her hair back and wrapped it in a vibrant, multicolored headscarf.

"You're taking cover shots for the Top 40 Under 40 in Tech. Can't you look more like a CEO?"

"I am a CEO." Ellie placed her half-eaten banana onto the desktop that Sandy had just finished buffing free from fingerprint marks and smudges. She giggled at the frustrated gasp that spilled out just a hair louder than the office's hissing white noise. Just to the side, a photographer kept his head down, prolonging the time needed to make final adjustments to his camera until the two finished their bickering. It was hard to tell which side of the argument his smirk supported.

"Whenever you're ready, Trey," Sandy relented. "This is as good as she's going to get."

Trey raised his camera and circled Ellie's desk, snapping random shots as she pretended to be lost in thought. Constant praise like "Beautiful, El" and "Gorgeous" offered little guidance to his subject. Trey often boasted that his reputation was from capturing true beauty. "I feature everyday people, not fashion models," he said. "Natural skin tones that bear the imperfections earned when people lived well and worked hard are better than pampered features and retouched images."

His preference for the oddities of a natural shine was in sharp contrast with the harsh studio lights that Medvedev used in his facility.

In the darkness of Capture Room 2, a young boy sat in one corner of the empty cell, curled into a ball, his legs bent with both arms wrapped around them, hoping no man could ever again roll his naked body flat onto the concrete floor. Snot and drool mixed with the tears that streamed down his face. Soft whimpers interrupted by short, quick gulps of air were the only sounds until a voice echoed from a speaker up in the ceiling.

"Press the button," the man said in low, guttural Russian.

The boy continued to sob as if he didn't hear a word.

"Press the button," the voice repeated.

"Please," he begged. His immature voice squeaked while extending the word until its sound faded into another gasp for breath.

"Press the button, and all this stops," the voice lied.

Released by his intertwined fingers, his right hand trembled and fell before fishing around the black space until finally bumping into a small object. Slight pressure charged that single LED on one end of the SCARS device. As promised, overhead light gave form to the concrete slab as a lock unlatched on the door opposite where the child cowered. He jumped up with nervous anticipation. Long, curly blond hair, tousled in knots, sagged to his shoulders. Before the heavy steel door opened and a sizable Slavic fellow reeking of vodka and tobacco entered the room, Medvedev excused himself. He exited the soundproofed staging area to avoid hearing anything that might spoil his appetite for the evening's special dinner.

After fifteen minutes, Trey was out of time.

"You'll just have to make do with what you got," Sandy apologized as she hurried Ellie off to the board room, where Nickerson Enterprises' chief financial officer was reporting performance numbers for the third quarter of the 2022 fiscal year.

"Glad you could join us, Madam Chairperson," Leonard Powell congratulated Ellie, offering a thumbs-up when she opened the glass door to the conference room. Its decor was the same minimalist design as the main office area, with seven people seated at a table that accommodated twice the number with ease. "Marcus was just about to share the financials with us." Ellie apologized, mumbling something about a dog-and-pony show as she took her seat at one end of the table, opposite Leonard and next to Andy Barnett, their angel investor with a twenty-eight percent stake in the company.

"We probably only have her for ten minutes or so," Leonard said. "Let's just get rolling."

Marcus flipped the presentation back three slides to a series of pie charts on the SCARS and Sensations markets.

"As I was saying, SCARS product development and sales were up 112 percent from last quarter. Revenue exceeded 4.5 million, more than doubling the total volume from all other competitors." Halfway down the table, Marcus grabbed a laser pointer to highlight his numbers on the chart. He bent his knees in a half-standing crouch, leaned forward, and extended his arm so the red dot could shoot straight into the numbers. His peach satin tie and charcoal business suit jacket knocked over Kaylee Morris's name tent and blocked her view of the slideshow. She jumped in on his presentation.

"What Pops is trying to tell us is that we are by far the market leader in SCARS device sales."

After nudging the company's representative of an earlier generation in his hip, she cocked her head toward his chair. He took the cue.

Waiting in line outside Capture Room 3 were eight people brought in from outside the North Caucasian Federal District. They spoke to no one unless they offered quick answers to the lab coat who collected survey information: age, sex, height, weight, any current medical conditions, and their history of alcohol and drug use. When told to move forward, they moved, keeping their eyes fixed on the concrete floor. Obedient volunteers followed instructions like their lives, or the lives of their families back home, depended on it.

When the red light above the door turned off, they made their way into a well-lit office space decorated with tasteful reproductions of Wassily Kandinsky's works on the light-peach walls. A buttery-soft, brown-leather reclining chair was the only piece of furniture in the room. Piano harmonies dazzled through air scented with hints of rosemary and lavender.

It was the second lab coat, entering through a second door, who instructed the occupant to sit in the chair as he wheeled a mahogany serving cart across the shallow burgundy rug.

"When was the last time you had anything to eat?" He extended the drop-leaf table and prepared items removed from a pullout drawer.

"Not since yesterday afternoon," was the typical answer.

The satisfied lab coat instructed them to lie back and roll up their sleeves. He activated a SCARS device, placed it back on the stainless-steel tray, then punched a hypodermic needle into the subject's arm that had the best vein. The lab coat continued repeating instructions to remain calm as he administered the hot dose of fentanyl, causing an avalanche of euphoria and sedation. He reorganized the cart in silence, careful not to stand between the subject and the SCARS device monitoring an intense, occasionally fatal, first experience with the powerful drug.

After recording the event details on a clipboard that hung from a brass hook on one side of the cart, the lab coat collected and tagged the device before speaking into a handheld radio pulled from his pocket. Two men not wearing coats entered through the second door and carried the subject out while the lab coat sanitized the area before following their exit.

"Kaylee, how about you jump in and report on your team's sales performance?" Leonard suggested.

Kaylee raised her hands and pulsed them in rhythm to the throbs pulled from her throat. "Ya hear that, Pops?" She bumped her rollaway chair against Marcus to the same beat. "That's the sound of money." Her pale white fingers flickered in an erratic display of green, purple, pink, and black painted nails. "Sales and Marketing be raining money," she shouted as her digits showered over the top of her jet-black crew cut. "It is raining all over Team Nickerson."

"You just keep bringing that money in," Marcus reassured her. "I'll keep on finding places to put it." He even cracked half a smile at his coworker's antics. Everyone there was in a festive mood.

"Deal," Kaylee said, then dropped her hands to open her laptop. After a quick scan of the room, she began her input for the meeting. "Okay. So, I don't have a slide highlighting any specific product line." With a *What-Else-Am-I-Supposed-to-Do* shoulder shrug, she said, "They're hella sweet across the board."

Kaylee held up a SCARS device. "Marcus is right." She hip-checked the CFO one more time. "Our physical technology remains the standard in this market space. But now, with our $200 *Capture-3000*, we are making Sensations technology affordable for the everyday user." She reached into the breast pocket of her denim jacket and pulled out a black disc the size of a quarter. "Our disposable *One-Release* has been a game changer since it rolled out two months ago."

Andy Barnett smiled when Kaylee changed the tone with an exaggerated, "But...." She paused, perhaps hoping others would share their appreciation for her theatrics, before continuing, "Those low-cost alternatives have not hurt our services." She asked Marcus to pull up his Production and Consumption slide. "We are still the leaders in creating the most realistic Sensations experience users can replicate on their own.

"You mean muscle memory?" Andy said.

Kaylee placed her right black-painted index nail against the diamond stud on the corner of her nose.

"That, too," she said. "But I'm talking about the whole shebang. Physical, mental, and emotional recall. That's why we are nearly exclusive providers to the healthcare industry. Clinics titrating individuals who are fighting drug addiction or those struggling with mental illnesses can't risk using a competitor's Sensations with failure rates as high as twenty to twenty-five percent."

When a red-stained lab coat burst out of Capture Room 4, blood-soaked rags loaded into a wheeled laundry basket, he froze at seeing his director standing in his way.

"Mikael Petrovych..." was supposed to be the start of a humble apology, but Medvedev would have none of it as he smiled and took an exaggerated step to the left. He found it best not to press for details when minor mishaps occurred in his capture facility.

"Nonsense, Demetri Mesovich. Please go about your way. Accidents will happen." Medvedev gave the lab coat a robust pat on his shoulder while offering the famous Russian blessing for "keep up the good work."

Mikael Petrovych Medvedev was a natural leader.

"Danette, can you give us a quick report on Legal?"

Leonard tapped on his eighteen-carat, white-gold chronograph wristwatch. "I'm sure the face of Nickerson Enterprises has another important appearance to make." Ellie smiled and shook her head as she shot her chief operating officer a middle finger. When the group taunted her with their impression of intimate photoshoot poses, she sprayed the crowd with both middle fingers, fanning them back and forth until she made her point.

"On that note," Danette interjected with a smile, "let me give you a quick rundown of our latest battles with the greatest enemy we'll ever face." Kaylee picked up two pens and began a blistering drumroll on the conference room table. Danette continued, "Yes, I'm talking about your friend and ours, the US government." Much to everyone's amusement, Marcus's balding head was Kaylee's cymbal highlighting the announcement.

Danette exhaled a quick chuckle and said, "Thank you, Kaylee." She then promised not to bring the room down with tedious litigation details. "So let me be brief," she said, then sucked in an extended draw of air before reporting. Leonard looked at his watch.

"As of today, there are 1,062 state and municipality lawsuits against Nickerson Enterprises. Most are related to FCC and FDA regulations we stand accused of violating, leading to undue burdens on local resources. My contacts within those agencies assure me that not a single case will move forward. Right now, the most pressing challenges are the rising sales taxes on SCARS device processing equipment and the service taxes on Sensations capture and replication. These taxes are doubling, tripling, and even quadrupling consumer costs, leading to an increase in cheap, low-quality products and services from foreign manufacturers. Ellie and

Andy will represent our company on this issue in
Europe at an international symposium on ethical,
safe, and reliable Sensations manufacturing." The
last seven words had no air pushing them from
Danette's mouth.

She popped into her seat as Leonard yelled for
time.

"Thirty-four seconds—a record, Ms. Reddy." The
room erupted with fanfare, with a smiling Danette
nodding in appreciation.

*
**

Capture Rooms 5 through 10 gathered humankind's
depravity under the rusted steel roof of Medvedev's
Surgut facility. During his rounds, their leader
prioritized spending as much time with new lab coats
as he did with those he had worked side-by-side with
over the last two years. Medvedev listened to their
feedback and incorporated recommendations for
productivity improvements. Accommodating their
favorite sins of the flesh was always a priority. The
director delegated his authority, allowing
procurement, production, cleanup, and disposal
crews to work independently under his facility's
charter. Medvedev provided large payments to
Russian citizens they brought into Surgut before they
were blindfolded and shipped to hundreds of
untraceable release points. He offered dignified
disposal of humans and animals who did not survive
their experiences. He ensured all lab coats were well
compensated and evaluated by mental health
professionals every month. Medvedev himself made
the tough decision to end the employment of those

considered no longer fit for duty. He honored and paid tribute to them at their disposal.

By every measure, Medvedev was an influential leader. Even as the landing skids of Sokolov's single-rotor helicopter touched down on the concrete slab, fighting the choppy October winds that bit through central Russia, he reviewed daily production reports on his tablet.

"Dema Zlovich, my friend." Medvedev's hand remained extended as Sokolov walked the final fifteen feet to join him by the single-frame door on the back of the windowless brushed-steel building. An ashy mixture of smoke and steam poured from one of three concrete towers alongside neglected storage vats that sat idle, trails of rust running down their massive exteriors.

Sokolov greeted the director with a friendly smile. "Mikael Petrovych," he said, "it seems that winter has settled into our homeland." He brushed his hand across the side of Medvedev's olive-drab winter jacket and offered an approving nod.

"My father wore this during his army service in 1955."

Sokolov removed his glove to appreciate its heavy cotton coarseness. He offered a favorable smile. "It has held up well."

"They do not think I know," Medvedev chuckled, "but my workers call me *vatnyk* when I wear it on days like this."

"You should not let them talk to you in such a way," ripped the smile from Sokolov's face, but

Medvedev dismissed his boss's words with a wave of his hand.

"A minor rebellion, my friend," he said, "but a wonderful legacy to Mother Russia. Come, let me show you the world you have created."

*
**

"I'm gonna cut you off before you even throw your first jab, Leonard," Ellie said when it was her turn to present. With a thumb and forefinger pressed to the corner of his mouth, Leonard zipped it shut and leaned into his chair as Ellie stood up and walked toward the front of the conference room.

"Marcus," she requested, "can you pull up my presentation? Skip all the 'Rah-Rah' bullshit I have for the rest of our investors and go to the '22 Market slide, please." Sudden windfalls of financial success projected against the wall.

"Let these numbers sink in and think about what they mean to you," she said, remaining silent for an unreasonable length of time. "I see over 250 million people worldwide who needed something humanity could not provide before we stepped in." She reached down and grabbed the wireless presentation controller. Every slide told a unique story of why she had developed Sensations.

The first was Ellie sitting alongside Anya Nickerson's hospital bed, their faces screaming with laughter as Owen strained to include himself in the group selfie. He captured one bloodshot eye and most of his ashy brown forehead, results of another double shift at the hospital. "My mother, bless her soul, was the guinea pig for what became our palliative care division." Ellie sighed and clicked her tongue before moving on to the next slide.

"Drug addiction and mental health illnesses require compassionate measures to bring people back into society," was her introduction for a photo taken at the Second Start Rehabilitation Center. Ellie munched an ear of corn, a paper plate resting on her bare legs, as a patient sat beside her on the picnic table. Their heads tilted into each other under a banner that read *My Shield and the Horn of My Salvation, My Stronghold.*

Andy Barnett scribbled in his notepad when Ellie flipped to the slide on memory retraining. "Patients recovering from injury and reconstruction, even artificial limb recipients, benefit from cognitive therapy Sensations provide." Ellie broke her pace, adding, "I want to note that the NFL contracts we have for muscle-memory training fund one hundred percent of our No-Cost Rehabilitative Patient Iinitiative."

"...and my Giants season tickets," Kaylee added with a sly grin.

"Our greatest setback has been my development team's inability to meet critical customer demands." Kaylee's happy-go-lucky smirk withered away when Ellie admitted, "I can't deny the benefits multiple Sensations recipients on a single stream would have. We've tried every configuration in the sandbox, but I'm afraid that project will not move forward into 2023." Andy expressed a noticeable sigh as he scratched through one of his five bullet points.

*
**

"When my engineers change a single line in the software code," Sokolov reached high into the air, then slammed his flat palm against the wooden desk, "the whole thing crashes and stops working."

Medvedev stared at the data Sokolov shared. "*Chernaya magiya*," he mocked the wicked spirits as he picked up the laptop to look underneath, then tilted it to look behind the screen. "How does that Nickerson woman do it?"

Red circles expanded beneath Sokolov's eyes from his constant attempts to rub away the frustration. "Nobody knows," he said. After draining his glass, he rested it in a brass caddy and placed the assembly beneath a decorative kettle. With the turn of the valve, steam billowed from the dark stream of tea filling his cup. He added excessive amounts of sugar and milk before offering to refill Medvedev's.

"I am good with what I have," Medvedev said while resting deep in his chair, allowing his boss time to savor that delightful first sip before pressing the matter further. As Sokolov's rapture faded into the reality of his dilemma, Medvedev rapped his knuckles on the table. "What if you simply ask her?" He grabbed his tablet and scrolled through random news articles until he found the cause of his inspiration:

Leading Experts to Review 'Sensations' in an Interconnected World
VIENNA 8.10.2022 (JOINT NEWS RELEASE)
International laureates in the field of sensory adaptation science will gather in Vienna from 13 to

15 October 2022 for the first European Conference on Sensations Addictive Behaviours and Dependencies ('Vienna Sensations 2022'). Under the overarching theme of global integrity, the event will showcase the latest scientific knowledge in this domain and explore challenges relating to unethical sensory manipulation manufacturing, Sensations dependence, and other addictive matters. It is the largest European conference on sensory addictions.

Sokolov continued reading the article as Medvedev said, "She agreed to attend as a participant rather than chairing the agenda."

"We will talk more about this over dinner." Sokolov forwarded the link to his email address. Before touring the plant, he directed Medvedev to reserve a table in Surgut's finest restaurant for "us and your most trustworthy and responsible workers."

"Of course, Dema Zlovich. They will join us." Medvedev grabbed his cell phone and rambled through a laundry list of instructions.

**

Giddy energy and emotion faded from the room when Leonard said, "Tell us more about this Europe trip, Ellie." The flat tone of his request and crossed arms mimicked an over-concerned, but even more irritated, parent demanding their child explain "exactly what they did this time."

"It's not that big of a deal," was Ellie's feeble attempt to downplay the conference. She left it there, hoping Leonard would drop the issue and go on with his meeting. Instead, he stared and waited for more.

Without animation or emotion, Ellie continued, "Dr. Mortimer York leads behavioral neuroscience studies at the Medical University of Vienna. They're hosting a fifteen-nation panel on the study of physiological psychology."

Kaylee leaned in toward Marcus and whispered, "Sounds pretty flimsy." Marcus chuckled when she parroted the name "Mortimer."

"And Mr. Barnett?" Leonard pressed.

"BravoTech has grants in several of Dr. York's research areas. Andy is also attending the conference and invited me to travel with him on their corporate plane." Ellie cut herself off from sharing any more information.

Marcus leaned over for his partner in crime to hear. "You can tell she's lying," he whispered to Kaylee. "She's not talking with her hands."

Kaylee's hushed lyrical rendition of "I smell an office romance" brought schoolyard giggles loud enough for everyone to turn their attention toward her and Marcus.

"Sorry," she said. "Inside joke."

*
**

The restaurant was empty except for one prepared oak banquet table set deep into the main dining area. It was draped with a ruby-red cloth with place settings for five people. Each eight-course setting featured intricate, hand-decorated Russian porcelain crafted in the original 1744 designs of Dmitri Vinogradov, ornate silver flatware, and heavy blue-crystal glassware. Hand-drawn name cards at the top of each place honored the five guests. Mikael

Petrovych Medvedev was already there, sitting at the head of the table. Dema Zlovich Sokolov, to his right, was the guest of honor. Beside Sokolov, Oleg Ivanovich Galkin would occupy a prized spot at the table. Alexander Sergeyevich Popov's and Leonid Romanovich Gusev's nametags were to the left of Petrovych. Decorated in the tasteful whims of a Russian tearoom, with dark emerald walls and satin-bronze-painted ceiling tiles, the restaurant would resume business the next day. Though capable of feeding over two hundred of Surgut's wealthiest in a single sitting, Oleksandr Nikolaevich Volkov had closed his upscale establishment that night for Sokolov.

Popov, Galkin, and Gusev arrived together. Any whispered gossip over why Medvedev had invited them stopped once they entered the restaurant. One man gulped hard at the sight of Sokolov. He scrambled to straighten his faded red tie.

"Who is that big man fumbling like a child?" Sokolov asked Medvedev.

"That is Oleg Ivanovich," he said in response. "The last time he saw you was during your first visit to our factory."

Sokolov paused for a moment, then remembered. "Oh, yes, the big Russian birch tree," he chuckled. "Does he think the bogeyman has come back?"

Their bellyaching laughs echoed across the empty dining room. "*Bugimen!*" was all the three could make out before Medvedev yelled.

"Comrades," he said, "hurry and take off your coats. Dema Zlovich is hungry." The three rushed to satisfy the director's wishes. Each shared respectful greetings and sat in their assigned chair, waiting for instructions on what to do next. Sokolov looked over the table the same way an officer inspects his troops, assessing their readiness before combat. Chiseled features disguised his thoughts as he peered into each man's eyes. When something inspired him to move on, he reached up and removed the folded napkin resting on the serving plate. Placing it in his lap set off a cascade of events. Medvedev raised his fingers, directing the staff to fill the room with pre-selected music.

"Very nice, Mikael Petrovych," Sokolov said. "My little Alisa wants to learn how to play just like Sofia Asgatovna Gubaidulina when she grows up."

"I remembered that was what she said when you invited me to your beautiful home. Thank you for sharing that special time with your family, Dema Zlovich."

Sokolov's nod either meant "You're welcome" or "You have a good memory." Perhaps he agreed that his home was beautiful. Regardless, his attention drifted long before Medvedev stopped trying to interpret the gesture.

As servers presented the first course, plump Khasan oysters, Medvedev erupted and demanded they remove every glass, other than the water goblet, from Sokolov's setting. The moment they corrected his outburst, Medvedev called for their finest Chablis for the remaining four place settings.

Sokolov nodded.

Festive events followed as the service *à la russe* offered succulent portions of the finest food Surgut had to offer. Sokolov slurped his oysters, meaty gems flown in fresh from the Black Sea, while learning what the men and their families enjoyed when they stepped away from work. A sinfully delicious meat-and-cabbage-stuffed pirozhki steamed untouched on his plate as Popov entertained the table with a story of his time on the Russian Olympic hockey team.

"That was the day I discovered," he said, "that money and power was something you must earn." He picked up the slice of Russian royal cake a server had placed in front of him, tracing one finger over its thin sponge layers filled with poppy seeds, glossy red cherry glaze, ground nuts, and chocolate chips. Then, presenting the cake to each person at the table, he explained himself. "They are not rewards handed out one at a time for being an obedient puppy until," he snatched the plate back toward him, "you no longer deserve the treat."

Sokolov smacked his lips as he followed the frosted chocolate decadence to Popov's place setting. "Then tell me, Alexander Sergeyevich," he challenged. "What is power?"

Popov cut off a healthy piece of cake with his silver dessert fork and savored the sinful blend of sweet flavor while the rest of the table waited for a response. He closed his eyes, rehearsing his response at a volume much lower than the soft orchestral tones humming across the open room.

After some time, he said, "Dema Zlovich, you groomed Mikael Petrovych on how to create power and money for himself." He dipped his head toward Medvedev while offering more compliments. "He is doing the same for me." Popov forced an exaggerated exhale through his nostrils, then said, "It is now my responsibility to use those skills to create my own power."

Bold words mean nothing when spoken by the weak. Popov demonstrated his vow by reaching across and swiping a thick glob of buttery filling from the middle of Galkin's cake, then sucking the chocolate cream off his finger. Galkin scowled at the insult but made no move in retaliation.

Medvedev enjoyed his dessert and the evening entertainment as his eyes scanned the table, waiting for the next strike.

"Comrades," Sokolov bellowed as both hands slapped flat onto the tabletop. "It is settled." Medvedev buried his surprise when he watched Sokolov reach across to grip Popov's right hand with his. "Tomorrow," he said, "you will take charge of the Surgut Capture Facility." He clasped Medvedev's right hand while declaring, "Mikael Petrovych will join me," Popov smiled at the words, "as a lieutenant in my organization."

Wishes of "Congratulations" and "Thank you" erupted in every direction. Sokolov raised his water glass, prompting the others to lift their oak red Kagor dessert wines high above the table center.

"As far as you both go, Oleg Ivanovich and Leonid Romanovich," he said, "we will hand you healthy amounts of money as reward for your loyalty."

"*Vashe Zdorov'ye!*" erupted. Oleg Ivanovich Galkin joined with an emotional, if not honest, cheers to their health.

*
**

After Ellie excused herself, Leonard pulled up the last slide of his closing remarks.

"As we blast full speed into this fourth quarter," he said, "my only concern is that we reported no downside for Nickerson Enterprises." Kaylee was the only one in the room who did not shadow his concern synced with a deep, worrisome sigh.

With an extended hum of each letter, she threw her emotions across the table. "O-M-G, Leonard, can't we take a minute to enjoy what we're doing here?" Nine minutes later, every Sensations success story from local, national, or international news seemed to pass through Kaylee's arsenal of marketing pitches. She had mastered her role as the optimistic upside of tomorrow, the perfect double rainbow arcing through Operations' gloomy preparation for some godforsaken event lurking behind every corner.

"Barring Danette's failure to hold those government fat cats at bay," she turned to flick a wink at their legal counsel, "or Ellie forgetting to sacrifice her next virgin to keep the lights on," she cast imaginary spells over each person, mocking the reputation Ellie's programming talents had earned, "what else could go wrong?"

Andy Barnett was the only one who could imagine a danger for which they had no plan. With a glimpse of his freckle-faced world beyond BravoTech, Andy cleared his throat loud enough to command attention from everyone in the room.

"Dema Sokolov."

Chapter 15

One month before the board meeting, Ellie and Owen had flown to Fort Bragg to meet with General Drew and Captain Hofer.

"It's been a while, Kenny," Ellie said as she wrapped her arms around Hofer. "Great to see you." Bitterness over the stunt with Hofer's parachute seemed buried in the past. Ellie leaned back to kiss Hofer on the cheek before reapplying her hug.

"You too, El."

Owen stood in line with his preemptive hand extended for when they broke apart.

"Captain." Hugging was much too informal for his comfort level.

"Hey, Owen."

Drew also did not seem to be in a hugging and kissing mood. Without so much as a "Hello," he turned on the overhead projector. An unfocused image showed a man standing in a well-lit warehouse. Hundreds of boxes, each about the size of a case of beer, sat stacked against a gray concrete wall. Piled five high, they reached the man's shoulders. The corrugated containers had no markings except a single piece of brown masking tape across each top to hold it closed and a magic marker swipe across every twentieth row. Just past the inventory, a group of workers loaded the boxes onto a standard wood pallet. A quick count put one hundred in the mass they were encasing in a cocoon of oversized plastic wrap. When they finished, the shipping unit would be ready for transportation.

There was nothing significant about the man inventorying the containers. His pale skin and short-cropped hair complemented the charcoal business slacks and white button-down shirt opened at the collar. Nothing in the picture hinted at the levels of untold violence and blood that blurry figure had on his hands.

"The man in this picture is Dema Zlovich Sokolov." Drew paused without qualifying his comment. Ellie looked at Owen for answers, but all he could do was shrug his shoulders.

She broke the silence with, "What does he have to do with me?"

"He is known in his world as both the creator and destroyer." Ellie inched her body forward but kept silent. Now that he had her attention, Drew continued. "This is the only picture we have of Sokolov. It was taken in an unknown facility in Russia where his organization used to manufacture counterfeit pharmaceuticals." The next slide showed an outlined image of the country with six light-colored circles labeled *Potential Manufacturing Sites* scattered across the middle. The overlapping yellow shades covered almost half of Russia.

Hofer added to the limited information.

"We believe he is now making and distributing illicit Sensations."

Drew played a video of a Russian woman who claimed she had escaped from a facility about one hundred miles north of Krasnoyarsk, deep in Siberia. She explained her work there, best described as that of a lab coat. Her blank stare and waxen features remained frozen as she painted vile images of events they staged and recorded with locally made SCARS devices. Her Russian words, stumbling through details of deprivation, were overlaid with the indifferent tone of a British translator.

"They assigned us to work in only a small part of the factory," the aristocratic voice translated.

A second voice, a male, spoke to the woman in Russian. The female translated that part as well.

"What was your assigned task?"

Ellie and Owen sat in horror as the frail woman described the repeated rape and abuse of a young married couple. One sat tied to a chair with their wrists bound behind them, forced to watch the other suffer horrid treatment. The lab coats switched victim/observer roles often, sometimes brutalizing both at the same time. Finally, with detached recollection, she described her specific duties of distributing and collecting the SCARS devices between sessions.

The male voice asked the woman how she escaped.

"I hid myself in a container loaded on a truck. We drove for several days. When I thought it was safe to get out, I was in Vladivostok. I do not know where the container was going to."

"Why did you go to the authorities?"

Tears welled in her eyes. Her lower lip quivered as her answer escaped. "I want to repent before God so that He may save my soul from damnation."

Drew paused the video. The woman's lips remained frozen on her plea for retribution. "This lying sack of shit," he said, "is being held in an Interpol detention center in South Korea. The video was the only thing that kept them from deporting her back to Russia—and a probable execution, from the sounds of it."

Ellie wiped the corner of her eyes before pleading with Drew for an answer. "How can anyone do something like this?"

Hofer launched into a hostile reaction. "What did you expect was going to happen?" As his growl strengthened, he tossed a handful of black discs across the table toward Ellie. She furrowed her brows to scowl at the insult. "You offer people unfettered access to emotions and desires. What the fuck do you think they'll want?" He reached over and grabbed one disc. Ellie tracked his aggression but kept her head still.

"Drugs."

He dropped the disc and grabbed another while she tucked her lower lip between her teeth.

"Alcohol."

He swapped the disc out for one more. Ellie's head swayed to the rhythm of his syllables.

"Sex."

He picked up the last few and flipped them back to the table one at a time like he was throwing poker chips into the pot. She pressed her eyes shut and slowly shook her head, hoping the words would stop.

"Sex. Depravity. Violence. More sex."

Ellie defended her work. "That's not the purpose of Sensations," she insisted.

Strains of sympathy in Captain Hofer's eyes betrayed the façade he had manufactured with General Drew. It was supposed to have been a tag-team assault on Ellie's stance against government intervention. Instead, Drew watched as the young officer began to soften, so he injected himself into their conversation.

"Sokolov is the absolute downside to your lofty ideals of individual freedoms and responsibilities," he said, then demanded to know, "What if one person's actions are so destructive that they threaten the livelihood of countless others?" Ellie did not have an answer. Her bravado crumbled under the weight of Sokolov's moral corruption. Perhaps she had never considered such a possibility. Drew's portrait of that reality caused her to recoil like a frightened puppy. She buried her head in Owen's chest.

"What is it you are asking from us, General?" Owen said.

"I want you to help us stop him."

Tearstains marked the front of Owen's forest-green pullover hoodie, just above the *Reshaping the Future*® logo. Ellie apologized as she pulled back and rubbed her thumb into the stains.

"*C'est bon,*" he assured her, then clasped his hand over hers. Ellie stared into his gaze and managed a lopsided smile before taking a deep breath and responding to Drew.

"How?"

"First," he said, "we need to shut him down and cut off his supply." The next slide was marked with fifteen asterisks scattered across a world map, points where agencies had confiscated shipments of Sokolov's Sensations release devices. "Each dot represents one hundred thousand of these little black discs," he said, pointing to the *One-Release* knockoffs.

Captain Hofer jumped in, "We have no idea how many they have turned out, but," Drew flipped to the next map, "devices already distributed are showing up everywhere." Some level of red shaded almost every nation in the world.

"Shut down their access."

After she wiped her eyes dry, Ellie sat tall in her chair and looked over at Owen. Intimate exchanges took place between the two before she nodded and turned back to Drew.

"I won't do that."

"Fuck," Hofer yelled the moment Ellie's last syllable trailed off. "You'll throw anyone under the bus to keep your goddamn cash cow fed. First, it was me." Bygone hostility was his only advantage.

Make it personal. Her thoughts reminded her he was only probing for a trigger.

As she replied to his accusation, "This is not about me," Hofer drowned her words with an assault unmatched in volume or tone.

"Now, you're going to abandon a trail of countless victims left rotting in the wake of your parlor tricks." Then, ignoring Ellie, he pulled a release device from the pocket of his camouflage fatigues and thrust it into Owen's face. "You see this, buddy?" he said.

"Fuck you," was Owen's reply as he turned his attention back to his fiancée.

Unfazed, Hofer continued. "They pulled this disc from a shipping container in Long Beach. Twelve little boxes in a Chinese container full of vacuum cleaners and kitchen appliances." Drew flipped the slide, showing a dingy-green, forty-foot high cube shipping container resting in a gravel lot. Hundreds of others sat stacked behind it, like they were an adult build-a-box set. Three cargo ships docked in the background were in various stages of unloading. The steel doors of the container were open, teasing just a guess as to the contents of its cargo. An unmarked cardboard box sat on the ground in front.

"Each contained 750 of these discs, serial numbered and indexed." He picked up a binder of photocopied papers. "We don't have the cross-reference to tell us what is on every disc. We don't know how many other random containers have added packages. We don't know how they get them in. We don't know how they get them out."

Drew took over the assault. "These sons of bitches are a well-run organization. My PSYOP team analyzed that disc Ken is holding."

Ellie cocked her head to the side. "Analyzed?"

"At least one person in my organization knows what it is like to be tied down and mutilated with searing burns to their genitals." The mental image caused Ellie to gag, but Drew would not relent. "Staff Sergeant David Rayan will take that home with him every night for the rest of his life. He will choose whether the memory of someone's worst nightmare or the image of his loving wife and four-year-old son will take priority at the dinner table."

Restlessness set in as Ellie waved off further graphic descriptions.

"You've both made your point," Ellie said. Then, fighting to regain composure, she looked at Owen and shared an *I'm okay* glance before moving on.

"I don't even want to know what sick fuck gets off on that kind of masochistic fetish." Owen grasped her shoulder as she continued, "They need to be in a hospital, and the people who make that shit should have the same thing done to them every moment of every day for the rest of their lives."

Owen parroted her disgust. "Every day."

Ellie directed her next measured words at Captain Hofer.

"I'm not going to give you that 'If they don't do it, someone else will' bullshit. It's true, but that's not the point." Ellie took a deep breath, convincing herself she wanted to move forward. "I'm not God," she said. "The moment I choose who should or should not possess the ability to capture emotions, I've opened Pandora's box on the evolution of humanity. We are not prepared to defend everything that happens next."

But unlike Hofer, Drew was ready to attempt a rational discussion.

"Ellie," he said as he took the seat next to her, "there are governments with laws established to protect people from these kinds of atrocities." He bumped his clasped hands against the tabletop to the same cadence of his appeal. She leaned forward, encasing his fingers with the warmth of her own.

"And yet," she reminded him, "those atrocities continue to happen." Although Ellie saw her only ally in the government continue to slip away, she continued to push. "Prosecute evil. Put them on trial in an international court. But don't let the United States unilaterally control what happens next."

Gentle breaths and soft sighs gave the impression that perhaps General Drew understood Ellie's point of view, until the disheartened parent pulled his hands back and turned away.

"I hope to God you can live with this," he said.

"So do I."

Hofer needed more. He wanted to know, "What can you do for us?"

Ellie wasted no time thinking of her answer.

"I won't shut it down," she said, "individually or across the board." She threw her hands up in the air. "Hell, I don't even know if that's possible. I can reverse engineer the discs to give you a location," was her concession.

"A geotag?"

She picked up a disc. "That's right, Captain. It can tell you where and when they made these."

"What about where they record the Sensations?"

"No." Neither Drew nor Hofer asked if the "no" meant *can't* or *won't*, but they both had the same simultaneous response.

"What else?"

"These discs are meant to be disposable." She pointed at a diseased token. "One use and it's gone. I can make the data permanent."

Drew nodded. "That would come in handy at a trial when we catch Sokolov." Ellie agreed with his assessment, but Hofer had a unique plan.

"They'll come in handy in the court of public opinion since he'll never make it in front of a jury."

Ellie's eyes scrolled through the calculations of her next commitment.

"I can get this to you in sixty to ninety days."

Commenting, "We need to round up friends outside our borders," Drew reviewed the Vienna Sensations Conference details.

"Andy Barnett has already RSVP'd for BravoTech. He's going to meet with intelligence agencies from eight allied nations. We'd like you to accompany him."

Ellie shook her head, insisting, "I'm not the police."

"You'll be a last-minute addition for optics only. Captain Hofer will meet with his peers separately."

After finalizing the details for their covert trip, Hofer reassured Ellie, "We won't have reserve chutes to deploy this time." He forced a sealed-lip smile that seemed to span the distance between her and Owen. "Try not to sabotage this operation."

Chapter 16

Ellie stood over the stovetop, reciting lines of computer code as she added a blend of fresh dill and pungent Hungarian sweet paprika to her mother's Russian beef stew recipe. The kitchen in their penthouse apartment was bigger than the entire Bowery studio. Though equipped with state-of-the-art technology and appliances, their home still echoed a familiar minimalist layout.

Wind chimes rang throughout the kitchen when a ninety-minute timer went off. Ellie closed the dictation app on her tablet before waving her hands over the large pot, pulling rich smells toward her senses. A nod of her head meant dinner was ready. "Andy told the board about Sokolov today," she yelled while ladling two hearty portions of stew into bowls. Owen was already in the dining room, setting the table.

He didn't seem surprised, only curious. "Did he tell them as Mr. Andy Barnett or Captain Kenneth Hofer?"

"Barnett." Owen's eyes widened at the succulent presentation Ellie walked in with two steaming servings of stew, fresh rye bread from Kornberg's Deli, and a white tapered candle set in a short lead-crystal holder. He cleared a spot for her to place the service tray down, then pulled her chair out before setting the items around the table and seating himself. Ellie lit the candle and poured two glasses of pinot noir before she continued.

"He read a security notice supposedly from Interpol. You remember. It was the one he wrote last week." Owen chuckled at the lunacy of their game. "Basically, it said, 'Sokolov bad, illicit Sensations, blah, blah, blah,' and told us to report any strange activity we observe in our supply chains to our local authorities."

With his first taste of stew lingering on his lips, Owen quipped, "I think that the entire conference you are going to will be a strange activity." The two giggled over the absurdity of an international conference where the inventor of Sensations was only attending as arm candy for some Southern California tech billionaire.

"Anyway, I'm just glad my day is over. Tell me about yours."

Elation washed over Owen's face as he jumped on Ellie's invitation, announcing, "Little Terri is going home tomorrow." She squeaked with each additional detail of the six-year-old warrior's triumphant battle over leukemia. "I am off tomorrow since I worked five days of double shifts this week," he said, "but I think I will go to the hospital when he is released."

Falling in love all over again, Ellie admired the dark chiseled features running under his fitted, long-sleeved, burgundy T-shirt before telling him there was nothing in the world she would ever desire more than nights like the one they were about to have. When she winked, the dazzling contrast of his smile offered a silent echo of his collusion. Ellie reached across the table and grabbed a leather binder that had remained there since they moved in three months before. They continued to plan their June 17 wedding between nibbles of stew. Before both bodies grew weary, Owen and Ellie tested the forty-five-minute Sensations Extended Capture device prototype.

In the morning, cold remnants of another interrupted feast sat abandoned on the dining room table. Wearing only red-and-black-plaid flannel pajama pants, Owen glanced at the mess long enough to develop a triumphant grin as he shuffled off to the kitchen. A full carafe sat underneath the coffee maker. Owen stuck to his morning routine and poured cups for himself and Ellie.

"Assistant," he said to no one in particular, "what is on for today?"

Technology concealed as an almost realistic but emotionally unavailable female responded.

"*Bonjour, mon cher* Owen," she said. Her French was terrible. "Today is Wednesday, October 12, 2022." Her stale English was not much better. "You do not have to go to work today. I hope there is something fun on your schedule." Unconcerned by her failure to seduce Owen, she continued her morning script. "Today will be sunny, with a high of seventy degrees and a low of sixty-one degrees. You have sixty-seven unread emails and fifty-eight unread text messages."

Midway through pouring the second cup, Owen paused for less than a second before he stretched his eyes wide and continued the routine. He grabbed both cups and headed to the bedroom. Light rushed into the blacked-out room when his shoulder pressed into the door. The only displays of wealth were the forty-by-forty-foot layout and the subtle impression that every item of the sparse design was limited-edition or custom. Wispy clouds of charcoal gray highlighted one wall, against which a queen-size bed rested on a polished oak frame. Two matching end tables held charging stations and small collections of books. A potted aloe vera plant in the corner on Owen's side stood nearly as tall as him. Ellie lay on the side where one end of a blackout curtain spanned the outside wall, holding back the city that never sleeps while she continued to slumber.

"Don't be quiet," Ellie said. "I'm awake." A gray top sheet, ripped free the night before, covered her rear but exposed her long, powerful legs and petite shoulders. Before she demanded, "Quit staring and bring me my coffee," Owen licked his lips while his eyes devoured the lusty ebony hue of her flesh. When she finally rolled over, her top-knot bun kept her long hair from covering her breasts, further distracting Owen. He stubbed his toe on the bed frame.

"Ouch," he puffed, then disregarded the minor mishap.

"Careful, there. Don't spill my coffee." Ellie smiled and winked.

Owen handed her a cup, then brought up the other matter of interest from the kitchen. "Hey, do you have a bunch of new emails? I have over a hundred notifications."

Two sips were necessary before she placed her coffee on the end table and picked up a tablet resting in its cradle.

"Shit," meant yes, she had a bunch of emails.

Except for a few articles about cross-country running, every email in Ellie's inbox pointed to the same story. Authorities had found Michael Slater, a twenty-four-year-old investment banker from a suburb of Milwaukee, dead in his home after neighbors reported hearing several gunshots. It was the third time in as many days that local police had responded to incidents at his two-bedroom condo in the affluent community.

One article, *Sicko Also Lost His Dear Lucy*, showed no remorse as it detailed the victim's tragic addiction to body horror. "Mr. Slater," it reported, "developed an insatiable reliance on experiencing disturbing, violent, and sometimes deadly events recorded through the adaptation technology commonly known as Sensations."

A man named Joe, who refused to give his last name, told the reporter, "He really got into those SCARS when they first came out. He had this one he called Lucy that he talked about all the time, but he never told me what it was or where he got it."

The last straw for Ellie was when she read Joe's theory. "I think he finally lost it when someone broke into his apartment the other night and stole that computer with all his favorite files, including Lucy." She closed the article and deleted any email referencing Michael Slater.

"Don't you wish it was still like those old movies," she huffed while wiping smudges across the screen, "when people could slam the telephone or throw a newspaper across the room when something pissed them off?" Permanently emptying her trash folder did not have the same dramatic effect.

Owen offered, "If you would like to throw your tablet computer at the wall, you can borrow mine until you get a replacement." Sipping his coffee, he raised one eyebrow in anticipation of her response. But he got a different answer.

"The FCC's gonna ram this one right into my fucking eyeball. I'm tired of my tech taking the blame for assholes being assholes." She waved her hand to introduce her next rant. "Come on in, everybody. Here's an invitation to do the same sick shit as before, but with someone other than yourself to blame." Unprovoked accusations from critics and pundits alike were an unfortunate side effect of the world Ellie had created. Rushing to defend her helpless child from schoolyard bullies was never a burden, yet the responsibility weighed on her.

Bursts of sunshine flooded their bedroom when Ellie pressed an app on her tablet, drawing an opening every five feet along the curtained wall. She rose and walked to the window. As warm sunlight melted the goosebumps on her naked flesh, she closed her eyes and inhaled as if she was filling her lungs with streams of the new day. Slight adjustments of her leg and thigh muscles kept her body still while she had an internal dialogue. Owen sat on the bed and watched, either admiring her physical form or amazed by her ability to self-soothe.

Without turning from the rays, Ellie spoke in a softer tone. "It's like this Sokolov character. Before Sensations existed, he was still a piece of garbage hurting people."

"Illegal prescription meds, the general said."

"Exactly." She turned to face her fiancé, his reward for the correct answer. "And before that, it was narcotics." She stepped closer to the queen-size frame. "Before that, prostitution and gambling." She raised one leg, then the other, then knelt on the end of their bed. "Before that, he was probably just a petty thief." She collapsed face down onto the covers next to Owen. "Now," her muffled groan vented, "I have to get on a plane tonight to hear how this is all my fault." Four minutes passed without another sound or movement until Ellie mumbled something vulgar into the bedsheets; her arms remained flat by her side, and her legs hung off the edge of the bed.

Owen caressed the small of her back. "What was that?"

She lifted her head. "I said I'm fucking done with this bullshit."

Owen grabbed Ellie's cup from the end table. "You piqued my curiosity. Go on," he said while offering her some tepid coffee. She sat up and waved it off, as her hands had too much to say.

"All this government cloak-and-dagger shit." Puppeteer-like fingers animated "the government investment in my company" and the "Special Forces developmental sandbox." Dueling fists mimicked "coddling one agency while the other tries to screw you from behind." Finally, Ellie extended her arms with her palms wide open. The magician showed that nothing remained up her sleeveless arm when she said, "They're of no use to me anymore, and every day is just a reminder of what we lose when someone enforces an arbitrary set of morals."

"What about the protection they provide from government regulation?"

"Do I look like I need protection?"

Inflamed by the need to defend the rights of everyone when examples of evil threatened them, Ellie declared herself invincible. Her nostrils flared to the same rhythm as her rising chest, each breath drawn slowly before its forceful exhale. Glistens of moisture formed across her upper lip, her abs, and down the insides of her thighs. Her perfect body paled compared to her extraordinary mind, the architect of the most remarkable invention the modern world had witnessed. When she shared her knowledge, that world only responded with, "How?" and, "Give us more." However, though remarkable, her mind was still second to her compassion. She lived her corporate mantra in almost every way: Care for the delicate and empower the world so humanity can thrive. That was the day she vowed to make her commitment whole.

By all measures, Eleanor Nickerson was invincible.

Spiteful silence marked the first seven hours of the flight to Austria. Before they departed, Andy Barnett had provided Ellie with an itinerary of events they would attend together. "Outside of that," he said, "you can do whatever you need to solicit new investors."

"Ken, come on," she pleaded.

Ellie tried to explain why she had told General Drew that their business partnership would end on November 1, but Andy interrupted. "Don't worry. BravoTech and Nickerson Enterprises will have a very public breakup after the announcement. Your dirty little secret will be safe with us." He spent the rest of his time at the rear of the jet, reviewing intelligence briefings on Dema Sokolov. Ellie played Sudoku and drafted programming scripts for ideas she wanted to test.

"Mr. Barnett," the pilot's voice came over the speaker system, "we are about thirty minutes out from Vienna Airport." Andy gave a thumbs-up in the general direction of the cockpit camera, then rubbed his strained eyes. He had spent nineteen minutes reading the same paragraph in his packet of witness statements. When he looked up, Ellie was standing in front of him.

"Why do you do it?"

Andy looked confused. He blinked, then pulled his cheeks up to force his eyelids together before stretching them open wide.

"Do what?"

Ellie motioned her ringed hand toward the empty chair in his row.

"Please," he said, extending the invitation with a wave of his own wedding band. The worn piece of jewelry was a new prop in his costume. Before she sat, Ellie brushed her fingers along his unshaven chin. If there had been more time, she could have counted each of the stray grays in his scarlet beard. There could not have been more than twenty or thirty. Instead, she took a seat and clarified herself.

"I know how Special Forces teams work," she said. "Detachment commanders don't hang around with an ODA for more than two or three years." When Andy smiled and rolled his eyes, she added, "They also don't spend their time babysitting a computer geek." Her last fact drew hearty laughs and corresponding head nods from both.

"Honestly?"

"Yeah."

"You're an asset." Andy's cold, hard truth was, "You and your technology are a national asset, probably global." Ellie sat back in her chair, resting her head on the plush bumper. "It's not that we need to own Sensations. We have to keep it safe, so they don't." He paused before leaning forward. "Some inside the government want it," he conceded, "but fuck them. Some of those clowns are worse than these tyrants." He flipped the intelligence packet onto the floor.

Ellie sat in silence, thinking about being nothing more than an *asset*.

"We never should have gotten this assignment in the first place," Andy said as he turned and sat deep in his seat.

"What?"

He counted off the alternatives. "FBI, CIA, Secret Service. Hell, any number of domestic agencies should have been picked before turning us into a Special Missions Unit."

"Drew?"

"Drew," was Andy's response. "You don't even want to know the shit he went through to get this, what he sacrificed."

Ellie smiled a bit. "I can just imagine."

"No, El, you can't."

Her smile faded.

Another flawless landing marked Andy and Ellie's arrival in Europe. Priority routing from ground control directed their jet to a remote section far from the international terminal. They finished gathering their items as the pilot unlatched the cabin's main door. Brutal chaos threw his body backward, his head slamming into the opposite side of the fuselage. Before Ellie could recognize the pop-pop-pop of machine gun fire, two concussion grenades bounced into the cabin. Grabbing Ellie by the throat, Andy threw her to the floor before the grenades exploded. Painful burning of acid smoke stole her vision, and a high-pitched wave of tone was the only noise she could hear. She knew Andy was on top of her, turning his body toward the front of the aircraft. She experienced his body fighting, pop-pop-pop to the left before shifting, then pop-pop-pop to their front. The last thing she remembered was a final pop-pop before Andy fell back. Warm liquid oozed over her midsection.

Ellie woke to gentle melodies that whispered in her ears while her head rested on what might have been the softest pillow she ever felt. She did not even try to open her eyes, instead basking in the touch of the talented fingers that massaged her temples in tender circles. *This is what I want. This is what you deserve.* Ellie agreed with the sentiment.

Shards of broken light penetrated a cloth covering her face when the music scratched like a needle dragging across an old LP. Her pillow crumbled underneath the weight of savage pain in her head, neck, and torso. Ellie tried to move, but restraints prevented any attempt. Besides, her jostling only amplified the agony throughout her body. His "Fix it now" command was directed toward someone else, not her. Before she could remember a response to his Russian, the pain was gone. Gentle melodies whispered in her ears while her head rested on what might have been the softest pillow she ever felt. She did not even try to open her eyes, instead basking in the touch of the talented fingers that massaged her temples in tender circles. *This is what I want. This is what you deserve.* Ellie agreed with the sentiment.

Chapter 17

Owen sat alone; a half-eaten plate of food had been pushed arm's-length into the middle of the dining room table. High above his seat, a single recessed fixture showered low-level light over everything in its path. It was just enough so he could read Ellie's handwriting on the pages of their wedding planner. A pathetic snicker of sarcasm escaped as he traced his finger along a note scribbled in red ink: *Installment #3 December 17.* Double underlines emphasized the significance of that milestone. When the doorbell rang, he tapped his finger along the top of her reminder before getting up to answer the door.

There was no need for Owen to check the peephole. "General, hi," he said, inviting Drew and Master Sergeant Sampson inside before the door was open more than a crack.

Both men recoiled when an offensive odor wafting from the condo struck their senses. Drew pushed the issue with a more theatrical response, waving his hands in the air, trying in vain to push the smell away from his nose.

"Goddamn, Owen. Have you just given up on doing laundry or something?" Nothing. Not a smile or even a chuckle.

"I made boiled cabbage tonight," Owen said as he led them into the dining room. "It is very healthy." His conversation shifted when he caught sight of the planner. "Today was the day we were supposed to pay our balance for the hall."

Drew exchanged glances of helplessness with Sampson before wrapping an arm around Owen's shoulder and leading him toward the living room.

"Make the deposit," he said. "We'll get her back."

Sampson tucked his chin and winced at the irresponsible promise but said nothing.

No longer did Owen ask if they had any news. Almost two months of visits from the general's team had set the aging routine—there were still no updates on Ellie. Likewise, he never had information to share. Owen followed the script and confirmed their cover story was still intact before promising to let them know if anyone made contact. Next, he agreed to "hang in there" while walking to the living room. He sat in one armchair and stared at the floor, waiting to see their next move.

Drew sat on the ottoman right in front of him and removed his wireframe glasses, buffing the lenses with one end of his black wool scarf. "We'd like you to fly out with us tonight for Andy's funeral."

Owen raised his eyes. "You are burying him as Andy?" His mouth gaped open as he looked up and stared.

"We have to," Drew affirmed. "Optics."

Squinted eyes betrayed Owen's confusion to Master Sergeant Sampson.

"If there is any chance Ms. Nickerson is still alive, we have to maintain their cover story."

"You never said 'if' before."

Chapter 18

Unnatural efforts pulled the skin tight across her forehead. Both eyes opened wide, but there was nothing for them to see.

"Am I awake?" she yelled, then exhaled a sigh of comfort when the words echoed. A somewhat familiar ache returned when Ellie tried to twist her head to one side. She reached up and touched a thick gauze bandage on the side of her head.

"One. I'm sitting upright, sort of, and my hands are free."

That time, someone responded.

"You might want to take it easy on those bandages," the female voice suggested with a comically obscene drawl. "The way you've been going through 'em we're fixin' to run out at some point."

Shallow gulps quickened as the awareness of her pain intensified.

"Who's 'we'?" There was no answer.

"Where am I?" Ellie demanded to know. When the pleasant Southern voice refused to answer her questions, she braced herself and tried to stand. That was when she realized she was strapped in the chair by her waist and legs.

Frightened pleas for help drowned the command for Ellie to "Calm down." She fumbled along the seatbelt strap, but there was no buckle to release or knot to unfasten. When she rocked her torso, the freestanding chair moved a bit. No one helped. No one stopped her. Violent spasms and indiscriminate sounds were all she could control. The screaming did nothing, but her jerking tipped the chair off balance and sent it crashing to the floor. Her head, the bandaged part, bounced a bit when it struck the cold tile. Desperate sobs replaced her rage as she lay still. Any attempt to move only aggravated her pain and sent high-pitched needles echoing through her head.

"Please," Ellie's submissive word waded through her sobbing and gasps of air.

"Are yous going to be a good girl?" the subpar Southern voice said.

"Yes."

Ellie was relieved when she realized the pain was gone as gentle melodies whispered in her ears while her head rested on what might have been the softest pillow she ever felt. She did not even try to open her eyes, instead basking in the touch of the talented fingers that massaged her temples in tender circles. *This is what I want. This is what you deserve.* Ellie agreed with the sentiment.

"Eleanor, darling, it's time to eat."

Motherly whispers woke Ellie from her slumber. Crossed arms supported her head as she sat at a table, trying to remember if the voice was the same woman. But that was so long ago. Muted soreness lingered after she shifted her arms and legs. With nothing tied down, she reached up and ran three fingers across her head. Dull aching replaced the intense pain, but there were no bandages anymore.

"Two," she whispered. "I can smell something cooking." Ellie opened her eyes. Squinting in disbelief, she raised her head and looked around the well-lit room. It was a diner, a real greasy spoon. The padded vinyl lining of the booth where she sat matched worn maroon seat cushions on the dining stools that lined a cluttered service counter. On her table, she noted how an off-brand ketchup bottle and chrome caddy that held sugar and artificial sweetener packets seemed to date the scene as much as the rest of its retro decor. Vintage movie posters hung in places usually reserved for windows. R&B tracks from the 1970s played at whisper levels. Ellie looked confused when she inspected the polyester tracksuit she was wearing.

Blueberry pancakes stacked high on one plate rested on the edge of her table, alongside a second dish with one strip of crispy bacon, two eggs over easy, and buttered toast.

"Where am I?"

The voice did not answer Ellie's question. Instead, she had her own agenda.

"You need to eat. It's been three days since you had food." The voice needed to know, "Don't you want to get better?"

Nothing in the empty diner offered clues as Ellie swiveled her head in search of answers. "I'm not doing a fucking thing until you tell me where I am and what you did with Andy," was the only offer she made to the shapeless impostor.

Crooning melodies from The Temptations caught Ellie's attention moments before panic set in as her world went dark. Hands crushed around the top of her neck prevented everything except the most pathetic gurgling releases. Although restraints kept flailing arms at her side, the body involuntarily continued to fight until it gave in and prepared to die. Without a moment to spare, the hands teased a release of their vice grip and allowed three gasps of air before reapplying a hold that crushed the victim's cartilage. Over and over, the cycle repeated until pain, fear, and surrender blended into one synonymous nightmare.

"Eleanor, darling, it's time to eat."

Familiar scratches from the 45 told Ellie that The Temptations were still playing on the jukebox. Long, shallow breaths soon chopped into hearty snaps of air.

She looked around and thought, "Three. There were five pancakes, now four."

She asked, "How long has it been since I ate something?"

"Why would you want to play this game again?"

Tilting her head down, Ellie pulled back her biting response before it sent her to that murky world. "I'm so sorry," she whispered while reaching for the breakfast plate at the end of the table. "Are you still alive?"

Without acknowledging her hunger, Ellie used her hands to scarf down three strips of bacon and a pancake before raising her arm to get someone's attention.

"Waitress," she called out into the emptiness, "can I get a glass of water? Oh, and a fork, please?" One quick chuckle acknowledged the absurdity of her predicament before she picked up another piece of bacon.

Designed to look like a two-way swinging door into the kitchen, a latch popped before it opened inward instead of out. Nothing would have surprised Ellie at that point, but nothing prepared her for the sight of a man dressed in a white lab coat entering the diner at a lazy pace. Oleg Ivanovich Galkin carried a small stainless-steel pitcher and a white coffee mug. Quick chomps on the gristly strip of bacon passed the time as he made his way over to her table and set the mug in front of her. Unsightly stains along the rim and down into the bottom were the marks of a used coffee cup Ellie had seen tens of thousands of times before. She looked up at the tall, boorish man and smiled.

"You guys forgot about something to drink, huh?" A wad of chewed breakfast meat hung from her lips. It had proven itself resistant to her chewing, so she sucked the fat and juice before placing it on the edge of her plate.

She watched him slowly pour hot tea into the mug. "My name is Eleanor." Galkin did not acknowledge her words. "But most of my friends actually just call me Ellie." She offered a pathetic smile.

"What's your name? Can you understand me?" When the mug filled, he grabbed a small towel from his coat pocket and wiped a few drips off the table.

"Can you understand me?" She repeated her question when he put the rag back in his lab coat and turned to walk back to the door.

"Can you understand me?" She repeated the question in Hebrew, but he continued to walk away.

"Can you understand me?" When she repeated the question in Russian, he paused a fraction of a second, but it was enough to spike the inflection of her voice.

"Who are you?" she demanded to know.

"How long have I been here?" she begged him to tell her.

"Where is Andy? What is it that you want from us?" her Russian words screamed for an answer.

"Eleanor, darling, you need to finish your meal."

She looked around the diner, but the man was nowhere to be seen.

Ellie lifted her head from her crossed arms at the table. "Four," seemed to be an appropriate response since her plate had shifted off to the side again, even though the chewed gristle was still there. Lifeless stares at the food set aside for her triggered pangs of hunger. She grabbed a skinny pancake, topping it with an egg and two slices of bacon before rolling the breakfast burrito and taking a chomp from one end.

Ellie said something that sounded like, "You never brought my fucking fork." Sprays of half-chewed pancake covered the table. She washed everything down with a gulp of lukewarm tea before taking another bite, then another. While staring off at nothing in particular, Ellie reached under the yellow tracksuit pant leg to scratch her smooth, bare skin. Random patterns explored both legs, then reached up across her stomach, over the saggy cotton sports bra, until she finally reached her armpit. Puffs of air forced through her flared nostrils when she pinched her fingers and tugged on a healthy tuft of hair. She dropped her hand and took another gulp of tea before mouthing another silent conversation. Gentle melodies once again whispered in her ear.

"Prokofiev!" was one of Ellie's "aha" moments, and she felt the need to share it with whoever was listening. "That's what you've been playing all those times. Sergei Prokofiev." Ellie stopped shouting in favor of a subdued tone. "My mother used to play his cantata for me when I was a little girl." Ellie closed her eyes just as her lips pulled into a childish smile. Her head swayed when she started to hum to the tune of "Seven, They Are Seven."

While The Temptations played their hit through the jukebox, she said, "I would like you to take me back to Prokofiev, please." The lyrical score charged her senses. Ellie followed the tenor's range while her eyes peered through cracked lids, straining to recognize when her reality would change. There was a subtle instance when one cello stepped over the jukebox's R&B track just as gentle melodies whispered in her ears while her head rested on what might have been the softest pillow she ever felt. She continued peering into the diner while basking in the touch of talented fingers that massaged her temples in tender circles. *This is what I want. This is what you deserve.* Ellie agreed with the sentiment, even as her eyes tried to resolve what her brain seemed to believe was real.

Chapter 19

In 1969, six hundred million people watched Neil Armstrong take "one small step for man." Fifty-four years later, Global News estimated over five billion views of Michael Yao's exclusive interview with Mrs. Melissa Barnett.

Except for a green light perched on top of camera two, the studio was dark.

"It's been eleven weeks since the synchronized terrorist attacks on the technology investment firm, BravoTech." A single soft-edged beam pulled one person from the black void. "Co-founder and managing partner Melissa Barnett is still searching for answers as to why her husband, Andrew, suffered brutal treatment before locals found his discarded body on the busy streets of Jakarta." Melissa fidgeted in place, her hands smoothing any creases that may have formed on her navy-blue blazer and brushing the annoying collection of blonde hairs that continued to fall from her fresh pixie cut. She didn't smile but made the point not to look distressed. This moment was not her first spotlight.

When the light came up on Michael Yao, he turned toward the new camera and continued, "Millions of people are asking, 'Who did this?' and 'How did it happen?' The United States and allied partners are asking why. But, even more voices, including Mrs. Barnett, want to know: where is Eleanor Nickerson?

"Good morning, and good day around the world. It's Monday, January 23, 2023. I'm Michael Yao, and this is Global News." He turned, drawing the viewer's attention again to the grieving widow.

"Mrs. Barnett, please let me begin by sharing my heartfelt sorrow and sympathy for your tragic loss." That day, insincere condolences were a common theme, as everyone in the makeshift studio held their concerns close.

Some, like the camera and lighting crew, were on edge since they had agreed to fly to the undisclosed location where Melissa Barnett was in hiding. She was the only employee of BravoTech not killed when a fiery explosion destroyed their Silicon Valley office three days after the attack at Vienna Airport. Neither local authorities nor the FBI had yet identified any persons of interest. The crew's work was professional, but they were eager to escape some psychopath's crosshairs.

The security team had one assignment: to protect Michael Yao and let him get his story.

Melissa Barnett had never met Andy, but she wanted the world to feel her suffering. So, she told Michael the story of how she first ran into her future husband at their business school orientation. In those early days, they shared eclectic passions for hobbies like deep-sea diving and snowboarding while they built a private equity firm that eventually funded technology startups worldwide. Choking back her tears, she joked how, "We always looked to let other people do the hard work." For security purposes, BravoTech withheld all identifying names and dates.

Michael Yao came across as sincere. Before he turned the story to the real focus, Ellie, he gave the Barnetts their long-overdue attention. Michael never asked Melissa her thoughts on what happened, either in Europe or at the isolated office building beyond San Jose's sprawling suburb. He never asked if she saw the gruesome images of Andy's body. Michael never got her thoughts on the popular theory that this was somehow related to Nickerson Enterprises and Sensations. He would save those subjects for his report after the interview. Michael was there to speak with Melissa. She offered nothing beyond the script.

"Way to go, Abby," General Drew whispered as he watched the charade play out on video monitors. He smiled when Melissa told the story of Andy's thirtieth birthday. Tears welled in the corners of her eyes. "Now, let 'em have it."

Broad vowels replaced her r-sounds when emotions triggered the Boston accent she claimed to have lost years ago. "We had a surprise party for Andy. We really got him last month," her smile claimed victory as she boasted, "because he always complained there was never time to be silly." Camera one captured her radiant smile when she said, "We rented out one of those old-school video game arcades." It also caught her head as it tilted to the floor. "That was the day he got the first death threat."

When the interview concluded twelve minutes later, darkness returned to the studio without Michael exploring the comment.

"How'd her makeup hold up?"

"Perfect, sir," a voice chimed in from behind the general. "Captain Highland's own husband wouldn't recognize her." Drew reacted with a single twitching nod. "I just wish we had control of the camera angles."

"So do I, Sergeant Jerez," Drew's response came with a hearty sigh. "But we don't want to get our scent on this Global News spin. Yao has his instructions from the FBI." He turned away from the remote feed as the security detail escorted Melissa Barnett from the undisclosed location. Even without their camouflage uniforms or branded equipment, it was obvious the other two people in the office with Drew were military. Sergeant Jerez used words like "PSD" and "TOC" without translating her intent. The pimply-faced kid monitoring the video feed fidgeted in his chair, bracing at attention every time he realized the general was standing over his shoulder.

"Relax, Private Lieberman." He placed both hands against the young soldier's arms, gripping them firm, but not too tight. "We're just here to do our jobs. Let's ease up on the protocol."

He could not.

"Yes, sir. I will, sir."

Jerez didn't wait for a break in the conversation, nor did she turn her head away from the laptop as she shouted over their conversation, "General, we have a situation."

Any euphoria from the well-planned interview faded. Drew shook his head, mumbling, "Why can't we get ahead of this fucking thing?" as he made his way over to the communications desk. He picked up a headset connected to Jerez's laptop.

Drew barked, "Go," into the microphone, then stood quietly for the next sixty seconds. His only reaction was to direct, "Contact me ASAP when you find him. Out," before removing the headset, picking up the laptop computer, and scaring the hell out of Private Lieberman when he threw it through an unpainted drywall panel in their makeshift command center.

Chapter 20

Can't or *won't* was never a consideration.

Ellie's arms hung limp until they creased at the elbow and folded across her lap. When the gentle melodies whispering in her ears stopped, and her head no longer rested on what might have been the softest pillow she ever felt, she scanned the familiar diner setting and took inventory of her surroundings.

Mouthing "Still four," she noted two eggs, three bacon strips, and two buttered toast slices on one plate. A stench, like the rest of that slaughtered pig was stowed behind the counter, wafted across the diner. Five blueberry pancakes sat stacked on the other plate. Ellie picked up one over-easy egg with a cheap, stamped metal fork and placed it on the pancakes. After adding a slice of bacon, she rolled the first pancake and took a hearty bite.

"I've got to have George add this to his menu." Most of the food stayed in her mouth when she mumbled something about calling them "Gulag Burritos." A clean, empty coffee cup sat next to a hot pitcher of tea.

The corner of Ellie's lips curled. "Can I get a glass of milk, please?" The Temptations were not loud enough to challenge her voice. If someone heard, they chose not to respond.

"Um, Mr. Waiter?" Her hand shot up the way it did when she was the prized pupil in Mrs. Brink's sixth-grade math class. "Ms. Hostess?" Everything in that refurbished prison cell almost seemed normal, expected. The windowless diner layout, the posters

on the wall, the service counter with eight stools
waiting for a breakfast rush that never came.
Everything was just the way she remembered.
Inaudible words identified everything in the room
before she turned her head to confirm her recall.
Four red leather booths—she was in the third from
the exit. She was positive the exit was not a door. At
every booth, there was one no-brand ketchup bottle,
six sugar packets, and four sweeteners. It was as if
she had been there a hundred times before.

"Three, two...."

On cue, the kitchen door unlatched and swung
inward. Galkin approached Ellie's booth, carrying a
small carafe of milk. Wasting no time, she unleashed
a barrage of random conversations at her unknown
friend. Every word was in Russian.

"Oh, milk! Yummy. It has been a while, but milk
sounded really good."

Galkin showed no reaction as he made his way
toward the table.

"Speaking of which, how long have I been here?
One month? Two? Thank you for taking care of me
since the accident. My legs are so smooth, but you
should learn how to shave American women." He
didn't react to her words but looked when she
pointed a finger into her armpit.

"When can I go home? What's your name? Do you
want money? I can pay. I'm sure I ran up a pretty big
tab at your fine restaurant." Ellie looked up as he
poured milk into the coffee cup.

"What is your name? How long have I been here?" Galkin placed the carafe on her table and turned to walk away.

"What do you want? How long have I been here? Am I waiting to meet someone?" His slight hesitation urged Ellie to press.

"Is it Dema Zlovich?"

"Oleg Ivanovich, I guess it is time to have a conversation with our friend." The Southern impostor chose to speak in her native tongue.

Galkin looked back toward the booth, replied in what could best be described as rural Russian, "You have been here four months," then waited for Ellie's dumbfounded look to fade before he turned and sat opposite her.

She picked up the mug and showed no reaction when the warm, thick texture slid through her lips.

"Thank you. That hit the spot." She raised the cup back to her nose. "It smells...sweet."

"It is very fresh."

She smiled and placed the mug down so her hands were free to talk.

"Hi. I'm Eleanor Nickerson. I guess you know that already, but you can call me Ellie. I don't have a middle name." Psychological operations. "My mother insisted that I not have one, either. If you like, you can call me Eleanor Robertovna."

"Eleanor is fine." Galkin's lifeless stare did not encourage her to keep talking, but it didn't cut her off either.

"My mother was Russian. Her family was from Petrograd. They left right before the Bolshevik

Revolution." She rolled another burrito and raised it to her new friend. "Would you like one? They're good." She swung her arms, dancing the food in front of his face before shrugging her shoulders in that *oh, well* way. Before she pulled her breakfast in for another mouthful, Ellie asked one more question.

"Why am I still here?"

Chapter 21

"Oleg Ivanovich is a smart man," Medvedev reassured his boss, but Sokolov continued to shake his head as the two made their way from his helicopter to the main entrance of the Surgut Capture Facility.

"Loyalty to your subordinates should never be blind, Mikael Petrovych. She has been here for much too long."

Medvedev scowled as he stepped through fresh snow that rose past his calf. The landing pad was clear only because the pilot had taken a moment to hover about one meter above the concrete, using the aircraft's rotor wash to blow a spot clean. By the time they reached the facility entrance, watermarks had stained the bottom edge of his coat.

"I agree, but yesterday was the first time she had fully regained consciousness. Alexander Sergeyevich assures me she will be ready to provide information today."

Popov greeted his leaders at the heavy metal door, encouraging both men to hurry inside and rescue themselves from "the dreadful embrace of General Frost." With one arm slung over Medvedev's shoulder, he welcomed the old director back to Surgut and praised his newfound status.

"Your short time away has improved your *vatnyk* dress clothes, Mikael Petrovych," he said while his gloved hand traced the outline of his now-sullied lambskin trench coat. Popov tightened the squeeze around his old boss and planted a gleeful tap on the top of the fur hat that covered his bald head.

"Take us to see the Nickerson woman," Medvedev insisted. Without exchanging words, he stepped to the side and gestured for Sokolov to follow behind the new director. Intrigue pulled him side-by-side when his boss began to tell a story.

"Never blind, my friend," Sokolov said as the two followed Popov through Surgut's maze of hallways connecting ten separate capture rooms, several staging areas, and the facility's administrative wing. "When I was a lieutenant under Grigory Chubais, I had a vision for the organization you see today." He wiped the imaginary image away with strokes of his hand. "But he would have nothing of it."

The corridor tightened, forcing Medvedev to step back, but he followed close so Sokolov could continue with his story.

"He did not want to go into the very profitable production business?"

"Grigory Chubais called them foolish imitations of another person's craftsmanship."

As Medvedev listened to the words, he looked around the dingy halls, with fluorescent light bulbs hanging from the cheap drop ceilings of the facility. When he first came to Surgut, the building was an empty vessel waiting for a great visionary to give it life.

"So, Grigory Chubais told me, 'Go and follow your dreams while you are still young. I will take you back if you want to return under my wing when you fail. In the meantime,' he told me, 'you will honor my patronage with fifteen percent of your revenue.' I was to be in debt to him for the rest of his life."

The hallway widened as the group reached Capture Room 7. Sokolov placed his hand over the handle just as Popov reached to open the door.

"Grigory Chubais was blind to my organization, content with his fifteen percent for doing nothing."

Sokolov extended one finger, dragging it across his throat while concluding his story. "He was unaware that soon I would be much too powerful for him to remain worthy of my vigorish." He curled the finger, drawing Medvedev's attention to the polished titanium ring. Fifteenth-century Slavic scripture surrounded an embedded oval Siberian amethyst. "Upon his accelerated death, everything he once possessed became my property."

Ignorant to the moral of Sokolov's story, Popov cleared his throat before announcing, "They are waiting for us, comrades."

"Hush!" Medvedev snapped in a tone neither man had ever heard come from the short, balding former lab coat. His eyes leered over the director until Popov recoiled and apologized for his behavior. Sokolov nodded his approval.

"Never blind, my friend."

"We will proceed when you are ready, Dema Zlovich."

Another nod instructed Medvedev to brush his subordinate aside and open the door to the waiting area for Capture Room 7. Sitting at a cheap folding table was an alarmingly tall woman. She had been a local beauty queen before harsh struggles in Surgut and the fragility of old age set in. Her duty was to watch the camera feed from the next room, where

Eleanor Nickerson and Oleg Ivanovich Galkin sat in the diner booth. Galkin was laughing as Ellie snapped her head back several times while she said, "Every time I looked back, the dog was closer and closer!" The woman's chuckles faded when she turned to see Dema Zlovich Sokolov.

Before she fumbled over whatever excuse she hoped to conjure up, Medvedev raised the palm of his hand.

"Alexander Sergeyevich, when you have control of your workers, prepare the Nickerson woman for tonight."

"As you direct."

Medvedev turned to Sokolov, but he had already left the waiting area and was making his way toward the warehousing and loading area of the Surgut facility.

*
**

Galkin wiped tears from his eyes with the sleeve of his gray, cable-knit sweater.

"And you never saw the dog again?"

Ellie shook her head while rolling another pancake.

"No, I don't think that demon animal wanted another...." She clicked her tongue and furrowed her brows, trying to remember the Russian words for "bop on the nose."

Sounding nothing like her fragile frame entombed in a white lab coat, the sultry voice stepped into their conversation. "Oleg Ivanovich, it is time to put an end to Eleanor's visit with us."

Lost in that last sentence, the two patrons sat across from each other and shared their gazes. Ellie reached across the table with both hands, curling her fingers into Galkin's.

"It's okay, my friend." Without knowing what would happen next, she told him it was what he must do. Refusing to submit as gentle melodies whispered in her ears while her head rested on what might have been the softest pillow she ever felt, her mind inventoried the diner. She counted and recounted the sugar packets while basking in the touch of the talented fingers that massaged her temples in tender circles. *This is what I want. This is what you deserve.* Ellie agreed with the sentiment, even as Galkin stroked the palm of his hand down her face. Two passes closed both her eyes; the third swipe was intimate when he trailed his fingers across her jawline and down her neck until it reached the top of her cleavage.

Mentally screaming and thrashing with fear, Ellie fought her body's urge to slip away from the nightmare as Galkin roughhoused her from the booth and peeled the dusty-blonde tracksuit from her corpse. Tortured by what might have been the softest pillow she ever felt, Ellie began to loathe the gentle melodies that whispered in her ears. It was impossible for her to separate reality from the other person's Sensations.

Who are you? her thoughts wanted to know.

As Galkin prepared her mannequin-like body for the evening, she described every action of his tender yet bumbling grasp and favored it over the biting touch of those talented fingers that massaged her temples in tender circles.

I hope Natascha is also enjoying her massage. My beautiful Natascha.

"Who is Natascha? What does she call you?"

That warm towel feels so good against my body.

"Careful, Oleg Ivanovich. My skin is very sensitive there. If you had your own woman, you could practice the art of intimate touches."

"Just surrender yourself, Grigory" is all I hear, so I do. I will do anything she asks of me.

Galkin had closed her eyes, and Grigory had no desire to try to open his, instead basking in the touch of her talented fingers. Vacant screams affected neither reality, so Ellie remained a reluctant participant in both worlds. Orgasmic thrills forced her mind to accept the brutal pleasures of their touches. Icy floor tiles stung her naked flesh every time she no longer believed the heated blanket continued to swath her body. The whetted blade practiced its unpracticed graze across her skin.

This is what I want. This is what you deserve.

Gentle melodies echoed in her ear. Music piping through Grigory's experience synced with Galkin's humming while he pulled the rough cotton material over Ellie's torso.

"Prokofiev," she said.

Kneeling over her body, Galkin nodded while continuing his work. "Yes. Sergei Prokofiev." He pulled the cloth down across her legs. "I remember when you told us your mother used to play...."

He froze, then snapped a look up at Ellie to watch the rested rhythm of her chest as it rose and fell with each shallow breath.

"Are you in there, little girl?" His fumbled expression seemed to demand a response, but one never came.

Yes! Yes, I am, muted thoughts screamed her validation.

A quick puff of air through his nostrils helped him shake away the hallucination. Galkin went back to his task.

"I wish you were there," he said. "I like talking to you." After smoothing the pleats of her simple peasant dress, he lifted her body back into the booth. Galkin looked up at a peculiar black patch spot in the middle of the grimy stucco ceiling. "Inessa Ivanovna," he said to the spot, "the woman is ready."

"Thank you, comrade," she said in Russian.

"Good morning, Eleanor," she said in English.

"I prefer your native tongue." Ellie inspected everything from her dream and found confirmation that it was not a dream. The rough cotton dress covered her smooth legs and armpits. "I like this much better than that ugly running outfit you had on me before." She avoided the urge to run fingers through her matted biracial hair he once again failed to groom, and her stomach wretched from the soreness his fingers left behind in her crotch. Nevertheless, she looked in Galkin's gray eyes and smiled.

"Thank you for taking care of me. I also like talking with you, but as you have discovered, I am not a little girl."

Careful not to react in front of that black spot in the ceiling, Galkin whispered, "That was you, was it?"

Ellie winked while adding a subtle smile the closed-circuit camera could never catch.

"Do you know what is going to happen to me?" she pressed but received no answer.

"Are you taking me somewhere?" Her question prompted another discreet puff from Galkin's nose.

Her question, "Is it Sokolov?" prompted a second blast of air.

Ellie looked up toward the disguised camera to plead her argument. Galkin's stare remained fixed on her body.

"Is there any chance you could let me walk myself to wherever we're going?" Before anyone had a chance to not respond, Ellie added, "I'm sure Dema Zlovich would like to see me fresh for our meeting." Then, she turned to Galkin and continued in English, "If we're not going there, I guess it doesn't matter where you dump my body."

Deep laughter erupted from her captor as he slapped both hands on the table, knocking the remaining two blueberry pancakes onto the floor. "Inessa Ivanovna," he said through bellyaching amusement, "I will escort the Nickerson woman to her event with discretion."

"As you wish, Oleg Ivanovich."

Ellie forced a broad smile at the silence that flooded the diner.

"You will wait here," Galkin said before getting up and exiting through the kitchen door.

Ellie flashed an "okay" sign as her captor disappeared into the void of the Surgut facility. She was careful not to look up at the camera while studying the studio for something she had missed before.

"There is nothing that identifies this place," she murmured while humming the chilling orchestral score that had haunted her mind for the past several months. The Temptations drowned her disappointment set to the tune of Prokofiev's cantata.

Galkin returned in a matter of minutes, carrying a white cotton satchel.

"That's some real cloak-and-dagger stuff, Oleg Ivanovich."

"We cannot let you inspect our facility, Eleanor." Presenting the two options was laughable. She preferred the sack over Grigory's moment of serenity, smiling as she stood and extended her arm to accept the gift.

"Thank you, Oleg." She winked. Galkin did not have the smooth complexion of a young man. His skin had aged beyond its years by hard work and the persistence of cruel Siberian winters. Regardless, when Ellie told the story to Michael Yao, she remained convinced he blushed at that moment.

She took a step toward Galkin and collapsed under the weight of her body. He was close enough to snatch her before she dropped to the black-and-white checkerboard tile floor.

"Oh," she said while wrapping her arms around Galkin's waist. "It has been a while since I did my own walking." The sight of the heavy felt-lined boots on her feet brought a chuckle. "These would look cute in white; don't you think?" Still holding onto Galkin, Ellie extended one leg to expose her muscular calf muscle and dark caramel skin while one hand gently caressed the extra pounds built up in his waist.

He could not take his eyes off her leg, even as he explained, "We will get you a winter coat before leaving. It is very cold outside."

"There," she said, stomping both feet onto the floor in a sudden display of confidence. "I am good, now." Standing eye-to-eye with Galkin, she had one last plea delivered with insincere puppy-dog eyes. "Will you hold me close so that I do not fall again?"

He swelled his chest. "Of course."

"Thank you," Ellie cooed as she reached for the cotton sack to pull over her head. "This will be very difficult to do."

"I will protect you."

The two made their way through the capture room waiting area. Inessa Ivanovna led them through the winding halls of the Surgut facility. All Ellie could see was the blinding white of the cotton material cloaked over her, but the bustling facility flooded her ears with curious sounds. "Step forward" and "Wait here" were commonly heard, as was the familiar sound of the diner's kitchen door latch. At one point, Galkin gave instructions for Ellie to step with care. His booming voice was almost loud enough to mask the soft whimpering coming from a young boy. When the child's cries faded away, the two continued in silence. Ellie walked with care, keeping one arm wrapped around Galkin's waist, caressing his side.

"Are we almost there?"

"We are close. I can remove your hood when we leave the building."

"Good. The plastic smell in this hood is starting to make me sick. What is it used for, Oleg?"

"They hold your SCARS devices before we use them for production."

Her subtle gasp was Ellie's last sound before they exited the Surgut Capture Facility.

Chapter 22

Smug satisfaction overwhelmed Oleksandr
Nikolaevich Volkov when he began turning patrons
away early in the afternoon. For the most part, his
customers were happy to return for a complimentary
dinner the next day.

"My apologies, comrade. Our restaurant has been
reserved for a special event this evening that is very
important for our country."

One particular individual, probably not
accustomed to hearing the word "No," refused to
accept Volkov's explanation. The short, portly man
whispered into the ear of his stunning companion.

"Wait here one moment, darling." He kissed her
cheek before leaving her in the entryway and went to
talk in private with the owner.

With his arm wrapped over Volkov's shoulder, the
man shared a desperate plea. "Oleksandr
Nikolaevich, I have very little time away from my
busy schedule." He then reached into his pocket to
grab a wad of cash. "Will one hundred thousand
rubles show that some men are more important to
you than petty visitors from beyond Surgut?" He
pushed the cash into the restaurateur's gut while
arching his toes to peer into the restaurant. He
noticed a dark-skinned woman, but the five people
taking their seats at the one table set deep in the
room were much too far to identify.

Volkov grasped the man's hand, guiding the
money back into his pocket.

"Semyon Iosifovich," he said with an icy stare, "one man is more important than the petty rubles found here in Surgut."

The man turned and snatched his beautiful friend by her arm to make their way out of the restaurant. They exchanged no other words except for a request by Volkov. "Please wish your wife the best from me when you see her again, comrade."

Shivers from the harsh weather swarmed Ellie as she took her seat, the first to do so. Galkin's concern was genuine when he asked, "Are you still cold?"

"I'm fine, Oleg, but thank you. It is nice and warm in here, so I just need to let myself warm up."

Sokolov waited for Ellie to pull her chair in before taking his seat on the opposite end of the table. Medvedev followed suit and claimed his spot at Sokolov's right hand while Popov then Galkin sat to the left. Ellie's eyes widened as she inventoried the lavish table setting.

"Do you have a preference for the dinner music?" were Sokolov's first words.

"I have always been partial to Ponchielli," she said, never taking her eyes away from her host. The slight insult had no effect on Sokolov. Instead, he turned his head toward Galkin and crooked his neck toward the kitchen. Galkin directed the restaurant staff to pipe in an opera from the Italian composer.

Volkov's staff did not serve wine during the meal, instead presenting a generous selection of Baltic teas throughout the first four courses. No one spoke a word as Sokolov sat lost in the simple dishes locals preferred rather than over-seasoned dishes treated as delicacies. The former lab coats picked at each serving while they darted their eyes across both ends of the table. Unlike those three, who each had a different reason for their troubled anticipation, Ellie and Sokolov devoured generous portions of dumplings, porridge, pirozhkis, and a cold stew made with chunks of ham and mixed vegetables. It was a matter of who would choose to go first, but Sokolov had the advantage in almost every category. Careful consideration preceded Ellie's first question.

Before servers presented the fifth course, she pressed, "Where is Andy Barnett?"

Dabbing the corners of his mouth with an ivory cotton napkin, Sokolov waited an uncomfortable amount of time before sharing his response.

"Is it customary in the United States to be so rude as not saying thank you when someone saves your life?"

"When that someone tries to kill you in the first place, I would say yes."

Sokolov rearranged his remaining flatware. Without looking up, he chuckled, "Yet here you are. Quite alive and healthy!"

A slap of her hand on the table startled the three onlookers as Ellie repeated her question. "Where is Andy Barnett?" Galkin leaned in to caution her on that tone of voice.

"Hush," Sokolov demanded before turning his attention back to Ellie. His tone subdued. "Your little soldier boy is quite dead."

She held a shallow breath that did not deny the accusation but pulled both hands above the yellow rose tablecloth as she said, "And what do you plan to do next?" She watched Sokolov pull a black disc out of the pocket of his cotton twill shirt.

"Do you know who I am?"

"The intelligence brief I read on the flight to Europe said your name is Dema Zlovich Sokolov."

"The rumor is," he said while reaching forward to place the disc in front of his setting, "that if someone experiences another person's death in this world that you created, the thrill also kills them." Ellie turned her head away from her friend's lasting memory while refuting the myth.

"Neither one of those accusations is true."

Medvedev, Popov, and Galkin all shared the same confused expression, yet Sokolov pressed for an explanation.

"Are you saying that the goddess herself, Eleanor Nickerson, did not create Sensations?"

Ellie turned to face Sokolov. "I am not a god." She delivered her reply without emotion or inflection, both hands idle in her lap.

"In my world," Sokolov said, "I am God."

He lifted one arm in the air and flicked its palm upward, commanding the staff to serve their fifth course. Sizzled skewers of cubed goat meat filled the room with opposing smells of savory oils, paprika, and seared flesh. As the server placed a kebab on Ellie's plate, droplets from the meat made a vile hissing sound when they struck the cast-iron skillet's hot surface and stained the cloth dark when blood-red juices fell to the table. Once the task was complete, he continued.

"I have no concern for the world beyond my rule." Ellie stared without reaction as Sokolov devoured his shashlik, then reached across the table with his fork to spear another skewer. With a rapid shake, it slid off the fork and crashed onto his plate, where he sliced the goat meat and began to wolf down sizable chunks.

Demands to know "What do you want?" and "What are you going to do with me?" went unanswered, as did Ellie's attempt to bargain with ransom money. Only when she became curious did Sokolov take a break from his feast.

"Where do our worlds collide?"

Garbled words poured from Medvedev while he reached down to the space between him and his boss, returning with a laptop computer. He opened the screen, unveiling the beautiful shower of computer code Ellie had given to everyone, even the evil men holding her.

"We have a list of features my team wants to add to Dema Zlovich's Sensations," Medvedev said. He pulled a computer printout of comments from his pocket, placing it to the side. "But first, we want to see the technical specifications for the version you created with the US Army."

Before Ellie had a chance to spin her lie that she did not have a military version, Sokolov wiped a spot of blood and gristle from the corner of his mouth before pressing the black disc on the table. She fought to keep half of her awareness in the restaurant while her senses took notice of another majestic setting of pampering.

"Let her sit while we enjoy the rest of our dinner," she heard.

I can't wait to tell Grigory about this wonderful experience. I hope he is having a great time.

While both heels of the masseuse's palms kneaded her sore, aching muscles, Ellie thought, *Is this Natascha? Can you hear me, girl? Grigory is well. He is safe. You will see him soon.* She hoped one day, after her ordeal was over, to meet the happy Russian couple she had spent so much time with.

What is that for?

Piqued by fear, Ellie savored Natascha's bliss as powerful hands slipped heated strips of cloth across their chest, the friction tingling sensitive flesh.

"Wake up! Please, don't let him do this." Her pleas were ignored as sensual gasps welcomed every added binding. He wrapped weighted coils over her quivering stomach, up between her legs, across her arms and neck, broadcasting their intent. Ellie was powerless to stop the pleasures she hoped would never end.

I want this.

"I need this to stop."

That's too warm. It's too tight.

Ellie struggled to push away the moments Natascha endured when someone pulled the top cloth away, exposing heated coils that lashed tight into her flesh and seared through the outer layers of skin. She lived an explosion of screams bursting from her lungs as Ellie's mind fought to reject the idea that any pain was her own.

I can't wait to tell Grigory about this wonderful experience. I hope he is having a great time.

While both heels of the masseuse's palms kneaded the emotion from her aching muscles, Ellie thought, *My God, Natascha. Please wake up! Where are you? I'll get Grigory.*

Sixty-one...

Ellie struggled to suppress the orgasmic ripples she welcomed and the suffering she knew would follow.

Seventy-three...

"Concentrate, Natascha. Concentrate."

That's too warm. It's too tight.

"What are you thinking, my love?" she heard him say.

"What was that, Oleg Ivanovich?" Galkin turned toward Sokolov, who appeared irritated by the first word in four courses of Russian desserts.

"I, uh, Dema Zlovich. I was wondering if we should recover the Nickerson woman." He pointed to her serving. "She may become more pleasant with a slice of this delicious Praga cake." He drove his fork through layers of rich chocolate and vanilla buttercream frosting, stuffing a hunk of sponge cake into his mouth.

Twelve feet of separation was too much for Sokolov to notice the tear that had developed in Ellie's right eye. He tapped his finger on the table while inspecting her mannequin stare.

"Hmmm."

Numb to the pain but disgusted by hissing sounds Natascha's blood made when it touched the binding coil, she watched Medvedev nod when his boss turned for his opinion. With the unspoken approval, he deactivated the last of seven used discs collected on the table. Nothing changed for Ellie, but Natascha was no longer there. She could not control the shaking in her legs, yet her appearance above the table remained fixed until the feeling that she would throw up passed.

"Is that your plan?" Ellie picked up her fork and threw it on the floor like a resistant toddler. "Are you going to pass me off to your vile Sensations whenever I say or do something that displeases you?"

"If I must," he vowed, turning his cake in search of its most appealing side, "but I prefer that we work together in partnership." He grabbed an eighth disc from his briefcase. "The choice is up to you."

"You're fucking insane if..." were the last words Sokolov heard from Ellie. He activated the disc before tossing it into the center, then rose from the table after instructing Popov to get their car.

"I want you to talk with her and review my expectations."

Medvedev nodded his head as he stood with an extended hand. They both turned to watch Galkin wipe the side of Ellie's face with his napkin.

"He is close with the girl," Sokolov whispered. Galkin was having a pleasant one-sided conversation with Ellie over how he would keep her safe and get her back to the facility.

"Oleg Ivanovich has been her primary caretaker for most of the time."

"Use that."

Galkin smiled as he told Ellie he would bring her to a room with a very comfortable bed that night. His words filled her with joy even as the massaging coils first turned their sensual pleasure into Natascha's nightmare that played out once more.

"If he gets too close and fails us, Oleg Ivanovich will become another horror for the Nickerson girl to experience firsthand."

Chapter 23

Leonard Powell was already frazzled, then everything turned upside down while inventorying critical assets for Nickerson Enterprises. Sandy urged him to "get someone else to do the job while you are acting CEO until Ellie gets back," but he went ahead with the task, insisting the time spent would help him keep his other thoughts at bay. Any resale of obsolete equipment, outdated computer servers, and office furniture was put on hold for fear that a purge might give outsiders the wrong impression about their expectations for Ellie's return. Of course, it was no surprise to him when everything was properly accounted for and in optimal condition.

Without knocking, he burst into the conference room and slapped his clipboard flat in front of Danette. The bottom of his pressed shirt had pulled out of his trousers on three sides. Sweat dripped past his cuffs onto papers on the once-organized tabletop.

"Governor, I apologize. I think my boss is having a moment right now." It took four more nods of her head, two "uh-huhs" and three "yes, sirs" before she could hang up the phone. "I hope you realize we just added about two hundred litigation hours to our Illinois state tax countersuit."

All Leonard could do was tap his finger on the inventory checklist while he caught his breath.

"I was checking out," he wheezed, "the sandbox."

"And?"

Leonard gulped heaping servings of air rather than respond to Danette's indifference.

"The sandbox is live." He described the mystical shower of green and amber lights that speckled Ellie's mysterious server farm. Abnormal heat output triggered the backup cooling system as temperatures in the room spiked past 105 degrees.

Danette gestured to pull more information from a man burdened with too many words trying to come out of his mouth all at once.

"Is it Ellie?" She popped from her chair.

All Leonard could do was raise his eyebrows and shrug his shoulders as he choked on another obscene mouthful of air.

"When did it start?"

The only improvement was the addition of a slow shake of his head to the drama.

Danette dropped back into her chair and demanded, "Jesus Christ, Leonard, calm the fuck down and tell me who is pulling data from our servers."

Thirty seconds later, he had enough control to carry on.

"No one is pulling anything. All the traffic is coming in."

"All of it."

"One hundred percent. Someone's writing straight into her database."

Chapter 24

The replica was unrecognizable. Leaving Melissa
Barnett behind, a soldier stood in her place dressed
in a tan, gray, and green pixelated combat uniform,
with captain rank and a nametag that read
HIGHLAND. Her striking blue eyes had reverted to an
equally remarkable shade of forest green. Braided
locks of jet-black hair, once tucked under a blonde
wig, fell to the blades of her shoulders. She knocked
twice on the office door before entering. The room
remained as barren as the day some unnamed
company had rented the space three months before.
General Drew sat behind an executive desk, a cheap
laminate leave-behind from the previous tenant. He
was busy on the phone detailing progress reports
that added up to nothing. Still, she motioned for him
to hang up.

"Sir, we have activity on our Sensations feed." It
was the first sign of anything since the assault on
Captain Hofer and Ellie's plane in October. Drew
kept his mouth shut, giving his full attention to the
young officer.

"At 1653 Zulu, my team detected an anomaly in
their SCARS feedback while conducting an AAR on a
current mission training block." She laid out pictures
of three operators. Two sat in the back of a utility
helicopter, dressed in full combat gear. The third was
the personnel file photo of a young soldier wearing
his pink and greens. Drew ran his fingers across the
baby-face image as Highland continued, "Staff
Sergeants Morales and Blake were analyzing the

capture of a casualty evacuation scenario when Specialist Scott transmitted GPS coordinates to them."

Before Drew could jump in with, "Who the hell is Specialist Scott?" the captain spread two additional pictures on top of the pile. A destroyed vehicle was in the first photo. Burned beyond recognition, its remnants were scattered along an unpaved road that ran through barren desert land. "Scott received life-threatening injuries when his convoy struck an IED buried in that road in Niger this past November." Her finger remained pressed into the wreckage. "He was wired for SCARS. We've been sending most troops outside the wire with capture devices for some time now."

"Why was this one different?"

Highland described Scott's heroic efforts when, despite his devastating injuries, he dragged three of his squad mates through forty feet of debris and burning oil. He pulled each soldier to safety one by one, hampered by two shattered ankles and muscles he didn't realize were torn until the medical recovery team cut the mangled uniform away from his body.

"Scott's Sensations will be a training standard for years to come," she said. "Evaluating and prioritizing casualties for relocation to a safe distance was nothing short of perfect."

Drew pulled the photo of Scott to the top of the pile, once again drawn to the young man's angelic expression. "Amazing grit."

Captain Highland brushed the general's hand away from those pictures, drawing his attention to the fifth and final shot.

"Sir, this is a lat-long overlay of the incident site." It had a thin grid square imprinted over the same black-and-white photo, taken from a height of about one thousand feet. "Both Morales and Blake reported that they, and I'm quoting here, 'heard Specialist Scott give precise coordinates to this location,'" she said while tapping the destroyed vehicle's center mass.

Drew rattled his brain for clarity, then pressed, "What do you mean *heard*? Sensations doesn't record voices."

"I know, I know." She threw her hands up and turned to pace the room before shooting back to the general's desk. "I said the same thing. So, I evaluated the clip myself."

The two officers stared each other down. One, not sure if they wanted to hear the answer. The other, afraid to confirm the impossible.

"The initial blast destroyed all communication and navigation equipment. Scott never had a position marker." Highland never blinked when she shoved the truth in front of her boss. "That kid had no idea where he was, but we got it off his feed. Perfect fucking coordinates, down to the fourth decimal."

General Drew stood and walked to the window. He welcomed his limp, aggravated by the weather, since he needed the distraction. "The last I remember cold like this was back in '04," he said, pressing both hands deep into his thigh. "That's when I got this trophy." He chuckled at the words "Operation Mountain Storm." Then, shifting his attention to the outside, Drew watched as cars, trucks, SUVs, and people battled to control the busy city intersection. The only winners were ice and snow, scattering vehicles up on the curb or into each other as pedestrians fought losing struggles to stay on their feet. Watching the mess created, he continued, "Geotagging on a SCARS capture. That was a capability Ellie told us would not happen. Now, it's in production on the Special Operations Sensations feed."

"No, sir, it's not."

The twist didn't catch Drew by surprise. Instead, he kept his attention on the comical struggles five stories below.

"It's not in the code..."

"...and hasn't happened before or since," he finished her sentence.

"Correct."

Drew filled in any blanks with the captain.

"I assume Specialist Scott cannot confirm your theory," he said without turning from the window.

She confirmed his hunch with a sigh. "Scott died two weeks after the blast."

Drew turned and twitched his eyebrows.

"Scenarios?"

Highland offered three plausible reasons. The first, "Programming error," was doubtful for a variety of reasons but always a possibility. Next, she explored how someone manipulating the code from within Nickerson Enterprises was the likely candidate.

"Or it's her," was offered with no other debate. "She showed us a capability that does not exist, only to prove to us she does."

"Well, Abby, it seems you already have the next steps planned," he said while grabbing the wrinkled collar of his black cotton polo. "Let me get changed so we can go upstairs to introduce ourselves."

Chapter 25

"You can take your hood off now, Ellie."

Dancing butterflies dressed in top hats and tails adorned all four rose-colored walls. Ellie gazed at the stencil drawings, then admired the brass candelabra chandelier hanging in the center of the spacious room. Each of the six bulbs gave off its unique pastel glow that combined into a rich mix, tinting everything in the child's bedroom.

"How do they say it in English?" Galkin entered and waved both hands in front of his body in the most awkward display of entertainment. "Ta-da!"

Ellie forced a smirk from her sagging cheeks. She tried to praise his excitement, saying, "That's right, Oleg. Ta-da," but the words trailed off into a hushed murmur. The soft, probably white, bed comforter was a stage set for the random collection of stuffed animals and fruit. Two jet-black gorillas wrestled for the banana that stitched them together. Ellie picked up the pair and stroked their wiry hair. The kaleidoscopic lighting made it difficult to identify the dried stain on one of the apes, but it flaked away when she rubbed it between her fingers.

"What kind of horrors happened in this room?"

"Nothing, nothing." Instead, Galkin's lie described his effort to create a "brand-new room just for you, so you can have a good sleep now that you are healthy."

"Come, sit." He nudged her frame down to the bed. "Feel how soft it is."

Ellie reached up and caressed his hand, sliding each finger between his until her grip coaxed him down to her side. Startled by her touch, he avoided eye contact and shied his head away from her stare.

"I'm scared, Oleg," she whispered when her cheek came to rest on his shoulder. "I'm scared."

Galkin patted the rough cotton material covering her knee, careful not to bend his fingers around her flesh as he closed his eyes and took in her scent.

"Dema Zlovich is a very reasonable man. Very smart. He will let you go home if you just give him what he wants."

Her voice softened to a childish whimper when she asked Galkin, "What happened to her?"

"Happened to who?"

"Natascha. The woman from my dreams."

His mouth gaped wide, but no words escaped. Ellie pressed for an answer.

"Is she dead?"

Galkin leaped from the bed just as the door latch slid open from the outside. "Hush." His nervous words garbled something about how that was just silliness. Medvedev entered, dressed in a white lab coat. He brought a laptop computer and a burlap tote bag filled with computer printouts, placing them both on a simple wooden desk set in the corner.

"Oleg Ivanovich, I want you to complete the daily report of today's production." He motioned for Ellie to come and sit at the desk. Galkin exchanged confused glances with her but nodded his head, urging her to comply.

"Is Alexander Sergeyevich not available to complete his tasks?"

Deep sighs held Medvedev hostage for a moment before he continued to arrange the papers in front of Ellie.

"Dema Zlovich and I had a brief conversation with the former director about the facility's lack of discipline. We have confidence that you," he said after turning to look at Galkin, "will not make the same mistakes."

Galkin snapped his spine straight and vowed, "Of course, comrade. I will get right on it." With a pathetic look meant to urge Ellie to "hang in there," he made his way to the exit.

"First," Medvedev instructed the new Surgut Capture Facility director, "check to see that Popov's out-processing is handled correctly. He is in Room 6."

Galkin promised to comply "at once" and raced out of Capture Room 5. His last glance into the room just caught Ellie's subtle wink.

"Miss Nickerson," Medvedev said when they were finally alone together, "I have a list of what you will provide us."

Ellie surveyed the harmless-looking fellow, starting with the stray hairs curling at the top of his balding head down to the fine stitching of Napa leather loafers that didn't seem to be his style. When she stood, she towered over him by at least eight inches.

"If you're done staring, can you give me the list?"

Snapping from his trance, Medvedev lifted his eyes away from her breasts and winced almost apologetically as he knocked over the sheets of paper. He struggled to bend and pick them up, returning the pile to a replica of what it looked like before his fumbling. He gave up and continued with the demands.

"Dema Zlovich and I will return to the facility in three days. We expect to review your progress at that time." His accidental step crinkled the top paper, and a small drool stain smeared the handwritten notes. Ellie swiped the sheet with her palm and sat at the toddler-sized desk, aware that he continued to stare down the scoop line of her peasant dress. She fished around the bag for something to write with until Medvedev pulled a pen from the pocket of his lab coat.

"Thanks, um." She cocked her head to the side, asked, "What's your name?" and began to review the list of Sensations demands.

He swelled his chest almost as far as his stomach protruded, then tucked his jowls and boasted, "Mikael Petrovych Medvedev. I am the coordinator of everything you see."

In English, Ellie mumbled how she "hadn't seen much of the dump" as she kept her head down and scribbled several notes before handing the pen back to Medvedev.

"Here's the deal, Michael." She flashed the paper against his nose while she stood and talked as fast as her Russian words would take her. "You win. I get that. I do this for you," she proposed, "and you let me go home."

Taking the sheet from her hand, the *Coordinator of Everything She Saw* seemed puzzled by her demands.

"What makes you think you have a say in the matter?" His eyes fought to stay locked with hers but flickered twice down to her breasts.

"Nothing." Ellie threw her hands in the air. "But if you want Sensations to continue working, you will see that I am returned to the United States by February 25. If not," her fingers balled into fists and dropped into her lap, "it all goes away." The bogus threat had no effect until her closed hand spread open like a starburst. She murmured, "*Chernaya magiya*," and watched as he stared off into a lifeless gaze. He seemed to want to dismiss her prediction but did not know if it was true, so she pressed. "What is today's date?"

Ellie accepted the response, "We will consider your proposal," expecting a follow-up after the little man's next meeting with Sokolov.

"Great," she said. She pointed to the paper and insisted, "Try and keep your eyes here for a second. I don't have a project with the US Army, so I scratched all that out." Overwhelmed by her pace, Medvedev remained frozen as she rattled off, "I can do one, three, four, and seven. The others all failed in development." Ellie tapped on the desk surface. "I need Internet access, blank capture-and-release devices, a private bathroom, and some healthy meats and vegetables for my diet." She smirked, enjoying the sight of her oppressor hunched over the desk, scrambling to write her flurry of demands.

When he reached back to massage the pain building in his back, she added, "And a desk that was not built for a six-year-old." Mere minutes of smug satisfaction triumphed over months of captivity and torment. Already frustrated, Medvedev was irritated by soft pastel rays when he arched his aching spine and looked at Ellie.

"We will replace those light bulbs," he said, then folded the paper twice before slipping it into the hip pocket of his lab coat. "No Internet" was his nonnegotiable display of authority.

Ellie pled, "I just want to go home." With an outreached hand, she tilted her eyes downward. "Partners, Mikael Petrovych?"

Superiority returned to his flabby chest and bloated jowls. He left the room without a handshake but did mutter something that sounded like, "Agreed." Ellie looked around the room, again silent except for the faint puff of air that flowed through vents along the baseboard. She offered a quick wave toward the camera perched high in the far corner before taking a seat and opening the laptop.

The computer clock read February 10, 2023.

"Fuck."

Chapter 26

Disjointed words filled three pages of notes Danette jotted on her legal pad.

"So, you're the famous Zachary Drew that Ellie always talks about?"

The general leaned forward, resting his elbows on the conference table, and quipped, "I guess you were expecting someone taller."

"At least twelve feet," she said before flicking her pen in the air to free her hands so they could yank on clumps of her dirty-blonde hair. For the last half hour, Drew and Captain Highland had shared about Eleanor Nickerson's secret relationship with the US Army Special Operations Command.

"And Andy Barnett was actually this Kenneth Hofer soldier?" The general's nod confirmed Leonard's question. "Jesus Christ, his family."

Highland slid a front-page article from The Boyarstown Gazette in front of the two stunned civilians. It read: LOCAL HERO LAID TO REST. "Captain Hofer was buried in his hometown with full military honors after he died in a tragic helicopter training accident."

Danette's swipe of tears left black mascara streaks across her left cheek.

"And you think this Sokolov guy is responsible for his death?"

"We don't know," Drew admitted.

"And he may still hold Ellie?"

"We don't know," Drew repeated.

"And he knows what happened to Owen?"

Drew hung his head. "Again, we don't know."

Kaylee Morris popped her head toward the conference room from the other side of the office when she heard Danette scream at two soldiers dressed in fatigues.

"Then, why the fuck did you pick now to come and pay us a visit?"

Her anger, which had boiled over in an instant, vanished the moment Drew responded.

"We think she sent us a message through Sensations."

Rewritten code. GPS coordinates. Server hack. Development sandbox. Military operations.

While Leonard shared details of the incident earlier that week, Danette reached to the floor, picked up the ballpoint pen, and continued adding nonsense to her list of incoherent sentences.

Chapter 27

February 13, 2023

A gentle knock paved the way for Galkin to press on the unlatched door, creating a slip only his gentle words could pass through. Before he finished asking, "Ellie, may I enter?" she welcomed him into her cell. For only the second time, she saw him wearing a white lab coat.

"I am almost ready," she said, catching his awkward gaze while her fingers crept the zipper of the stonewashed jeans up to the button. "There! How do I look?" Ellie extended both arms outward and twirled in place to give him a complete look at her body. He was speechless and blushed as bright as her red polo shirt when she said, "I guess you're still not used to seeing me with my clothes on." However, her subtle wink seemed to relax him a bit. It always did.

"They are ready for us."

After two more quick bites from an apple she had picked from the wicker basket resting on top of a stainless-steel service cart, she buckled her knees a bit, rolled her eyes, and said, "Okay, I'm ready." Galkin grabbed the laptop and attaché case from the sleek iron computer workstation and then followed Ellie out of the room. When they entered the first corridor, she turned back and said, "My ass can barely fit into these jeans these days, but thank you for getting my old clothes." Galkin seemed to have lost the power of speech as she ran her finger along the Nickerson Enterprises stitching across her breast, so she kept talking to fill the dead air.

"I'm glad you finally let me walk to the bathroom by myself," she reached up to pinch her nose, "because that hood stunk so bad." She could never enter any of the capture rooms and only spoke with subjects she used for her SCARS development.

When she turned in to the hallway that led to a conference room, Ellie looked back. "Did Alexander Sergeyevich really play for the Olympic hockey team?"

"That is what he always bragged about," Galkin grumbled, only to smile when Ellie turned her body and crouched into a face-off position. She stared into his eyes while swiping the imaginary puck past his sloppy defense.

"That's so cool!" She dropped her stick and poked him in the belly in jest. "But, nothing compared to loading those big containers onto ships." She looked down, pretending to concentrate. "Where did you work? Vlad-is-top?"

He shook his head. "No, no. Vladivostok."

"Vladivostok."

"Very good."

Ellie bounced on her toes and giggled with excitement. "Vladivostok! When we have dinner tonight, will you tell me more stories about growing up in Russia?" But Galkin only frowned at her girlish charm.

"I don't know what Dema Zlovich will want to do tonight."

Her elation faded as she asked, "Should I be worried?"

He stared into the echoes of that frightened woman who had endured countless hours experiencing the Sensations of Sokolov's graphic horror.

"Give him what he wants," Galkin assured her, "and he will let you have what you need."

With a disturbing scowl, Ellie tipped her head once to confirm his advice before she vowed, "I will give him everything he deserves," overpronouncing every word. She resumed the behavior of a defeated woman while Galkin rehearsed his introduction three times before opening the door.

"Comrades," he announced, "I present Miss Eleanor Nickerson."

Unpainted drywall panels sectioned off part of the facility warehouse for that day's presentation. Instead of a ceiling with fixed lighting, floodlights hanging from the corrugated sheet-metal roof high above filled the room with that familiar harsh glow. Ellie spotted Sokolov and Medvedev. They sat in two of the five folding metal chairs arranged in a semicircle around the front of the room. A lab coat she did not recognize sat next to them. The last two chairs in the arc were empty, intended for Galkin and herself. A young man and woman sat in the middle on an elevated stage. They remained still, staring at an empty back wall. Her breathing was quick and shallow while he fidgeted with the jacket zipper on his matching red tracksuit pants pocket.

With no introductions, Sokolov declared, "Our friends have volunteered to evaluate your Sensations improvements." He never looked back at Ellie. "Do not waste any more of my time."

"Yes, Dema Zlovich," she rushed her words while stumbling past the two empty chairs, mumbling "Hello" to the nervous couple, then posting herself behind a small folding table. Galkin followed and laid out her computer and a small paper bag. Three stacks of paper were a mix of printouts and handwritten notes, dog-eared and highlighted with four separate colors.

Tedious displays of nervousness and confusion wasted several minutes. Finally, Ellie repositioned her materials and stepped to the side of the table before debating whether to cross her arms in front or let them hang at her side. With a surprised, "Oh," she stepped back behind the table and pulled eight black discs from the bag. As she struggled to align them in perfect order, Medvedev leaned over to his boss and whispered in a not-so-subtle tone.

"How long do you want me to let this foolishness go on?" His words seemed to echo throughout the entire warehouse, which was silent except for faint sounds of workers making their way through the hallway maze. Operations were on hold during their scheduled time.

Sokolov waved off the need to take any action. "It is obvious that she is not a very competent speaker. Give her time." He pulled a disc from his shirt pocket and pointed it in Ellie's direction as he assured Medvedev, "If she does not respond as obedient cattle should, I will strike her with this special charge of motivation."

Ellie stopped any further meddling with her material.

"My apologies, Dema Zlovich."

Her final decision was behind the table with both arms crossed in front of her body.

"I am going to assume that Mikael Petrovych reviewed the capabilities I am not able to provide."

With the disc placed back in his pocket, Sokolov grunted his understanding. Ellie tilted her head downward in humble submission.

"I think you will be quite happy," she said as a smile formed, "with something I have been trying to perfect for more than a year." Galkin and Medvedev leaned forward in their chairs, but it was not until Ellie declared, "multiple Sensations recipients on a single stream," that Sokolov finally showed signs of anticipation. He jumped on his desire to know more.

"How many simultaneous releases?"

"Right now, I can only do two. But," she teased, "I should have that number increased to seven before tomorrow afternoon." Sokolov scribbled notes on the pad he pulled from the attaché case by his side.

"Show me."

"At once, Dema Zlovich," she said, moving forward before anyone could ask important questions. Swiping a finger across the eight SCARS release discs, she explained, "I prepared a meditation exercise to use as a demonstration." Ready for her next step, Galkin rushed to the stage and grabbed four copies of handwritten notes to distribute. "Oleg

Ivanovich is giving you a copy of the emotions I intend to reproduce in our subjects here." After he handed out three of the copies and took his seat, Ellie gave them a moment to review the eight-page document. "We can stop the two-hour exercise anytime you prefer, Dema Zlovich. You can then ask the subjects any questions you would like to evaluate my Sensations capture." She gave him time to review the material, comforted by the slow, constant nods of approval as they scanned her work.

Without waiting for the other three, Sokolov rested the papers on his lap with his notepad on the top. "Very good, Miss Nickerson." He looked over at Medvedev and waited for his obligatory agreement.

"I agree, Dema Zlovich. This will be a glorious victory for you."

Galkin was the only one who noticed Ellie's cynical huff. He remained silent.

With Sokolov's directive, "Proceed," she noted the time on her laptop. It was 10:08.

"Everything will be okay," she assured the couple while pressing the first release disc. Waves of serenity overcame the recipients of her prototype.

I cannot move. I do not want to see. There is nothing else that I can feel. There is nothing else I want.

They agreed with her sentiment because her thoughts and emotions were their own. Ellie held her breath as she scanned the classroom. The Russian couple sat lost in a captivating world created in her mind, joined by Galkin, the lab coat, and Medvedev. She stepped off the stage and stood in front of

Sokolov, but he did not want to see her. He didn't react when she poked her finger in the center of his forehead because there was nothing else that he could feel. There was nothing else he wanted.

I want to share what I know about Dema Zlovich Sokolov, this disgraceful imitation of a man who thinks of himself as both the creator and destroyer.

Confident she had subdued everyone in the room, Ellie rushed to the exit and pressed her ear up against the door. The expected silence was incentive enough to move forward with her plan. Three lab coats stood motionless in the hallway. She stepped out and approached them without incident. They remained lost in three identical versions of her experience.

He fancies himself a god, but like the mythical Poseidon, he only rules over an empty void, not like the other, more powerful gods he dismisses as unworthy. He lives in the dark world of illicit Sensations, the only place where his rule is absolute.

She retraced her steps taken during those frequent bathroom breaks, then re-created the pace count of her hooded escort through the facility. Ellie made her way to the main entrance. Her first setback was crushing when she realized the Surgut facility had no phones. None of the computers connected to the Internet.

"How the fuck am I supposed to get in contact with anyone?"

She ransacked the break room before considering going back to find Sokolov's phone.

"There's no time."

Maybe I should have pity on him. He was born in the dirt of Chelyabinsk, Russia, the industrialized city of World War II turned depressed by 1971, as the Soviet war machine appetite depleted the city's usefulness. He was raised in poverty there with his mother, father, and younger sister until 1978. Sokolov's parents abandoned him on the streets when his sister died from disease. From that day forward, they were all dead to him.

Icy blasts of Siberian winter forced her back inside the moment she exited. Luck was on her side, a gift from a lab coat about her size who had just stepped into the facility. With no resistance, she stripped his parka and zipped herself up. A key fob in the pocket sent her rushing outside to search for the car. No one felt the need to close the door she left open. As blowing snow piled onto the desks and several noses, the workers shared in the extract of Sokolov's imagery.

Crime and violence kept Sokolov alive. But, more so, they gave him life and purpose. He was a strong worker, tending to menial jobs as entertainment for local criminals. He quickly turned into a loyal page, then a trusted soldier.

Ellie scrambled across the parking lot, clicking on the fob in desperation until the distinct chirp captured her attention. She shouted an exuberant "Yes" while hopping into the black sedan that was still warm from the lab coat's arrival. When she pressed the start button, a digital dashboard clock lit up, reading 10:16.

Sokolov rose in the ranks of an old Soviet vory v zakone criminal organization. They peddled in prostitution and drugs, weaving their way through a violent world with no permanent footing. He was a trusted lieutenant to Grigory Chubais, who wanted nothing to do with the "foolish games" of manufacturing. He gave permission to Sokolov to branch out on his own in exchange for a fifteen percent cut. Too weak to do the job himself, Sokolov had Chubais murdered for no other reason than that he did not want to share power with anyone.

Sokolov's biography was a combination of military intelligence briefings, dinnertime conversations with Galkin, and her creative imagination. Narrating the piece gave Ellie a chance to fill every SCARS release recipient with her peaceful reflection on a boy who turned to crime because he had nothing else. Surgut's Capture Facility was silenced and stripped of emotion. When she pulled out of the parking lot and onto the single-lane road dusted with snow, Ellie smiled while her mind replayed the story that was fast becoming fact to everyone in the facility.

When our worlds were poised to collide, he was very much in command of the global Sensations black market. The vory v zakone Sokolov controls has no formal name. They are soldiers who report to his lieutenants, who in turn report directly to him. Sokolov is aware of all details within his organization. He is a logistics mastermind who sweats every detail, ensuring near-perfect operational throughput.

"Come on, come on," Ellie sang nonstop as she edged deeper into the tall evergreen forest. Drifts of snow all but masked the highway markings. Visibility worsened and forced her to slow the car. She glanced at the clock, which read 10:20.

"Fuck."

With a stereotypical Russian build, Sokolov does not "look like a gangster." He appears clean-cut, but tattoos cover his entire body. The vory v zakone tattoos, those initiation marks, rites of passage, and secret badges of honor, tell his story when he undresses. They are not on his face but are noticeable around his neck, wrists, and hands when he is dressed.

Trails of smoke just past the next turn caused Ellie to bang on the steering wheel in celebration, convinced, "That's got to be a restaurant." As the clichéd image of a Russian tearoom grew larger, she rehearsed her appeal, hoping to soften her American accent.

"Hello. I am lost and trying to contact my friends. May I use your telephone or Internet connection?"

She parked the car in the lot and rehearsed one more time.

Sokolov has no vices. To him, they are signs of weakness that make a man vulnerable to whoever possesses the source. That is the reason he has never experienced his own horrendous creations. I am curious how he will react to my Sensations. Will he still be able to pretend that he is a man in front of his soldiers who now know the truth?

"Hello. I am lost and trying to contact my friends. May I use your telephone or Internet connection?" Ellie appeared worried but not frightened as she explained the situation to the man entering the restaurant. Semyon Iosifovich was by himself that evening.

This worm who claims he is God in his world has only one weakness: his family. His wife, Ksana, was a gift from Grigory Chubais, a reward for ten years of faithful service. But, she is only a vessel for his children, one girl and one boy. Sokolov will take care of her lavishly so that she may raise his children in a sprawling mansion built in the Pushkinsky District on the southern edge of St. Petersburg. They are far away from his criminal ventures, and he intends to keep it that way. For their security, Sokolov is only able to visit two or three times every year.

"My dear," he said. "What is a beautiful creature like you doing out on such a terrible night?"

Ellie fought back every natural reaction when the stranger slid his arm under hers. Instead, tears welled in her eyes. She pressed up against his obnoxious neon-green ski jacket. Without bending over, the best she could do was wrap her hands over his shoulder and belly as she cooed, "I think they might be in danger. I'm scared. Please help."

"Let me help you find somewhere safe."

I know that when the time comes, he will kill every person in this facility if it suits his greedy ambitions. He will destroy every innocent soul just as he did to Natascha and Grigory. I will not give him the chance to do that to me. I will leave today, but only to return and destroy the false god, Dema Zlovich Sokolov. You do not want to be here when that happens.

Every lab coat turned Ellie's version of reality into what they knew to be true. But, just as their minds embraced the fact that they would return and destroy the false god Dema Zlovich Sokolov, their arms twitched while the world scratched and hissed.

I want to share what I know about Dema Zlovich Sokolov, this disgraceful imitation of a man who thinks of himself as both the creator and destroyer.

From the passenger seat of Iosifovich's SUV, Ellie watched the clock tick past 10:23.

"What are you doing so far out in the country, little girl?" Showing little concern for the worsening weather, Iosifovich spent more time looking over Ellie than attending to the road. His erratic weaving almost sent the car into deep snowbanks several times.

"I don't know," she lied. "My friends brought me out here to travel with them while they are on a business trip."

"Who are your friends? I am a very important man in this area. I can help you find them."

Ellie smiled. "I don't know that either." She traced her fingers up across his arm and down his side. "If I can contact my agency, they can help me locate my friends." When Iosifovich snapped his head in her direction, she winked and pointed out toward the road. "Drive, silly boy."

"Where are you from? We do not see many Negro women in this part of our country."

Her response, "London," brought a smile to Iosifovich's face. When he reached across to rub her jeans, Ellie hiked the bottom of her parka for him to spread her legs just a bit. Such a welcoming invitation inspired him to creep his hand along the denim fabric covering her thigh.

With a newfound focus, he gripped the wheel with both hands while insisting, "We must hurry and get you safe, then." Ellie sighed and sat deep into the soft fabric. "Your friends must have spent a lot of money for you." He glanced over as she nodded her head. "They must not be disappointed."

Ellie gazed out the window as she reassured her savior, "You will be handsomely rewarded, comrade." She watched the trees wisp by, each needle of Siberian pines collecting a hefty mound of snow before brisk winds blew them clear only to collect again. Every minute increased her separation from the Surgut Capture Facility and brought her closer to home. When exhaustion finally overtook her body, Iosifovich heard her gentle moan, "Owen," as she drifted off to sleep.

Crime and violence kept Sokolov alive. But, more so, they gave him life and....

Sokolov's knockoff disposable release devices exceeded Nickerson Enterprises' competitor's Sensations failure rates when the third disc cut out and failed. Two hundred and thirteen lab coats and capture subjects awoke to the sudden realization of the pitiful excuse for the man known as Dema Zlovich Sokolov. Some found joy in their knowledge, while others feared the reprisal of a wounded dog. The transient subjects just questioned who Dema Zlovich was and why they knew so much about the man. Sokolov needed less than a moment to regain his awareness. Mournful reflections on his childhood led to protests that what he thought about himself was just not true. All those feelings faded as he blew into a rage and rushed the stage, smashing the eight discs into crumbled pieces of plastic. He grabbed the man sitting with his wife and yanked him to his feet.

"Where is the Nickerson woman?" His face flushed red with rage while shaking hands squeezed the man's neck.

Medvedev, Galkin, and the lab coat remained seated, closing then widening their eyes in confused disbelief as the man gasped, "I don't know! I don't know!" His wife pleaded for mercy. When Sokolov tossed the man aside like a rag doll, he crawled back to her for comfort.

Vengeful orders spewed from Sokolov as fast as his hurried breaths of air allowed.

"Find her," he demanded, sending Galkin running out the door. Only after he was in the hallway did the man pause to try to understand what had happened.

Medvedev was already on his feet when his boss barked, "Take that laptop and find out what black magic she created." The logistics mastermind who sweated every detail, ensuring near-perfect operational throughput, wanted to know how this betrayal would work for his organization.

Without hesitation, the other lab coat jumped to the stage and retrieved his two subjects when Sokolov pointed and instructed, "Kill them."

Chapter 28

Matching green Nickerson Enterprises polo shirts and khaki slacks helped the three contractors fit into their new environment, even if the costumes were more than a little obvious. New employees starting in the wake of their leader's disappearance was a better impression to give any curious onlookers than a constant military presence on-site. Indulging in self-pity, Drew stood at the window and watched Manhattan's traffic play its synchronized dance.

"It still feels weird to sit at her desk," he huffed when he caught Highland's reflection in the window. "I'd still rather just stand here than sit on my ass without a goddamn thing to do but wait," his frustrated sigh attached to the final words, "for something."

"Good news then, sir," pulled him from the gloom. The captain smirked when he turned to show his *What's so Good About It?* face, handing him a single-page computer printout. "Jerez pulled the changes that she wrote into our operational Sensations." There were three lines of code on the page. "These additions aren't in the public release version."

She explained how the code "seems somehow to pull location data through the recorded subject's senses," Sergeant Jerez and Leonard Powell burst in from the server room.

"We're getting more data coming in," one of them yelled from across the spacious main office area.

"Lots of data," yelled the other one.

Chapter 29

His underlings scoured the facility while Sokolov remained in the classroom, praying to the gods he once considered foolish, childish fantasies.

"Please, please make this go away," he whined, coiled in the corner as he pounded against the side of his head. Sharp knocks on the door pulled him to his feet and gave him a few moments to put himself together.

Despite hearing his voice on the other side of the door, Galkin shouted, "Dema Zlovich, are you in there?" By the time he entered, Sokolov had composed himself until he saw the man in charge of Ellie's caretaking while at Surgut. He lunged at Galkin, demanding answers.

"What stories did you tell her?"

Sokolov grabbed his throat with crushing force, but Galkin did not resist. Nor did he offer any lies, instead redirecting the focus on the information he had to share.

"We have searched the entire facility, comrade. She is not here."

Sokolov's grip relaxed.

"All other personnel are accounted for and have recovered from her evil enchantment."

Sokolov dropped his hand when he realized the entire facility had experienced her Sensations release. His exclamation, "The entire facility," was more an appreciation for the power of his new SCARS programming than any fear of how many people knew about him.

Galkin inspected the man he once worshipped before he continued feeding information.

"We inspected the parking lot." He raised a finger. "One car is missing."

*
**

Pulled over to the side of a secondary road, Iosifovich watched Ellie sleep for over forty-five minutes. Other than sweeping long strands of black hair away from her face, he spent his time mesmerized by the rise and fall of her chest and the gentle flare of her nostrils with every shallow breath she took. The snow had stopped falling, and a lack of wind suspended any lingering activity in the thick Russian forest. For forty-five minutes, he only had the rumbling hum of his vehicle to keep him company while debating his next moves.

Shudders from tires that gripped icy pavement when the car pulled back onto the road snapped Ellie from her slumber. While rattling the cobwebs from her mind, she looked outside the window as if there was the slightest chance she would have known where they were.

"Are we close to your second home?"

He pointed to a fork in the road up ahead. "We are going just past that turn."

Ellie finally smiled with the realization that she was going to be safe. She sat up in her seat and ran her fingers through her hair, pulling the rest of its length from her zipped-up parka. Three concrete towers came into view when they turned in to the clearing area.

"No, no, no, no, no..." trailed off to inaudible sobs until she whimpered, "Semyon Iosifovich." It was her mixture of a question, plea, and damnation to hell for what he was about to do.

Without looking over or acknowledging her shattered disbelief, he drove toward the gaggle of workers standing in the parking lot of the Surgut Capture Facility. "Like I said, little girl, we do not see many Negro women in this part of our country."

Startled lab coats scattered like the snow when the wind finally blew the moment they recognized Ellie sitting in the passenger seat of the black SUV that rolled in. Some were afraid to approach the sorcerer, fearing that she had returned as promised to invade their thoughts one more time. Others ran to find Sokolov or Medvedev. They wanted to be the first to announce, "We found her." Most remained leaning up against the side of the facility, smoking cigarettes and placing wagers on what would happen next. Finally, Ivanovna approached the vehicle and gently tapped her knuckles against the driver's side window.

"I see you have found our little lost pet." She waved her bony arm wrapped in a ridiculously puffy white down coat. "Hello, again," she said in English. "We are happy you decided to come back."

Tears welled in Ellie's eyes as she did nothing but stare forward, her hands tucked down her sides so no one could see their uncontrolled shaking.

Before Iosifovich had an opportunity to present his prey and declare undying loyalty to Dema Zlovich

Sokolov, the towering Ivanovna barked orders at the lab coats remaining in the parking lot.

"You and you, take the Nickerson woman to Room 7."

Looking down at the driver's bloated smile, she shattered his arrogance with the instructions, "Go home to your wife, Semyon Iosifovich Vochenko. I will be in contact."

She turned and walked away from the car, trailing Ellie back into the facility.

Chapter 30

For the first time in her captivity, Ellie feared reality. Standing in the middle of Capture Room 7 with both hands tied behind her back and one of those putrid sacks over her head, she waited for the unknown to strike. Even though everything in the room before had been removed, careful steps inched her feet across the tile floor, prepared to bump up against something. The only thing she eventually crashed into was a wall.

Like the sharp thunderclap of a vicious summer storm, the first bang came from behind her. Noise pounded both eardrums and sent her crumbling to her knees as she howled a terrible cry when trying to raise one shoulder enough to cover her ear.

"Do it again," Sokolov commanded from the monitoring area outside the room. Ivanovna tapped her keyboard and sent another boom they could hear from the other side of the well-insulated walls.

"Do it again." Ivanovna complied.

"Again."

From the video monitor, the crowd of onlookers stared in amazement as Ellie struggled to her feet again and again, only to have the next jarring whomp knock her down faster and more severely than the time before.

"Again."

As Ivanovna inflicted carefree torture with the stroke of a key, Medvedev looked on with fascination. Ellie's body lunged from the screaming and crying, sounds that were not heard outside the room. Trails of vomit ran out of the hood and down the front of her corporate polo. Still, although every attempt was more challenging than the last, she rose to her feet after every assault.

"Dema Zlovich," Medvedev raised his issue, "if you want information, it might be best to leave her functional."

Frantic clumps of air snorting from Sokolov were the only sounds made until he turned to the senior group of facility lab coats. "Finally, you are failing to live up to my expectations." Once again, Medvedev spoke on behalf of the lab coats who could not offer any opinion on the matter.

"Her wizardry is more powerful than any of us." His words elevated Ellie's mystique to a dangerous level. "But I believe you are the secret to taking command of her technology." Blatant flattery was the only shot he had. It worked.

"Explain yourself."

Describing a mind so powerful, Medvedev painted Ellie's ability to manipulate her thoughts, feelings, and emotions in a way that crafted the story she wanted to tell. He insisted, "It must be training from the American military."

He called it "psychological operations."

"It is how her lies became the truth you all witnessed."

Smiling and nodding in agreement, he opened the laptop when Sokolov said, "I need to create the truth to broadcast."

"Yes, Dema Zlovich." Medvedev turned to the other lab coats, encouraging their enthusiastic agreement.

"Yes."

"Absolutely."

"It must be you," said Ivanovna.

To test their breakthrough, Medvedev needed a capture.

"For thirty seconds, comrade, please let us into the mind of a god."

With blazing efficiency, he captured a moment of Sokolov's choosing. In fact, he captured three moments.

"Wait. Erase that and let me do it again," his boss murmured after the first try, like he was a teenager trying to take the perfect selfie. Finally, on that third attempt, Sokolov agreed he had not cluttered his mind with anything but the message all his followers needed to feel. Medvedev then ran the program, broadcasting his manifesto. Every person in the capture facility appeared to agree.

Tomorrow is the day the entire world will begin to fear the name Dema Zlovich Sokolov. Then, with the full power of his Sensations spewing forth from Surgut, he will triumphantly return home and welcome his wife and family to come and sit alongside him on his throne.

They believed their declaration to be true because it formed in their mind. It appeared just like the perfect vision Sokolov shaped of himself flying over the historical Catherine Palace in St. Petersburg on his way to his sprawling estate on the Pushkinsky District's remote southern edge. It was there his family waited.

When the release ended, he praised his lieutenant, saying, "Once again, your work is impeccable, Mikael Petrovych," and waited for his expected turn.

"My program only shares the reality you have created, Dema Zlovich."

After two sharp pats to Medvedev's back, Sokolov extended the invitation, "Let's go talk to our pet."

Different noises caused Ellie to recoil but did not knock her to the ground that time. The latch slid, and the door swung in, filling the pitch-black room with the ashen glow of fluorescent lighting. She peered through her mask for a shadow or movement but saw nothing. Struggling to keep balance, she turned around several times in search of something. Nothing was there. Metal scraping across metal made an unmistakable sound when the upper slide of a handgun pulled back inches from the base of her neck.

Ellie froze. Her chaotic breathing settled into a gentle pulse.

"Hello again," the voice whispered in her ear as he ran the handgun across her hooded cheek with horrid seduction. Her scared, slumped frame rose straight for the first time since her return to the facility.

With no answers, Ellie exclaimed in defiance, "Kill me if you want, Sokolov. I'm done playing your games."

The barrel pressed up against the back of her head.

"You've already lost."

Sokolov turned to his lieutenant and smiled before pulling his arm back and striking the side of his pistol against her head, sending Ellie straight down to the floor. His foot pressed hard into her back, just above her bound wrists, as a sign to not try to stand up.

She did not struggle.

"Do you need an explanation of what the Russian God can be?"

She did not respond.

"Of course not," Sokolov sighed. "You have forgotten what it means to be Russian." Crushing her head between the floor and the steel barrel, he growled, "Maybe you never had any idea what Pyotr Andreyevich Vyazemsky said." Her only reaction was the gasp of air released when he bounced his foot off her body. "He knew I would come someday," he said, then struck her side with a swift kick. "That is why he wrote his poem about me."

Ellie gasped, coughed, then insisted, "I will not give you anything."

"I already have everything I need." Sokolov walked back to the door without looking down. "Tonight, let me show you what a god can do. If you survive to the morning, you will know what it means. If not, so be it." Medvedev followed him out of the room.

The door latched.

Darkness returned.

Ellie still did not move.

"Inessa Ivanovna," Sokolov said, "make copies and play this release." He pulled the black disc from his shirt pocket. There was a sequence number written on the back. She asked him how many times, offering a delighted smile when he said, "Until I return tomorrow." Neither Medvedev nor any of the other lab coats knew what was on the disc.

"Absolutely no one is to go into that room," was his last instruction before leaving. "Do I make myself clear, Director?"

Honored by her new promotion, Ivanovna's gangly frame sprang to life with the energy of her younger self.

"I won't let you down, Dema Zlovich."

You could almost see the spittle of drool forming in the corner of her mouth as she focused on the computer and pulled sequence 90263 from the Surgut facility's database.

With the release activation, Ellie sensed his racing heartbeat lay over the top of her own struggling rhythm.

God, please let her be safe.

He did not struggle or beg for his own life. He pushed the pain from his broken leg, arms, and ribs to the back of his mind, but every sensation he experienced collected in the tiny space of one instant at the front of hers. She felt someone hold his head high, facing it into harsh lights as they demanded answers. Still, she was his only worry.

"Kenny," she fought to call out, but he would never hear those words. Sokolov had already told her he was dead. Was this how he killed Andy? Tied in a chair, their head slumped low with remorse as confusion set in.

Ellie, I'm sorry.

Tastes of his blood mixed with her own flavor every time they struck his face. Vile traces of vomit and bodily functions released when there was no more strength to hold them, blending so well that she could not tell if they were her own or his capture.

Fear spiked before that shocking awareness of plastic wrapped over his head and face. Any effort she made to take a breath only pulled the film tight against his gaping mouth. Her mind cried in vain, for she could only endure the pain of his broken arms tearing themselves free from their sockets during his fight for survival. She could only participate in the collapse of his lungs and throat as they lost the battle for one more gasp. As he lay face down on the floor of that dark room, she could only sit in the chair and feel life slip away until one final emotion soothed him with euphoric bliss. His love for her.

I will always be there, mon chérie.

The moment his heart stopped, hers lost the will to beat. When Ivanovna replayed the Sensations release, Ellie sensed his racing heartbeat lay over the top of her own struggling rhythm.

God, please let her be safe.

For the second immersion, and every experience after, she suffered confusion and then despair over losing her dear Owen. She could do nothing as she lay motionless on the floor, aware of her dark, rotting reality. Nor did she have a chance to understand where he was or how her fiancé fell into that fatal moment. One clarity was the unexpected connection their souls held. Her beaten body lay drowning in his suffering. His tortured frame sat lashed to a chair, punished by her unanswered fate. Ellie realized she would have the rest of her life to know it was all because of her creation.

But that was not the time for regret.

That was the time for suffering.

Every iteration of the twelve-minute release further piqued Ivanovna's interest. Ellie's broadcast of her truth about Sokolov was her only frame of reference for the capability of that technology.

"What are you thinking? What beautiful world has Dema Zlovich created for you?"

She joined Ellie for the eighteenth experience of Owen's torture and murder. The final realization that she did not die, that her lungs continued to savor healthy gulps of air, came as another shock when the release ended. Fright turned to disbelief that she was safe, transforming into a wave of ecstasy that soon became masochistic envy as she watched on the monitor as her prisoner's conviction began again.

Hours later, a knock on the outer door startled Ivanovna. She rushed to welcome the interruption until she realized Galkin had come to pay her a visit.

"Oleg Ivanovich, you should not be here," she said while blocking his sight of the monitor.

He dismissed her comment with a wave of his meaty paw.

"Nonsense, Inessa Ivanovna. I am simply here to wish you a much-deserved congratulation on your promotion." She was happy yet confused when he informed her, "I, myself, have been selected to accompany Mikael Petrovych and take over a new facility we will soon construct."

She welcomed him into the control room when he presented a celebratory treat of fresh tea and honey spice cookies.

"How is the criminal doing in there?"

"Sleeping," she said with a snicker before returning to her chair, spinning around to face Galkin while he poured cups of tea for them both. Its herbal essence blended with the warm cookies, overtaking the rancid stench of Capture Room 7, a change that seemed to disappoint Ivanovna.

"To your health!" Galkin toasted. Before she tasted the brew, Ivanovna dipped a cookie in her pungent tea while he peered at the monitor in wide-eyed curiosity.

"Amazing."

She turned to see what caught his attention when Galkin let go of his ceramic teacup. Before it hit the floor, his hands, molded by years of hard labor at the Vladivostok shipyard, reached up and broke Ivanovna's neck with one swift twist. The only sounds made were a sickly crunch of cartilage and the snap of tendons separating from the bone. Teacups crashing on the tile floor muffled those final harmonies.

When Galkin canceled the SCARS release playback, he watched Ellie struggle to take the next breath her mind believed would never come. A sudden flood of light and the sliding bolt jolted her back into a reality where she, not Owen, was in danger.

Pleading, "No! No!" she writhed across the floor, trying to sit up but failing each time. A familiar voice spoke from the silhouette.

"It's okay," they said. She recoiled from his touch, but there was nowhere to go. His hands were rough, reigniting a sudden familiar intimacy.

Probably trying to say, "Oleg? Is that you?" Ellie's words could not overcome the frantic gasps for breath mixed with gags of bile that battled the realization of what she experienced.

"Hush, little girl," he said while struggling with the knots in her hood. Finally, he ripped the bag in two, then wiped the vomit from her face like he was cleaning food off an overfed newborn. As her vision slowly focused on reality, her thoughts returned to the memory of his ordeal.

Through panicked breathing, she could only cry, "Oleg," while he apologized and promised he was trying. Finally untying her bound wrists, Ellie wrapped her battered arms around her savior.

She howled, "They killed my love," but Galkin could not understand what she said. He reminded her not to speak English. Ellie stared into his eyes, unsure of what she should say. Then, her appearance softened as she raised a tender hand to his grizzled beard.

"They killed my partner," she purred in fluent Russian. "I was so scared. I thought it was you." She buried her head into one man's chest while sobbing for the other.

"It will be both of us if we do not leave immediately."

Galkin had hatched an elaborate plan before he ever stepped into the monitoring area of Capture Room 7. When Ellie emerged from the room, Ivanovna's contorted body was tossed to the floor, already stripped of its brown cotton slacks, blue work shirt, industrial boots, and the dreadful white lab coat. He instructed her to change out of the Nickerson Enterprises polo and American clothing. She stripped without hesitation, extending the time she stood naked before donning the coarse cotton panties and bra. Galkin savored the last time he would get to see her undressed.

It pained him to say, "Please hurry," but the words finally forced themselves past his tongue.

"Put on her parka and gloves." He pulled the hood tight over her head and ensured they tucked every hair inside. "This will keep you from looking like a Negro as we go through the building." Ellie did everything he instructed while she focused on calming herself.

Galkin dumped the former beauty queen's body into Capture Room 7. He pulled a match from his pocket and passed it over the container he had claimed was tea before tossing it into the room. After re-engaging the latch, he grabbed Ellie's arm. One slight whisper escaped her lips, "Forgive me, Owen," before she shut her mouth and followed Galkin into the hallway.

Operations were normal in the facility even as fire spread beyond the single room. Smoke alarms and fire suppression systems were never part of Sokolov's hasty construction. With only minutes before someone would discover the blaze, Galkin and Ellie zigzagged through the hallways as fast as possible without drawing attention.

Galkin gave an expected nod when an announcement blasted over the central speakers.

"There is a fire in the processing section," the night shift supervisor announced. His priority was not on evacuations or life-saving measures. "Secure all cargo from the warehouse."

The warehouse was their destination, and they arrived just as the announcement diverted everyone in that direction. Galkin held Ellie up when they reached a green shipping container like the one she had seen in General Drew's briefing. It was loaded on a trailer, ready to leave the warehouse. He opened its heavy steel doors.

"Climb in and go toward the back," Galkin said, handing her a small canvas pouch. He told her there was food, water, a flashlight, and warm clothing in a cargo box. Ellie mumbled something that he took as his confirmation.

"It is important to keep quiet, no matter what you hear." A nod of her head was all she could offer.

"There is a cell phone in the box. When you arrive in Vladivostok, call the number programmed in it." He began to close the container when Ellie pleaded for more.

"How will I know I am there?"

Galkin closed his eyes like he was drifting off to another time. "When they slam your cargo on the ground, you will smell the beautiful salty air of Vladivostok."

Ellie reached for his arm and pulled Galkin closer. "What about you, Oleg?" Her question fell short of describing his obvious danger.

Gentle taps on his temple brought a devilish smile to his face, "There is too much information up here. When Dema Zlovich discovers that Inessa Ivanovna and I have executed you and set your body on fire, he will come looking for us to discover why." Confident that his plan was solid, he continued, "My car will drive in the opposite direction, away from the cargo shipments."

He assured her, "They will not find me alive."

Ellie begged for him to get in with her, but he knew of too many reasons he could not go.

"The container can only be secured from the outside."

"My car must be seen leaving Surgut tonight."

"There is not enough food for both of us."

"I cannot go free. No, I must pay for everything I am part of."

Genuine tears of sorrow formed in both sets of eyes. Then, with one last caress over his jaw, Ellie placed a soft kiss to his lips before choking out the words, "Thank you, Oleg."

"You are welcome," was his rough English response. She watched him wipe the corner of his eye before closing the heavy doors and securing their outside latch. With sharp slaps that echoed across the metal wall, he yelled for a driver. "Someone get this container out of here before this whole warehouse burns down."

Once again, Ellie was in complete darkness. She crawled over and around boxes securely strapped to the metal floor until she reached its front. Well-stocked with provisions, she settled in for another experience that had no clear end in sight. Her body began recognizing its pain just like her emotions had realized their suffering.

In the canvas bag, wrapped in swatches of oily rags from the motor pool, was Ellie's half-carat diamond solitaire ring.

Encased for those first few hours, then days and weeks, of freedom, Ellie brokered a deal with the bittersweet, silent reminders of everything she would carry for the rest of her life.

Chapter 31

Another day in the desolation of uncertainty weighed on Danette until she triggered a shockwave that spanned two continents.

Every person in the office had a task assigned for when that day would arrive, but instead, they all ran to her desk the moment she jumped from her desk and screamed, "Holy fuck, Ellie! Where are you?"

Two hours later, a joint South Korean-US Special Operations team swarmed the small Port of Sokcho on the peninsula's eastern coast in search of a victim.

What they discovered was a phoenix risen from the ashes.

Six Korean dockworkers huddled around a makeshift campfire burning in the dark, laughing at stories Ellie told them about their old friends Oleg Ivanovich Galkin and Volodymyr Iovich Kaza.

"Then he said, 'I don't think you want to travel in that shipping box full of fertilizer, although it does smell better than you.'"

The group roared even louder.

"I told Volodymyr Iovich that the yarn and twine container sounded like heaven."

"Tell him we got her," an American keyed his microphone while Ellie shared her goodbyes with the final links in a complex multinational smuggling ring that dabbled in the rescues of human trafficking victims. When the soldiers turned blind eyes, and her saviors disappeared into the darkness from where they came, she figured Volodymyr Iovich Kaza was as made up as the name Toi Story.

Promising rays of a new day cracked the misty veil blanketing the East Sea as wisps of steam drifted off dozens of steel cargo containers. Ellie looked down to watch the same miracle rising from her skin. Her breath finally showed signs that yesterday's residue was also peeling away.

"Master Sergeant," she said, "what's today's date?"

Soldiers from both nations dropped to one knee, maintaining a 360-degree lookout when their team leader raised his fist high without interrupting her moment.

"March 16, ma'am."

Its bottom arc finally cleared the horizon. A seam of rust from the morning sky lifted the sun above the calm blue waters, satisfying her peaceful trance.

"I haven't seen a sunrise since October 11."

**

The voice of reason grimaced like he was one more bad answer away from an aneurysm.

"It's been almost twenty-four hours, so when do we get to see her?"

General Drew ran a clammy palm across his sweaty face and leaned back into the chair.

"I told you, Leonard, we have protocols for this kind of reintegration."

He couldn't tell whether it was Danette, Sandy, or Kaylee who yelled, "Protocols, my fucking ass!" They were all standing behind him. Even Marcus was almost ready to use salty language from his Navy days. Captain Highland and Sergeant Jerez moved to the conference room, using secure communications as their excuse to avoid the team's rage.

Danette stepped forward to claim the voice, adding, "Complete your little procedure crap and get her back here immediately, or we go public." Her kittenish, powder-blue eyes bulged fiery tones of red when Drew leaned back in the chair, clasped both hands behind his head, and smirked.

"That's exactly what I told them, too," a voice cut through the standoff.

That smirk became the widest smile Drew could muster when every Nickerson Enterprises employee snapped around in unison. She wore a gray sweatsuit with a heavy windbreaker. It disguised every notable feature when the hood was pulled up over her head. They all needed that half-second pause for their brain to decide if Ellie standing in the middle of the office was just a pipe dream. The next ten minutes were a barrage of screams, crying, laughs, kissing, hugs, and teasing.

"So..." Danette teased the next words, "how was your trip?" She smiled and asked Ellie what she had bought her on the trip.

"Fine, and nothing," she said. "Why do I smell better than everyone else?"

"We didn't realize you were going to take a shower before coming back."

Danette looked back at Drew, mouthing "Thank you" before returning to her friend.

The conference room glass wall, a token of full transparency at Nickerson Enterprises, frosted over for Ellie and Drew's private conversation. Soft wails echoed through the walls as a reminder to everyone that Ellie's ordeal was far from over.

Inside, Drew held tight when her knees buckled and refused to straighten. He could only glide their bodies down together until he was in a chair, her frame slumping to the floor. That was her time to lay her head in his lap and cry.

Stroking her hair, he whispered, "Take all the time you need." Ellie lifted her head to look at him with bloodshot eyes and a smile struggling to surface from underneath her sadness.

She confessed, "I had one moment when I wondered why you had abandoned me."

"Never" was the only reassurance she needed. Then, struggling to her feet, she shed the crippling weight of her captivity and wiped her face dry. The proud father watched her stand tall. He offered a simple nod before Ellie pressed a button on the wall, again turning the opaque glass clear. No one tried to hide the fact they were watching, and they rushed at her invitation when she waved them in.

Drew pulled his chair close to the table as everyone filled the conference room. With no desire to control the euphoria wave, he offered, "Just let me know when it's my turn to say something."

Kaylee's wide-eyed stare at Leonard only received a shrug of his shoulders in response as silent buzzing replaced typical office chatter. Each person grabbed a chair to join the general, but they were short. When Sandy scurried to grab one, Ellie broke the silence.

"Don't worry about it," she said with a dismissing wave. "I need to stand, anyway."

Everything was right again, with Ellie standing at the helm of Nickerson Enterprises, poised to move the company forward. She took her time, whispering thoughts no one else could hear while staring into each face.

Sincere apologies for earlier secrets and heartfelt thanks were not part of her plan. Instead, "Let's discuss what we need to do from today forward" was a two-hour, one-way conversation. Every set of eyes shifted from Ellie down to the pad where they took notes and then back. She left no time for anything else.

Before the meeting ended, Ellie promised, "If, when all this is finally over, you still have questions, I will sit down and answer them all."

Humble disciples filed out of the conference room and returned to their environments. Leonard and Sergeant Jerez jumped on the phones and woke IT team members. Sandy made the initial contact with Global News. General Drew and Captain Highland left for their secure office location. Kaylee and Danette each had a long list of contacts and instructions. As those two walked back to their desks, Kaylee broke the silence.

"I don't think this is a bell she's gonna be able to un-ring."

"I don't think she wants to."

Chapter 32

April 24, 2023

Three digital clocks hung from the far wall of the operations room. The red block numbering of the center ticked up to 0118. At first glance, the room could pass for a typical corporate call center if not for its occupants.

"Sir, Talon reports crossing Checkpoint Bravo," a soldier called back over her shoulder while tracking three dots on a digital map. Grid squares overlaid neighboring countries of Estonia, Latvia, and Russia. Bold splashes of blue interrupted varying shades of green. Within that thick forest terrain, a maze of road and river networks scattered in every direction. That soldier was one of five tracking the dots on their computer monitors, each listening to a different channel on their headset.

Two familiar faces sat at a small round table behind the stations. Unlike Drew's, the fatigues Ellie wore had no rank insignia or nametag. When everything went quiet, she furrowed her brows but did not speak. She was a spectator, nothing more. Drew rolled his chair to get a better view of the middle screen.

"Our birds just crossed the border from Estonia," he said while waving Ellie up. She pedaled her feet forward to join him. "Russia gave us clearance to penetrate and hit the Sokolov estate, but that's it. They've got bigger shit to worry about on their western front." He rambled off a short list of things that could go wrong, describing possible maintenance issues, bad weather popping in from the Gulf, or hostile contact. His head hung low when he admitted, "Anything happens, and they are on their own. Moscow will deny its support and label our guys as terrorists of the state." His cheeks huffed, then pushed a blast of frustration.

Ellie's mouth went dry. She blinked only when holding off that distraction any further finally became impossible.

*
**

Pungent waves of musty meadow dew mixed with the aroma of birch saplings washed through the two trailing helicopters' open cabins. Master Sergeant Sampson closed his eyes and inhaled through his nose once, twice, three times before leaning over to his commanding officer.

"Just enjoy the ride, ma'am," he yelled over the roar of turbine engines while the constant snaps filled their senses with a fresh dose of Russia's springtime bloom. Captain Highland nodded her head and gave Sampson a thumbs-up. Not even a deep exhale seemed to settle her nerves. Sampson smiled when she pulled on her chinstrap to verify its tension for the seventh time in the last twenty minutes before re-running the exit scenario through her mind. When the helicopter leaned to the right, she followed that course with her hand and counted nineteen seconds until the predicted sharp bank pulled the aircraft on its new heading.

*
**

Drew broke the room's silence by spotlighting Ellie when he said, "Their biggest risk right now is the accuracy of your route into his compound." All she could do was wave off his doubt.

"That arrogant bastard would never allow his workers to have the lasting memory of my Sensations release." She shook her head to reinforce the words, but Drew's eyes remained focused on the moving map, so she leaned in. "I knew he would have to record his own rebuttal...."

Drew finished her thought. "So, you programmed the capture to record details of everything he was aware of."

"Like I said," she smirked, "arrogant bastard. He likes to sit up front in the copilot chair...."

"Giving us muscle memory right into the backyard of his little happy hideaway." He took his eyes off the monitor for a second to smile at Ellie. "Fucking genius."

Rapid pulses invaded the thick forest from every direction. But, only when the three helicopters passed overhead did the surroundings erupt with the roar of those engines as they churned with the numbing beat of rotor blades. They arrived without warning and moved on faster than your head could turn to catch a glimpse. The three Special Operations helicopters hugged the terrain, flying so low they appeared to rest their bodies on the plush vegetation outside their doors.

"Two minutes to target" was the first radio call to come in since they went dark. Highland confirmed the pilot's warning into her headset. As shadows rustled around the cabin, she broadcast final instructions to her team.

"You heard 'em," she said. "We just passed Foxtrot. When we hit the LZ, Chaulk One takes their split between security and first zone." She watched Sampson nod his head when she commanded, "Chaulk Two takes second and third zone."

Highland went off-script from the mission brief, reminding every soldier, "We know he's there, so we're not pulling out until we neutralize our target." One final affirming nod was Sampson's show of support. "When the target is confirmed, rally at the birds. Last one back eats the cookie. Prepare to move!"

Fighting to suppress his laughter, Sampson pulled the night-vision goggles down just as miniguns from the lead aircraft rained fire into the night.

✻
✻✻

Ellie closed her eyes, replaying the computer simulation rehearsals in her mind, finding comfort whenever she looked up to see the dots in the precise locations where they were supposed to be.

Once again, Drew tried to pull secrets from Ellie.

"Your intel confirmed six hours ago that Sokolov was still with his family. He's been there since the Surgut Facility burned to the ground in February."

Her focus was on the mission. She showed no desire to entertain Drew's curiosity. "He's scared," she said instead, "plain and simple." Ellie turned her head just enough to project her voice without interrupting her view of the mission. "He thinks I'm dead, yet he can still feel me inside his head, sharing every thought with his enemy."

Six soldiers poured from the helicopter moments after its wheels grazed the manicured lawn of Sokolov's estate. They moved quickly through the darkness, their reality transformed into an illumination of green digital patterns.

"Security set" was the first call that came in over everyone's headset.

On the lawn, they counted five bodies, well-armed mercenaries ripped to shreds by the miniguns of Chaulk One. To Highland, nothing looked real through the lenses of night-vision goggles. Expanding pools of fresh blood were simply emerald masses oozing beyond dozens of other green pigments.

Concrete fragments and a couple of bullet-riddled SUVs were minor obstacles as they made their way to the front entrance. When Highland raised a fist, four others stopped, looking to the left, right, and behind as the fifth approached the Russian-oak door. No less than ten feet high, it looked like the royal gates of a medieval palace. The soldier stuck thick rolls of putty on one side as high as he could reach, then down to the pavement. After doing the same thing to the other side, he joined the team behind the riddled vehicles. Simultaneous massive explosions ripped the doors off their hinges, and they fell in shattered pieces inside and out.

Zone Two was the upstairs rooms of the main dwelling. Highland had no need for goggles, even in the middle of the night. Their not-so-subtle entrance had alerted Sokolov's crew. Every light in the house was on.

Although Drew kept Ellie updated on the team's movements, he had no reason to translate all the radio updates. But when a voice squelched, "Zone Three," through speakers mounted close to the center monitor, he confirmed, "That's all of them." She never acknowledged his words. Instead, Ellie was sitting back at the table, her eyes still closed, with both hands crossed on her lap. The only subtle movements were the rise and fall of each shallow breath.

"Can you feel me?"

Everyone in the room remained focused on the operation. Her whispers were lost to the chatter of mission updates from their twelve soldiers on the ground, yet she did not seem to mind.

"Where do you hide when you're scared?" An evil smirk stretched across her face. "I'm sure you promised Ksana everything would be all right as you ran from your bedroom.

"You lied."

Gaudy artifacts were set in no particular order around the grand ballroom. Recessed into the walls along the grand marble staircase were stone statues carved in the likeness of bogatyrs posed in graphic portrayals of combat. Sokolov often explained that those mythical medieval warriors were the Slavic legends emulated by his organization. After the mission, Highland noted in her after-action report that the house "reeked of the tasteless displays of new money."

Right at the top of the staircase was the first bedroom. The group of three hugged the wall, their automatic weapons covering both directions down the hallway. When Highland gave the hand signal to "breach," one pulled the pin on a small canister while the other grabbed the door handle. Then, with a quick flip of its latch, the heavy door opened just enough to toss the flash-bang grenade into the room, creating a deafening roar that stunned a young female crouched behind her bed. Two cleared the room while Highland bolted through the smoke and headed straight toward the woman.

"Where is Dema Zlovich?" her angry Russian demanded to know, but wailing and crying were Ksana's only response. Highland grabbed the silk nightgown she wore, twisting the fabric tight around her neck as she lifted and pulled the woman until she landed on the thick cotton mattress. "Where is your husband?"

Nothing she said made sense in any language. They left her face down on the bed, her hands zip-tied behind her back and her mouth covered with tape.

"Did you kiss your children goodbye?" Ellie wanted to know. "Did you lie and tell them everything was going to be okay?"

Negative updates continued to flow into the operation room. The outside grounds were secure; nine targets were neutralized. The secondary building was clear. No reported contact. Chaulk One soldiers made their way toward the main house. Two bodies fell to the ground before the bright flash of a rifle faded into darkness. One US soldier lurched backward, bleeding from a sharpshooter's mark that struck just above his protective vest. Blazed gunfire from the other five weapons dropped the shooter in an instant. Chief Sasaki ran to his soldier while the others secured the target.

He vowed, "We're gonna get you out of here, Santiago," but it was already too late. Sasaki paused, honoring his soldier with the only moment he could afford before ordering two soldiers, "Get him back to the bird," and moving forward as a small force of three. They left the body of eight-year-old Maksim Demich Sokolov where it fell, his blood staining the natural stone walkway that meandered back toward the house.

✳︎✳︎✳︎

The incoming update, "Zone Three, clear," pulled Drew to his feet.

"Dammit." He began pacing behind the monitors, occasionally looking down at the table where Ellie remained in her trance-like state.

"Sokolov is in one of the upstairs bedrooms," she said without opening her eyes.

"Or away from the residence completely," he worried.

She looked out to see him staring down, his face wrinkled with doubt. Without trying to ease his fears, she extended her hands. "Come sit with me, Zach." The general pulled a chair up across from her. She spread both arms over the table so he could curl his fingers around hers.

"He is in one of the bedrooms."

*
**

Sokolov was hiding in plain sight. He sat cross-legged on the floor of his daughter's bedroom. Alisa was across from him. With the door wide open, Highland could see the girl as she cried and pleaded with her father. A laptop computer was part of their little circle, its screen open and facing Sokolov. He told her to shush before calling out in English.

"Can you hear me, American soldiers?" He assured them he did not have a gun. While the other two secured the hallway, Highland stepped into the girl's room.

She surveyed the childish pink-and-white space before saying, "You have caused us a lot of trouble, Dema Zlovich." His eyes widened when she added, "I'm here at the request of Eleanor Nickerson."

"It doesn't matter," he said, "you will never bring me to her." A simple digital timer on the screen continued its count from 18.97 seconds.

In anticlimactic fashion, Sokolov's story ended when Highland pumped a three-round burst into his head and torso. Frozen with fear, Alisa remained silent as Highland broadcasted an evacuation order. She then ran out of the teenager's room, a place of peaceful sleep and magical dreams, now a chamber soaked in her daddy's blood. The girl wiped the trail of blood from across her cheek before leaning over to tap *Cancel* on the touchscreen.

As soon as the sixth set of boots pulled into the helicopter, Chaulk Two lifted into the air and pulled into formation.

"Tell her we got him."

*
**

When the transmission burst through the speaker, Drew and four soldiers glued to their digital moving maps pumped their fists in celebration. The fifth delayed Ellie's gratification.

"Copy Tango," was her calm reply. She added, "Misty is open," directing the operation to the shortest route for their fuel-starved aircraft. Then came the moment of satisfaction.

Long-overdue glee never reached Ellie. She looked across the table, staring into Drew's face. Deep creases underneath his tired eyes tracked into the wrinkles framing his burdened smile. She tilted her head to the side just a bit, searching for the best approach to satisfy her curiosity.

"What was his name?"

Drew's grin faded, its remnants wiped clean when he reached up to his chin and pulled the skin tight with a slow, somber clasp.

"Staff Sergeant Hector Santiago joined ODA-3412 six years ago," he said. A different smirk appeared when he chuckled, "He was the one who campaigned to get this team assigned to the Sensations project." Ellie's curious twitch turned into a snicker of her own when Drew said, "He fancied himself a bit of a computer geek.

"I guess it's time for Eleanor Nickerson to come out of the shadows, don't you?"

She nodded her agreement but had more to add to the general's thought.

With words that matched the slow pace of her finger tapping on the table, she said, "When Abby returns, we will hold a joint press conference." Confusion broadcasted across Drew's face, but he never got the chance to ask a question. "Melissa Barnett and I will announce BravoTech's liquidation of their holdings in Nickerson Enterprises."

Although the news was not unexpected, Drew sighed at the confirmation that her original plan would still move forward. With a look that mirrored undying love for a child who had disappointed their father, a smile returned when he stood from the table.

"When vengeance is repaid, the god shall return to her world of abundance."

Chapter 33

A bed of purple-frosted petals surrounded the slab in every direction before taking hold on one side of its rounded lavender edge. The winding flowery staircase climbed to the impassable frosted white peaks that guarded its glossy surface. Icing spelled out *Happy Birthday, Ellie* across the cake top in the darkest red imaginable.

Michael Yao narrated the shaky handheld video clip of Ellie carving massive slices, then handing them out to a small crowd gathered at the picnic grounds. Three cedarwood log tables with benches built into the frame rested in the short, green grass. Tall basswoods sprouting their heart-shaped foliage were the perfect background. Further past that was a partial view of the Second Start Rehabilitation Center.

"That was the scene today when Eleanor Nickerson made her first appearance since the tragic events surrounding BravoTech." The smartphone recording showed her laughing and smiling while doling out slices, occasionally setting them down to share hugs and kisses amidst more laughter. Without an explanation for her absence, Michael told his viewers it was "most likely related to the FBI's tight seal on any details while investigations into the attacks continue."

Ellie stood tall behind a makeshift podium in her typical blue corporate polo and denim jeans. With one arm wrapped around Mrs. Barnett's waist, she thanked everyone for the incredible birthday surprise before turning to the camera and adding, "During this difficult time, we are grateful for your respect of our privacy while we continue to grieve for the losses of Owen, Andy, Nancy, Jorge, Bart, Brenda, and Mary." Fading into the news video's final moment was a photo of the women posing with their loved ones and the five fictional employees they lost.

*
**

Bright rays showered the campground, but Ellie refused to wear sunglasses.

"I never want to hide from the sun again," she joked with Melissa when they stepped back from the crowd. A young Hispanic girl, eleven or twelve years old, ran up to hand each of them a bright yellow paper plate with a slice of birthday cake and a plastic fork.

"Here you go," she said with a nervous squeak before running away to join a gaggle of kids her age, telling her friends how she "got to talk to both of them." A mixed group of races and genders, some wore jeans while others had shorts or skirts under their oversized green T-shirts with the Nickerson Enterprises logo on the front and the Center's heart-shaped cloud design on the back.

Purple sponge cake dangled on the edge of the fork Ellie pointed toward the children.

"All those kids were placed in foster care or living on the street while their parents battled their drug addiction demons," she said before popping the buttery dessert into her mouth. In between chews, she added, "They are all reunited now, living together as families."

Melissa smiled at the sight of one boy chasing another, both weaving through small pockets of adults in their lighthearted game of tag. "Incredible" was the only word she could find.

Ellie's eyes widened and puffed out as far as her stuffed cheeks. She placed the unfinished plate onto the table, her every movement under the watchful eye of a lanky young boy whose skin was as dark as hers. One quick wink was the only incentive he needed to grab the slice and continue filling his belly.

"Multiple Sensations recipients on a single stream," she said, "is the first development integration I'm rolling out." Her hands animated the conversation as they walked through the campground. "Imagine the impact we can have when we start helping entire groups of patients finally rationalize what it feels like to be clean, sober, and happy."

"I'm not the one you need to convince, Ellie." There was no hesitation when she flicked her wrists. "He's just going to have to understand that this is how we're moving forward." They took a worn grass path, moving closer to the tree line and away from prying eyes and ears.

"It's like this, Abby," she offered in a hushed tone. "Danette is developing programs with local agencies for better tracking, monitoring, and regulating of the ethical use of Sensations." Her eyes widened when she added, "Without using Sensations as a control mechanism."

Abby shook her head only once, refusing to commit to either side of the debate. "What about lot number tracking?" She raised the issue often discussed since her return. "They do that on drugs, food, hell, even paper bags at the grocery store."

"In the capture-and-release devices, yes. But..." she hesitated. With no desire to have that discussion again, Ellie turned to walk back toward the party.

"I'm not fucking putting a geotag in the code," was loud enough to catch Kaylee's attention from across the campsite. "I will not force-feed a goddamn tracker into human emotion." Ellie caught the frantic expression of her marketing manager, who was jerking her head toward the group of children who had lost focus on everything else but her yelling.

Ellie paused and looked around. Eyes stared at what she just did while mouths talked about what she just said. She welled with emotion and turned back to Abby, already running into her arms.

"I'm so sorry, Melissa," she said in between fits of wailing and sobbing. "I just miss them so much." Partygoers cleared the table as the two women approached, their heads leaned in close together.

Abby whispered, "Just keep it together a little longer, El." They sat on one side, away from the crowd. Kaylee distracted most people by starting a conga line with the kids. "You and Drew have more talking to do, but not today. Go home."

Ellie looked up in awe as if a plane was skywriting that message across its crisp baby-blue backdrop.

"Home." She followed the words as they dripped from the canvas, splashing at her feet letter by letter. "I haven't been there since we left for Europe." With her lips pressed tight, she forced a smile watching

Kaylee lead her disorganized line of children, with the occasional parent, past the grieving women.

"I bet she's relieved I'm not couch surfing at her place anymore. I think I was putting a dampener on her sex life."

Finally, genuine smiles returned when both women joined the silly display dancing past them.

Chapter 34

Gathering storms shoved other memories aside when the car pulled up to the front of Ellie's condo in SoHo. The crowd was a mixed bag of zealots. Some were there to catch a glimpse of their savior, likening her return to the second coming that would save humankind. There were colorful *Welcome Home, Ellie* and *We Missed You* messages hand-painted on poster boards. Earlier in the day, the followers raised them high above the mass, hoping she would notice and reach out with her cure for whatever demons haunted them. Others wished she had never returned. Accusations like, "You killed my baby," placed the blame on Sensations for addictions that fed a variety of destructive acts committed in the pursuit of euphoria.

Kaylee suggested, "Ya know, we don't have to do this today," while continuing past the building without the twenty-some-odd gatherers noticing her peppy electric sedan. Ellie reached from the back seat and cupped her shoulder.

"No, dear. This isn't going to go away anytime soon. Might as well do it now."

"Security will keep the building safe," Abby added.

One slow loop around the block brought them back to the parking garage. Tired and weary after a long day perched by the main entrance, none of the gatherers noticed the lime-green vehicle pull up to the gate, where an attendant was ready to buzz them through.

On the quick elevator ride to the penthouse apartment, Kaylee walked Ellie through everything again.

"Danette and I are the only ones who've been there since General Drew cleared everything." Her pause had no takers with questions. "We tried to keep everything clean and dusted, but," watery eyes betrayed the brave front she had carried all day, "you've been gone a long time." She hugged Ellie and squeezed like there was no intention of ever letting go. There could have been more emotion, but the elevator ding pulled them apart.

Mellow contemporary music hushing from every speaker greeted Ellie's return. The fresh-baked protein bread's sweet-scented aroma invited her to take those hesitant first steps into the apartment, where soft lighting created a crown of glowing light atop Danette's curvy figure. Ellie stood in the doorway, scanning the apartment for its staggering familiarity and changes.

"Thank you" was her only critique before wrapping both arms around her old friend while whispering her gratitude countless times. She made no mention of the first paint applied around the door that had been replaced or the new area rug emblazoned with bold red, black, yellow, and blue patterns woven into the thick cotton.

"Happy birthday, E." Danette pulled away, stretching her eyes wide as her hand fanned the threat of tears. "Your pantry and fridge are stocked with all that health food crap you like." That lightened the mood a bit before her words turned somber. "I didn't pack up any of Owen's clothes," she said, dipping her head toward the floor. "I didn't know what you wanted to do with them."

Ellie reached with her left hand to graze the tip of Danette's chin, the brilliant shine of her ring sparkling like a radar beacon every time the blue-eyed beauty blinked her watery eyes.

"How about I come in, and we just sit and talk for a while?"

Giggles erupted after Danette stepped to the side, welcoming the three women in for a long night of reminiscing, storytelling, wine, laughter, and tears. But all too soon, they were gone. Ellie sat up in bed, her back against the headboard. She grabbed Owen's tablet, still nestled in its charging port, and entered his password. Three quick taps to the screen gave her access to their personal Sensations folder, filled with hundreds of data files. She clicked on the first, *OWEN20200518*, then smiled as the wave of his sensuality struck her mind.

Is this what love feels like?

"It is, my dear," she whispered aloud as her hand grazed its palm across her chest. "We will discover that together."

Will you guide me?

Their first capture, an eight-minute introduction to eternal passion, nourished Ellie with the rush of new romance. Settled into the bed, they writhed together in a way she had never coded her technology to recreate. Her body responded just as he did at that moment, just how her urges pulled ecstasy from them both every night they were together, and in the way she still loved him. Ellie was able to look around the room. She recognized her empty SoHo bedroom but felt his skin tighten under the cool breeze blowing through her old bedroom window. When he had no more to give, she sat up and relived the countless times she ran fingers through those loose coils while he lay nuzzled in her lap.

Will it always be like this?

"Always, my love."

But Ellie would not avoid the pain of everything she knew. Instead, she welcomed the horrors and invited every demon they conjured up. Ellie invited them into the bed where she and Owen rested.

First, her body recoiled when harsh Russian words, *Ya lyublyu tebya, Natascha,* echoed his profession of love.

Then, Ellie embraced her tender response.

Ya lyublyu tebya, Grigory.

"Please show me your suffering."

Ellie closed her eyes and drifted into the worlds she created. She whispered soft reminders of affection while her mind revisited Natascha's brutal torture. Her voice slipped back into those foreign words.

"I am here with you."

As the heat first burned through Natascha's muscles and tendons again, Ellie fought her need to push the horrid pain from her mind. Instead, she embraced the dying woman and shared in her suffering.

Please make it stop! Please make it stop! Please make it stop!

The world once again became an explosion of screams bursting from her lungs. Alone in her New York City apartment, the cries blended with a hushed tone of reassurance.

"I can promise you peace."

Ellie's mind fought to embrace all the pain as her own until Natascha's screaming stopped for the last time.

An underweight, pimple-faced kid sat in the bulletproof booth of a dimly lit flophouse hotel. It was decorated with peeling lime-green wallpaper from three generations ago. Without music or videos to keep him entertained, the twenty-something-year-old picked his nose, deciding which ones he would eat and which he would wipe on his shirt. He recognized the heavyset, gray-haired man who barged into the office.

"Whoa, Grandpa," he snickered. "That was quick." When the man was there eight minutes earlier, he had worn the now-tattered tie knotted and tight around his neck. He did not look amused.

With a well-educated Midwestern accent, he barked at the kid. "Your junk from the vending machine doesn't work. I want my money back." He placed the black *One-Release* disc in the metal tray that the manager pulled into his booth.

His reaction was a good sign that failures were common in their line of Sensations: "Let's see what we got here." The kid flipped the disc to look at the back—*NATASCHA, WITH LOVE*.

"Dude! That's some hard-core shit. You are ballin' with that." Grandpa did not appreciate his compliment.

"Just give me my money," the man demanded.

The marketing-whiz tweaker was all out of Natascha, but he kept his customer with *OKSANA GO SWIMMING* and a complimentary *SASHA'S FIRST DATE*.

Ellie had left the building for her first run three hours before Kaylee pulled into the parking garage. Armed escorts were a requirement Leonard had demanded before agreeing to let their CEO return home. The guards replaced General Drew's forces, providing twenty-four-hour security for the executive team. Running through the streets of Manhattan and Central Park was, once again, her time to think about nothing but the next footstep.

Lunch box in hand, she hopped into the passenger seat.

"How far did ya go this morning?"

Ellie hung her head in shame before admitting, "Only five."

Five miles after more than six months of captivity and recovery was enough incentive for Kaylee. She snatched the Boston cream donut perched on her dashboard and flicked it into a bag of trash in the back seat of her car.

She huffed, "Where are we off to today, slacker?"

Saturday morning was a visit to the hospice center at JJ Peters, where Sensations were now a routine part of end-of-life management. Pain and suffering were no longer demons haunting patients on their final journey. Doctor Shyla Cauthen escorted both visitors through hallways splashed with pastel colors and messages of hope inscribed on the walls. Delightful smells from breakfast still hung in the air. Ellie praised the improvements since her mother had been a patient three years before.

"Anya's experience has become a model for our palliative care treatment," the doctor said.

Tales of her antics with Owen brought Kaylee and Doctor Cauthen to tears. Giggles rattled through the quiet halls, drawing the curiosity of a frail older man who shuffled out of his room wheeling an IV pole with two bags that fed their solution into his arm. He introduced himself as Benjamin.

His question, "Are you the savior we can thank?" caused Ellie to smile and shake her head.

"No, Benjamin," she said as her hand toyed with the gold solitaire on her finger. "I'm just here reviewing the products my company sells to this hospital." Benjamin took note of the Nickerson Enterprises logo on her purple polo shirt before returning to his room.

"Well, if you ever meet that lady who makes those little emotion things, tell her she is a godsend." Benjamin closed the door to his room but continued his conversation from the other side. "And try to keep it down out there."

Kaylee reinforced his demand with a firm finger pointed at the doctor, then snickered, "You might need to adjust Benjamin's pain medication tonight."

Waving the other two toward her office, Doctor Cauthen hushed her tone when talking. "Benjamin's suffering from stage four pancreatic cancer. It's a miracle he is alive, let alone jumping out of bed to scold us." White noise from the air-conditioning vent finally kicked in to dampen their words. "He's not on any pain medication, though."

On cue, both visitors turned back toward Benjamin's room like they needed some way to prove what they had seen was real.

"Those bags are just IV nutrition and antibiotics. Ben's only pain management is the Sensations treatment he receives four times a day."

Ellie listened to the words and thought that it was good. That afternoon and evening were spent at the office, programming the changes her mind had mapped while hiding in a steel container hauled across Siberia and Far Eastern Russia.

When nighttime fell, Ellie once again reset her connection with Owen.

Will it always be like this, mon chérie?

"Always."

Holding on to the tenderness of their simmering passions, she delayed the next command three seconds before fulfilling her desire.

"Please show me your suffering."

Lucy's torture raged throughout Ellie's mind for one last time, with her begging for the fix he dangled in front of her. Threatening to tear their body apart from within, she cursed the day she ever met H. Ellie believed the promise that everything would be different if she could have just one more fix, even though she knew Lucy was lying. As it punctured her skin, the needle prick stung as a reminder of the magic that would take away all their suffering. Instead, she was suddenly aware of that vein under her skin as poison burned through the network, filling her with nausea and disgust until it all faded into nothing. It was all she wanted. For those last moments, Ellie experienced rapture. She welcomed the bile burning through her nasal passage as her stomach churned, trying to reject the foul poison from her body.

Her pain never went away; it just did not matter anymore. Nor did the struggle to breathe.

Without warning, Ellie was alone with her thoughts. She knew that the surges had stopped passing through her body and heard the fading beats of a heart that had failed for the last time. A single tear tracked the contours of her cheek, coming to rest in the corner of her mouth when her lips pursed to whisper the words, "You can rest now, Lucy."

For five more days, Ellie followed the same schedule. She ran seven miles, then eight, ten, twelve, then fifteen. She visited psychiatric wards, rehab clinics, treatment centers, physical therapists, and counseling centers to observe jubilant transformations in a world brought on by her technology. She spent her afternoons and evenings shaping the new future she envisioned. At night, she called on Owen to help her relive past horrors of the world she made. The pain became hers. Their creator took on the eternal suffering of others so that they could finally rest in peace.

When Friday arrived, Ellie rested.

Chapter 35

"Come, my dear, tell me what you think of our new home?"

Medvedev's bloated chest swelled with pride as he exited his olive-drab armored SUV and surveyed the residential community. Built into plush, green, sloping farmland were three rows of dual-family units. Each harmonica house had an identical white stucco exterior with a red tile roof. A modest front garden spilled out until it bordered an unpaved road. Above this tiny community sat one dwelling that was larger but built in the same design. It was for Medvedev and his new bride.

But she did not seem as eager to get out of the vehicle, instead fighting back tears while whining, "How long do we have to live here?"

Medvedev ignored her comment, only raising his head to take in the country air through his nose. But the heavy stench of natural fertilizer made him frown, so he turned back toward the car and reached in, yanking young Alisa by the wrist as she yelped. Finally relaxing his grip once she crawled out of the vehicle, he smoothed the gray pleated skirt that did little to cover any part of her adolescent legs and turned her shoulders to face the community housing. His tight grip around her waist kept the girl from falling each time the heel of her patent leather pumps stuck into the soft dirt.

"By the time we say goodbye to our friends and return to Russia," Medvedev smiled and kissed her cheek, "you will not want to leave this beautiful country."

A frigid summer had left heavy traces of snow in the mountains that served as a backdrop for the Medvedevs. News of their arrival spread through the tiny community. Russians and North Koreans poured from their homes to greet their leader and his young bride. More than a few of the faces that gathered had also worked in the Surgut facility.

"Ah, I see my friend, Leonid Romanovich Gusev."

Gusev battled through a growing crowd of well-wishers who carried gifts and food to share with the couple.

With a courteous nod, Gusev said, "Alisa Demanova Medvedev, please excuse me, but I need to have a moment with your husband."

*
**

"*Chernaya magiya.*"

Medvedev could not hide the dreadful look on his face. He leaned back in the SUV, sweat trickles building around his cheek and chin folds.

"Read me the data one more time, Leonid Romanovich."

"Of course. July production: 226 captures, 7,862 releases produced." Medvedev pursed his lips as the tan coat read production numbers that were far below the heyday of Sokolov's operation. He justified the numbers with the excuse of the prior month being his first "back in operation after Dema Zlovich made those fatal mistakes."

When silence hung in the air, Medvedev spun his finger until Gusev continued. "When the first shipment arrived in Germany, our customer complained that none of the discs worked." His impatience boiled over at the words selected.

"Did not work?" he demanded to know, "or were altered?"

"Altered, Mikael Petrovych."

Scans of all the production reports and shipping documents showed that everything seemed in order. Quality control verified that the releases matched the descriptions of when they first captured each scenario. With no idea what to do next, Medvedev grabbed the sheets to look at all the data again.

"How were they altered?" He leaned into Gusev for answers. "Did you evaluate the problem yourself?"

A gentle smile pulled Gusev's chapped lips wide. He tilted his head back as shallow breaths calmed the nervous facility director, who now wore a tan lab coat with a lapel pin of a fluttering North Korea flag.

"I did."

He closed his eyes and drifted with the memory set into his mind. "It was beautiful when she assured me, 'Masha Stepanovna is at peace,' she said. 'She is no longer part of the unholy world created by Mikael Petrovych Medvedev.'" When the vision faded, fear stepped into its place. Gusev's ears pounded with pain caused by the three rounds his leader fired into the reinforced front windshield, spider-webbing the glass as it kept the bullets and smoke inside the vehicle. Medvedev spilled out when he opened the door, cursing Ellie's evil trickery but not his tantrum. Lab coats ran to the car and helped him to his feet while Alisa looked on, satisfied chuckles rushing past her sealed lips. Her husband's trousers, split open in the crotch, were an entertaining distraction while she shivered in the soft dirt of that foreign countryside.

Medvedev brushed some dry, dusty dirt from his legs before sticking his head into the vehicle. As Gusev stared at the handgun pointed at him, he lost the ability to blink.

"You find that Nickerson woman," Medvedev growled. "You find her and kill her."

Alisa realized her mistake of standing too close when he snatched her arm and trampled through three rows of modest gardens. It was a new shortcut to their cookie-cutter house built into sloping farmland, where soybean crops grew in a nutritious blend of pig and chicken shit. Before he left on his search for the Mother of Sensations, Gusev handed the lab coats a cardboard box filled with altered SCARS release discs.

Chapter 36

Secret meetings once held in secure rooms, behind a swipe card, four-digit PIN, and sliding bolt inside the reinforced door frame, were now on full display inside a fishbowl. Gathered in the Nickerson Enterprises conference room, General Drew and a disguised Captain Highland sat on one side of the table, dressed in casual khaki slacks and unbranded forest-green polos. They were flanked on both sides by unfamiliar faces molded into charcoal business suits with just the right amount of wear that they did not look like yesterday's purchase. Ned Fuerst sat at the far right, wearing the same suit he'd had on three years earlier. Seated across the table, Leonard and Danette swapped versions of the same confused expression.

Breaking the silence, Danette swiveled her chair around to face Drew. "I guess we still have a few minutes."

The comment prompted Drew to look down at his watch, but he showed no reaction. "The meeting's scheduled for 10:30."

Danette drained her mug before going to a rolling service cart carrying two carafes of coffee and a platter loaded with donuts and sticky buns. "Can I get anyone anything?"

Fuerst took her up on the offer by raising his eyebrows almost as high as he lifted his coffee cup. His mouth was full of a sizable powdered-doughnut chunk, at least the part that didn't cling to his beard or sprinkle down to the table.

At 10:29, Ellie opened the conference room door for a petite woman carrying a briefcase. It was impossible not to give attention to her royal-blue eyes that contrasted her dark African skin. Ellie followed her entrance.

"Sorry for the delay."

She did not offer an explanation, instead introducing Michon Neuman as an executive from her bank. "Michon helped me secure the loan for today's sale."

Drew introduced his team.

"Michael Berger and Noah Wattles are lawyers with the GAO." Both men politely stood and exchanged smiles and a "Hello" with everyone in the room.

"Of course," he looked at Ellie, "you remember Ned."

She nodded but otherwise ignored the donut-crusted Health and Human Services director. When Drew said, "Mrs. Barnett and I are eager to sign these final documents," Leonard looked at every face, trying to figure out how many were lying.

"As am I, Mr. Drew. As am I." Ellie opened the portfolio she had brought with her and wrote something on the notepad.

"Will you have any of the other investors here?"

She looked up and offered an expressionless response, "There are no other investors. I bought them out as well," then resumed scribbling random lines of computer code.

A cold business transaction followed.

BravoTech sold its stake in Nickerson Enterprises at the 2020 purchase price. No one acknowledged Ned Fuerst's comment that he got "a better return with my checking account." Ellie and Melissa signed the paperwork in silence; Michon notarized the documents and completed the transaction in less than fifteen minutes. As everyone gathered their belongings, Drew remained in his chair.

"Can I have the room with Ms. Nickerson for a few minutes, please?"

Almost four months had passed since the two last spoke. Separated by much more than the boat-shaped conference table, Ellie canted her head to avoid looking at him.

"I'm sorry it had to be this way," she said in between the silent conversation she was having with herself, adding, "I'm sorry everything has to be this way." Drew reached both hands across the table. It was far too wide to connect, but she still pulled both arms into her lap.

Time had accelerated beyond imagination after the attack that killed Sokolov. He gasped when he caught that first glimpse of the woman his little girl had become.

"What happened to you?"

It was not the physical effect of her months spent in Surgut that worried him. Ellie's body was once again flawless. Her dark skin, healed from the marks left by beatings, bindings, and malnutrition, flashed radiance. Her frame swaggered with the strength of a cross-country runner who had returned to her peak. Ellie ran at least ten miles a day, six days a week. On

Fridays, she rested. No one saw anything but a superhero who had endured the worst evil could throw at her and rose above it all. But fathers see what the rest of the world can't. When he finally convinced her to look up, Drew saw eyes screaming with pain and torment. It was a look he bore witness to countless times in soldiers who gave everything they could, only to come home expected to give up everything to the life they once fought for. No one knows that pain until it's too late, except those who have seen it before. They recognize the eyes.

"Have you had a chance to talk to anyone?"

Ellie looked away and snickered while she pulled deeper into her lap as her thumb started chafing the band of her engagement ring. Muttered words insisted, "There's nothing to talk about," before she mocked the suggestion. "Besides, even if there was, who would I talk to?"

Her reaction proved she would not welcome any answer to her question.

"No one has any idea what I am going through." The muscles in her arm snapped tight when she raised her hand to stop the next words.

"Don't offer to send me to your team of counselors again."

*
**

Schoolyard rumors ran throughout the office as every person went about whatever tasks they were pretending to do while sneaking peeks into the fishbowl. Marcus and Kaylee reviewed client contracts and billing.

"They're probably talking about those horrendous terms the general agreed to," he said.

"I bet it's about keeping the Army on as a silent partner," she guessed.

Abby was sitting with Danette while she waited for her boss to finish.

Danette figured, "She's probably getting ready for the regulatory battles we're about to have."

Abby spilled a different secret.

"He's telling her that Sokolov's operation is back up and running."

When Kaylee caught Danette's wide-eyed reaction, she pushed both legs against the floor to roll her chair across the open floor as quickly as possible.

"What's up, Buttercup?" she squeaked.

"Tell her what you just said."

All three government regulators and Ellie's bank executive, having finished the only task that brought them to the office, had left to complete the work elsewhere or do their actual job. No one knew for sure. Abby still looked like Mrs. Barnett but spoke like Captain Highland.

"We have confirmed reports that the Mikael Medvedev character Ellie told us about is now running the operation." No one asked how long it took to get back up, nor did they ask what Abby meant when she said, "Eighty-five days." The same stood when she admitted, "We have no idea where in Russia, if it is there."

Rational theories and wild guesses ran through the air. Alone at her desk, Sandy did not hide that stare tracking her boss's every movement. A troubled expression deepened every time she watched Ellie cover that ring.

"No," she revealed, "it's something else."

Drew did share the news about Medvedev restarting the Sensations ring in Russia. Sparkles of light flickering through the glass wall glimmered around Ellie while he offered every incomplete detail collected. All the while, violent impressions of victims ran through her soul. Their numbers were not countless. Logistical wizardry groomed into Medvedev put the total for his new operation at 8,144. Nightly encounters with victims and the oppressed around the globe had given Ellie a much higher count. She had wept with Yuri as he finally surrendered his body and begged, *Please kill me when this is over.* Tatiana never realized the toll corrupt indulgences took on her purity, and she never had the chance to regret their savage beatings on her mind. Ellie had claimed the addict's suffering as her own, but that only made it possible to commit the same hedonistic blunder again. She had experienced the satisfaction of Gerald's explosive rage as he committed acts that should have caused her to loathe the concept of free will, hoping he would find redemption. No one was immune to the maze of atrocities pouring from her digital world. Ellie had searched and wiped away their suffering and sins by making each her own.

"I know," was the only revelation she could share.

People often dismissed the covert realities of Drew's world as exaggerated stories, but it was impossible for him to ignore her simple comment.

Tired from years of fighting, he danced with excitement over the connections made. He stated a fact, not a question, without asking how it could even be possible. "You do know where Medvedev's operation is staging from," in a tone that even seemed to surprise himself.

Ellie did not deny the accusation. Instead, she finally reached for his grasp, curling her fingers as if the table width did not keep them from physical touch.

"You know," she said, "picking off puppets of evil one by one won't stop the source of their design."

"Neither will singular salvation."

Ellie invited Drew into a world where she guaranteed nothing but pain and torment. "But," she promised, "if your mind and soul carry the intent needed, you will find your way to save others from the consequences of sin."

She guaranteed that answers would only lead to more questions. He understood that more questions would only lead to incomplete answers. Ever-present fears of psychological operations and betrayal would cloud any truth. Drew studied the crease in Ellie's mouth as she described the world she experienced inside Sensations.

When he begged, "Show me," she tapped the control panel to frost the fishbowl glass and pulled a black disc from her jeans pocket. With one press against its top, Owen guided them both into a world midway between the bright, unblemished haven of Nickerson Enterprises and the violent last moments of Emma Saneho.

Chapter 37

Snapshots of Ellie flashed across the screen, overlapped by the curious tone of Michael Yao's commentary.

"It's been nearly six months since the unexplained resurrection of Eleanor Nickerson. A growing procession of followers and critics have moved beyond her SoHo residence, establishing footholds in most major cities across the United States."

Smartphone images faded, replaced by a tall, middle-aged man standing on a residential city street. He smiled for the news camera. His gaunt, sagging cheeks were a sad byproduct of the years addicted to opioids and other illegal drugs. But the sparkle in his eye hinted at a promise of hope. Clean-shaven, with a fresh haircut, he held that overextended smile while Michael explained the source of his miraculous transformation. The caption underneath read TOM BUERGER – DETROIT, MICHIGAN.

"They're calling it the Sensations salvation." Michael described how individuals chased the perfect high so they could record and sell the rush to drug-free addicts. Those too scared to inject themselves could reap the rewards whenever they wanted, alone or in groups.

"I tried to kiss the sky," he said, "but it almost killed me right there." He pointed to the row house behind him to show his viewers where "right there" was. "When I was in the hospital," he shook his head with an enthusiasm that only a person who loves telling their story will use, "that detox was hell." Michael filled in the blanks, telling his viewers Tom spent five days in Mercy County General, recovering from respiratory depression caused by an overdose of synthetic opioids. The microphone went back to Tom.

"All I needed when I got out was another fix, but my girl, she took all my money so I wouldn't buy no more drugs." He waved to Cassandra, who stood just outside the camera view. The short, robust redhead wore black cotton shorts and a purple tank top with the block-letter words SENSATIONS SAVE across its front.

Michael jumped into the story again. "With nowhere else to turn, Tom remembered his Sensations capture from the night he overdosed. When he transferred the release, Tom's miraculous reaction has become a familiar story these days."

"She told me that I am saved, that I am loved, and my pain is now hers."

"Nickerson Enterprises has not commented on whether the voice Tom heard was that of their founder, Eleanor Nickerson. Full disclosure: Tom was not using authentic Nickerson SCARS devices." The camera followed Tom as he ran over to his girlfriend and began an impromptu dance party in the streets.

"It has been six weeks since Tom last used any drugs or Sensations recreations, and he claims to have no desire whatsoever."

The overhead projector went dark as lights began to brighten in the fishbowl and the entire corporate floorspace. Frosting the windows was unnecessary since everyone had already gathered. Marcus puffed a chunk of air before picking up his pen to start a list he titled FINANCIAL SCENARIOS. Leonard and Danette both chose to keep quiet. They would wait to see what everyone else thought before showing their cards. Sandy beamed like a proud mother hen. She later told Ellie, "I always knew you were going to change the world."

Kaylee was the one who could not stay quiet.

"You," she questioned while slapping all ten multicolor fingernails on the table and thrusting her chair back.

"You," she accused as both palms slid down to her brown corduroy slacks when she stood to face the head of the table.

"You," she declared while pointing her right index finger, the scarlet one, "have been a busy little beaver."

She turned to look into Drew's eyes. "And you're in on this?"

Raised eyebrows and a cocked head said more than words could, but it wasn't enough for Kaylee.

"What does *this* mean?" she pressed with exaggerated twitches that mocked his response.

"Zach got approval from the Army to fast-track his retirement," Ellie stepped in. Her eyes softened when she turned to look into his. "He's joining us as a global military and law enforcement agencies liaison."

Simple answers were not enough for Kaylee. Her voice grew angry as her patience, as thin as it was, dried up.

"Bing, bang, boom, that's it?" She scanned every face in the meeting room, asking them, "And, you're all okay with this?" But they seemed too stunned to speak.

Marcus reached up and tugged the sleeve of her blazer.

"What?" she barked and pointed at Ellie. "We've got our CEO playing late-night savior." Then, her scarlet dagger shifted to Zach. "Now, she's recruiting disciples. For what?" Counting the rest of the room with, "One, two, three, four, five," she paused but could not contain an irritated chuckle, "You're going to need a few more."

"I'm not a god."

Doubt and fear crashed against the wall Kaylee used as support, knocking her back down into the chair. Her legs slid straight, and the dancing fireflies on her fingertips sagged by her side. Tears welled, then flowed from her eyes as she begged to know, "Then, what the hell are you?"

Answers to her questions came when Ellie invited the room into a world unlocked by the single quick press of a black disc. Pain, suffering, rage, and agony blended with hope, harmony, ecstasy, and love with no anticipation of the next moment. Owen guided each person on the specific journey they needed, giving them every answer they wanted. They marveled at colors that had no complexion, shapes without form. *There is so much more to discover* was the only thought the release fed them. Days, minutes, or years passed by in their individual experiences. The most convenient way to put it is to say everyone grew wiser. When they were ready, everyone returned at that exact point to watch Ellie lift her finger from the one short press.

Without hesitation, Marcus leaned over toward Kaylee.

"Are there any other questions, Thomas?" Sarcasm earned him the orange finger, the middle one.

"I guess that makes you the tax collector, whatever his name was."

"It's me, Marcus." Every head turned and stared at Danette when she interrupted the banter. "I'm the one who has always doubted my friend until now, when I thrust my hand into her side."

An exchange of smiles replaced sentimental memories and answers to the question, "And then what?" Ellie tipped her head as she rolled her chair to the side toward Zach, surrendering the rest of the meeting to Danette. Without hesitation, the lawyer stood up and walked to the end of the table. Her instructions were simple.

"Nothing changes." Kaylee's *That-Was-Easy* reaction pulled a few tension-breaking chuckles from the room. Danette rolled her eyes.

"As I was saying, nothing changes." She paused to see if there was any more sarcasm before continuing, "until Ellie rolls out her vision. Remember, this is just computer code. Ones and zeros. Everybody uses the same program as Nickerson Enterprises." She paused again, looking to Ellie for the next words.

Ellie crossed her heart and promised, "There is no code out there besides the stuff I've released." Zach's raised eyebrows reminded her to add, "I removed anything we had that went against my goal of individual freedom." Her declaration, the cause of so much conflict between father and daughter, made him smile.

Pumping up the team like the head cheerleader of a high school pep rally, Danette spoke to Zach, Leonard, Kaylee, Marcus, and Sandy, "We're the face of Sensations." She pointed at their leader and insisted, "Not her. She'll share any new source code immediately. Then, you guys share the news about it through your channels."

When she stood, Danette stepped aside for Ellie to describe the future as safe, beneficial, moral, ethical, and legal uses of Sensations.

"We can lead them there," was her glorious simplification. It left one point unsettled, and Leonard was quick to speak up.

"What about everything you showed us?" His question was a shocking reminder of the visions that had started their discussion. "How long can you do that in the shadows?"

Her parting lips made no sound as she glanced toward the ground until an answer came. A deep breath pulled her focus back to the team.

"Until I am needed no longer."

Chapter 38

Seductive displays of the most sought-after innovations poured from every booth at the convention center. Artificial intelligence robots competed in epic rap battles with the day's top hip-hop stars. Advanced automation prototypes entertained spectators with demonstrations ranging from playing patty-cake with little children to making the perfect French macaroons from scratch. Heralded as the largest gathering of developers, engineers, and programmers worldwide, one more event was scheduled to close out the celebration.

Attendees were shoulder to shoulder trying to get a view of the keynote panel discussion on "Morality of the Mind." Lights dimmed around the convention center, drawing eyes to a mini stage set on the floor. It was empty except for five chairs lined across, waiting to have a purpose. Anyone who couldn't see the space directly had hundreds of monitors around the center to view the event.

The moderator, a fair-skinned woman with a choppy-layered pink bob hairstyle and a convention T-shirt tucked into her khaki slacks, introduced herself as Alish Post. She excelled at keeping the audience energized, even after three long days of caffeine-laced electronic overstimulation.

"Who's ready to meet our panel?" she howled with a pitch most people lose before they turn twenty-five. The crowd responded with cheers and an assortment of "Woo-hoo" catcalls.

A psychologist who specialized in Sensations-related addictions and treatments received courtesy claps. Damon "The Thrill" Juntz energized the crowd when he bolted on stage, drawing long, drawn-out chants of "Juuuuuuntzz!" His high-energy rhythm and thrill-seeking motivational captures were some of the hottest Sensations products of the year. The crowd offered a mixed reaction when Alish introduced Joseph Hale, a recovering Sensations addict from Milwaukee, Wisconsin. Rounds of applause followed, mixed with shouts of "Good for you!" as well as snickers about his weakness as a man. Joseph hung his head in shame when someone yelled, "Hey, Joe! Where's Lucy?" Obscene gestures from "The Thrill" further entertained the crowd.

"Are you ready for our last two panelists?" Alish smiled and brought a hand to her ear, urging everyone to cheer and scream louder. She held her pose long enough that it was almost impossible to hear her announce, "From industry leader Nickerson Enterprises, Chief Marketing Officer Kaylee Morris and Chief Operating Officer Leonard Powell."

They waited behind a short man wearing the same T-shirt-and-khaki uniform as Alish. When Leonid Romanovich Gusev heard the introduction, he turned around and faced Kaylee.

"The Nickerson woman will not be here tonight?" Gusev struggled to pronounce every word. When Kaylee said, "No," and some explanation afterward, he shoved his way past the backstage crew and exited through a fire stairwell.

Spectators on the opposite end of the now silent 2.6-million-square-foot convention center might have heard Kaylee whisper, "I told you this was a bad idea." The crash of heels clicking while she walked on stage was a constant reminder of the crowd's stunned silence.

Booing began the moment they sat in the last two seats.

Alish waved high in the air while trying to speak over the crowd.

"Yeah, yeah, I get it. You're disappointed, but Eleanor Nickerson doesn't make public appearances." Then, she gave the crowd a motherly smile while scolding, "You know that, guys." Even when technicians raised the volume on her headset microphone, the words did not help the situation.

There was no slow simmer. Mixed fevered chants erupted, pulling together into a ground-shaking demand for their beloved icon. Soon, "Ellie, Ellie," was all anyone could hear as the mob worked themselves into a frenzy. Kaylee and Leonard, along with the psychologist and roundtable MC, escaped through the back area before chaos spilled up to the stage. With a manic stare plastered across his face, "The Thrill" stood and faced the crowd with his arms stretched wide. His wire-thin frame, covered by tight denim jeans and a long-sleeved black-and-white camo shirt, rallied the group with more antics. Pulling a SCARS capture from his pocket triggered a fantastic roar from his fans. He activated the device and then slipped it back into his pocket. With one hand raised to his forehead like he was peering through the submarine scope, he scanned the crowd before turning his attention back to the stage. Joseph Hale sat frozen in his chair until "The Thrill" yanked him to his feet and jumped, sending both men stage diving into the mob. Joseph did not survive the swarm.

Zealots smashing booths and tearing down product displays in the name of their desire to see the Mother of Sensations became the lasting image of Tech Expo '24.

Chapter 39

In a silent, imageless world, he waited.

Countless tortured souls waited.

Horrors from the past gathered to fill that empty void, but she always sought him first.

Is it time to share my torment, mon chérie?

"Not yet, my darling."

Will it always be like this?

"No, but without you, I may never return."

The same irresistible moment overwhelmed her senses every night. The allure of his passions tempted her to escape the nightmare ahead.

Without regret, she always begged, "Please show me your suffering."

Time and again, Ellie endured Owen carrying her into a world where nothing existed but the suffering of others. There were moments when she learned their names as she felt them crying out to curse the choices they made. However, their captures often lost those defining characteristics forever. Only flashpoints of fear, loathing, pain, sorrow, and regret remained. It was all they had to offer when someone placed that simple device in front of them and captured their agony. The device didn't care why or who. All it did was take the worst part and hold it forever. She visited that dimension to liberate the oppressed, reliving their dark flash one final time. Unspeakable acts of violence and depravity poured into Ellie. Because she did, no one would ever experience them again.

She would never describe those atrocities but could never let go of their constant reminder.

Gentle chimes echoed through the room as soft lighting rose from every corner. Ellie lay in the center and fought the alarm's effort to roust her out of bed.

"Good morning, Ellie. The time is 3:30 a.m."

The charms would not stop until she did something. Burning bright through her lids, the lights would not dim on their own.

"All right, all right," she relented. "I'm up. Turn off the alarm."

Silence returned.

Only when Ellie opened her eyes did the flood of torment she had battled overnight strike back. They grew wide and refused to blink as her lower lip quaked. Lying above the covers, she popped up and rolled to one side, where a bucket waited for her to vomit the empty contents of her stomach. With a rag sitting on the end table, she wiped bits of blood and bile off her face before taking the bucket into her bathroom for a well-practiced cleanup routine. With one tug of the top-knot bun, her hair cascaded down on the back of the same oversized green T-shirt she wore every night. She looked down at its logo across the front, tracing her fingers across *De Oppresso Liber* before spitting the water rinse into the sink. On her way to the kitchen, a shadowy outline sitting on her couch didn't seem to be a surprise.

"How'd you get in?" she asked without interrupting her path.

Abby chuckled. "I still have your key. I would've turned on a light, but I didn't want to use the wrong command and wake you up."

Ellie's whisper, "Turn on the living room lights," brought a smile to both faces. Abby hung her head, shaking it back and forth as she walked over to the kitchen. A fresh cup of coffee was already waiting.

"I hope you don't mind a running buddy this morning." Nothing she wore gave any indication of her military background. Colorful splash leggings and a neon-yellow jacket would blend well with the cross-country pack running through Central Park in early March. Ellie gave a *Not-At-All* wave of her hand while she took her second sip.

Minutes passed in silence as they stood in the kitchen and waited for the caffeine to work its magic. Just as Ellie tipped her cup to drain the last bit, Abby marked her question with a noticeable sigh.

"So, how long do you think you can do that?"

"Do what?" There was no other reaction.

Abby reached and laid a hand up against Ellie's arm, easing the slight tremor.

"El, I could hear the screams."

Ellie's reaction was more technical than emotional. On her way to grab a tablet from the kitchen counter, she commented, "I've never had someone in the room with us overnight." Abby bunched her brows in confusion over the comment but said nothing.

"Was I loud?" She started typing random bullet comments.

"It was soft, muffled."

"What did I say?"

"You mostly sounded like you were in pain."

Short, quick questions popped off one after the other. The moment Abby stopped talking, Ellie asked the next. Her head remained focused on the tablet. Her frantic typing never slowed.

"Did my pain drift off, or did it drop quick?"

Abby threw both hands up in the air, her palms pushing against the surge of frantic words.

"Stop. Stop," was all she could say. Ellie started to ask another question, but her gaping mouth closed when she looked up and saw Abby's eyes.

Temperatures hovering close to freezing did little to deter loyal followers from joining the predawn run through Central Park. Abby never asked if it was safe for her to be out in a crowd like that. Ellie never commented on the four security guards who wore matching cold-weather gear, even when they surrounded her like orange traffic cones marking a pothole on Fifth Avenue. The police stationed along random sections of her route never reminded anyone that the park did not open until 6:00 a.m. In fact, talking was a luxury few could afford if they wanted to keep up with her pace. By mile ten, only a dozen or so stragglers remained. The rest usually stopped under one of those lampposts or by a park bench as steam rose from their exposed skin and the night chill bit unprotected lungs. A few had planned well to protect themselves from the elements, so they carried on.

Added to her running buddies were a steady stream of spectators lined along the asphalt trail meandering through the park. Some offered words of encouragement and praise for their savior, while others shouted obscenities at Ellie for her crimes against God and His creations. Most simply woke early in the morning to stake their spot along the trail, hoping to catch a glimpse as she ran by, like a passing parade float on Thanksgiving. Camera flashes only picked up red dots peering through a black wool-knit cap and wraparound scarf protecting her face. Ellie often glanced to scan the crowd for familiar onlookers. One of those faces sent her to the ground, cowering in the fetal position. Both arms covered her face and head. A pathetic cry, "No. No," triggered the four security guards and three other joggers to draw pistols that had been tucked into their sides and point them at anyone they thought might be a threat.

Abby collapsed over Ellie and started probing for information.

"What? What did you see?" She repeated the question four times before any answer became coherent.

"He was there," she wailed. "I remember."

Abby looked around the shrinking crowd. Those who did not run at first sight of guns tracking their movement were either pointing their guns or indifferent New Yorkers waiting for a reason to react.

"He was where?" she wanted to know. The only word Abby could understand was "Russia." She pointed at a tall man wearing light-gray sweatpants and a matching hoodie.

"Take one. Go north."

She pointed at another with black compression clothing under his red athletic shorts and insulated vest.

"Take one. Search west into the wooded area."

After both teams took off, three other joggers approached the women and helped them to their feet. The orange-clad guards only seemed to get in the way. Abby wrapped both arms around Ellie's waist, propping her up and leading her toward the nearby SUV. If anyone else tried to touch her, or if they even came too close, her knees would buckle under the weight of a fear that drew wretched howls. Abby stroked gentle caresses across Ellie's tear-stained face, humming soft melodies until her wailing turned to sobs, finally quieting in the back seat of her military escort. For the first time in over six months, she slept without reliving encounters she could only wish were nothing more than nightmares. All it took was a trigger from her own hellish experience.

Nothing roused Ellie from her sleep. Her body decided it had rested enough, a reaction she wasn't familiar with anymore. Slight breaks in the curtain brought a touch of the city's nightlights into her bedroom. When her arms snagged underneath the covers, she frowned before lifting the comforter to slide her legs over the edge. An unnecessary bucket sat waiting on the floor. She stood in front of the dresser and stared at her reflection, tracing a finger along the bun of hair on her head before pulling the olive-green T-shirt tight across her chest.

"Like it never happened."

Murmurs from the living room matched her whisper, so she threw on a pair of black sweatpants to join them under the glow of a lone floor lamp.

Zach did not get out of the accent chair when Abby jumped up, only to be waved off by a dismissive hand.

"No, it's okay," Ellie said, heading to the kitchen. "Go back to what you were doing."

They were waiting, so they went back to waiting. She brewed a coffee, returned to the living room, and sat on the couch across from the others. Two sips were needed before she placed her cup on the white marble coffee table. The click of its ceramic edge striking the stone kicked off the next words.

"Abby," she said, "thank you." With her hands tucked in the folds of her oversized turtleneck sweater, Abby nodded her reply.

"I guess your visit was a little more than an unplanned coincidence."

Zach jumped into the conversation.

"We picked up chatter that Russian Sensations operations were running into," he used air quotes to describe "critical infrastructure breakdowns." Ellie didn't ask for clarification. "You are targeted as the cause of those failures."

A smug grin splashed across his face when she reclassified the accusation as fact.

"I am that cause."

"Captain Highland and her team have been shadowing you for about a month now."

Abby leaned into the circle.

"Do you know who was in the park?"

Ellie closed her eyes and pulled her cheekbones high, but the strain only produced a slow shake of her head. She began to rub the ring still on her finger.

"No, but I saw him before. In Surgut."

Questions that everyone knew the answers to, and those that would always remain a mystery, never made their way into the living room that night.

"I don't think you should be in the open like that for a while." Zach reached up and stroked his gray beard. He wore it full but well groomed, with no stray hairs that stood out or hung over his lip. "Danette and Marcus are heading down to D.C. to meet with regulatory and tax agencies."

In the past, Ellie had dismissed those meetings with an *I-Don't-Give-A-Shit-About-That-Stuff* look. Her response was yet another example.

Abby took the handoff and added, "We'd like you to join them."

Muted dialogue took over as the three exchanged glances across the living room. Ellie pulled her coffee close, drawing deep breaths of the complex aromas hidden at the bottom of her near-empty cup.

"What time are they leaving?"

"Six a.m.," they both said. Abby added, "It's almost eleven right now."

Since it was no longer a point worth arguing, both Abby and Zach held their tongues when Ellie walked them to the front door. Her simple explanation was, "That'll be here before we know it. I have to get back to bed."

Chapter 40

Bureaucratic mavens filled the arced row of lawmakers lining the oak podium to hear testimony on the taxation and regulatory oversight of Sensations. Spaced apart, each setting had its resident's nameplate, microphone, and side shelf to hold their beverage. Behind the senior staff was an arsenal of aides, interns, and lawyers, prepared to feed bounds of tedious data at a moment's notice. The Nickerson Enterprises representatives sat at a bare plywood table with a single gooseneck microphone to share between the three.

Ellie sat without speaking for three hours, peering into the crowd of familiar faces as they ran through scripted messages calling for government ownership of Sensations.

"Ms. Beacon," she interrupted the FDA Deputy Commissioner. The figure she had met years earlier looked like she had lost the battle of bureaucratic deterioration. "Um, Olivia, if I may?"

Danette slid the microphone over to Ellie as she whispered, "Be nice."

"Ms. Nickerson, it's a pleasure to have you finally join our conversation." Beacon's jab prompted more than a few whimsical grins.

"I'm concerned about your intent with these proceedings today." *Intent* sparked unusual reactions in that meeting. Rapid breaths from Danette did not help to calm her anxiety. Marcus closed his eyes for an extended blink before shifting his weight in the uncomfortable wooden chair. Three officials sharing the front row with Beacon pursed their lips tight to contain any smirk. Every eye turned to the deputy commissioner, who ran her hand across the pleats on the green version of her grandmother's favorite dress. After a moment to consider the question, Beacon responded with a three-pack-a-day snarl.

"My intent," she said, snapping the venomous word, "is to understand your company's need to dominate this technology."

Ellie dropped her shoulders and relaxed her head to one side. Smiling was a knee-jerk response while she waited for a single chuckle to bubble up from her stomach. However, her answer was much more passive.

"Olivia," Ellie's hands animated every word, "all SCARS technology is registered under either free-to-use or open-source software patents. There are no restrictions to make, modify, use, or sell any component of the designs or code."

"But only your design works consistently," was the accusation.

"That seems to be the case."

"I don't understand," Beacon said. "Why? Why are you doing this?"

Damnation never melted away. Painful moments in others' lives that became hers swarmed through the darkest channels of Ellie's mind. Whether she was awake or asleep, they waited for a reason to jump to the forefront of her thoughts.

Why? Why are you doing this?

A panicked woman begged the man she loved. His words and the foul stench of whiskey on his breath hurt her more than anything the others did to her body. She was a gift, a plaything for them to enjoy that night and relive whenever they wanted.

How many other times was she violated on full display for his special guests without the enduring keepsake of Ellie's SCARS technology? Was she punished because of her love for that man, one that led to a legacy of one brutal moment? Horror achieved victory that day, plaguing both of their memories when Ellie could not respond to simple questioning.

"Why? Why are you doing this?"

Danette tried to deflect Beacon's focus by raising the "614 regulatory measures implemented by either the FCC or the FDA," but that only led to a heated exchange.

"I would prefer to hear Ms. Nickerson's answer first."

Unfazed, Danette continued, "Unregistered Sensations include products that have entered the global market without government oversight or regulation."

"Ms. Reddy," was Beacon's last attempt using the subtle tone of her raspy voice.

"While it is estimated that over eighty-five percent of these products record or transmit valid Sensations, counterfeit SCARS may be categorized as..."

Heated words stepped over Danette's unyielding remarks.

"That is not the question I asked, Ms. Reddy."

"…dummy SCARS that do not contain any valid Sensations at all."

"Shut up," was Beacon's heated demand, delivered with a slap against the rim of her regulatory amphitheater.

"Or counterfeit SCARS that may be lower cost, ineffective modeling or depraved, violent, illegal, or otherwise sinister actions."

Spectators of that clash sat frozen, their stares waiting for more. Ellie felt Beacon's knotted expression. She relieved the burning sting of bile retched in their stomach, spraying it across the barren table. Beacon watched Marcus and Danette scramble to catch Ellie as her eyes rolled back and her body fell limp to one side.

"We're done for today," Beacon said, waving her arms to scatter the flies. "Take her back to that ivory tower." With a smile of long overdue satisfaction, Beacon whipped her focus back to Ellie, "Go home to your safe world, little girl, behind a keyboard where nothing can hurt you."

Chapter 41

A typical gaggle of protesters and supporters gathered outside Ellie's building. It seemed as if their only roles were as a permanent presence of fanatics who hoped that someone would take notice and give them a chance to be heard. Focused more on the unexpected cold weather, they showed no concern when Marcus's green sedan pulled up to the service entrance just past nine o'clock at night.

Danette pleaded again for Ellie to get checked out at the hospital.

"If you won't do that, E, let me spend the night to make sure you're okay."

Ellie flicked her wrist in her friend's direction from the back seat.

"I told you I'm fine," she said with a frustrated breath, "just like I told you an hour ago, two hours ago, and three hours ago."

Danette rolled her eyes. "Whatever. Four hours ago, you were passed out at the HHS headquarters with fucking puke running down your cleavage." She turned around and dropped her head to the side, a pool of drool streaming over the center console. That brought the first giggle from Ellie in weeks.

"Dork."

"Loser."

"Isn't there a better woman you would rather have in your bed?"

Danette spun back around and grabbed her phone. "Better? No." She typed a text message while bragging, "But, definitely more fun."

Marcus stayed out of the banter and drove the car. When they reached the garage elevator, guarded by two of Leonard's security personnel, he put the car in park.

Ellie reached her hand out to where Danette's waited. When they curled their fingers around each other, they shared a silent, intimate conversation.

"I promise," Ellie said.

A fresh shower and a change of clothing were all Ellie could think about. It was unnaturally dark when she closed the front door, cutting the warm beams that strayed in from the hallway. Drawn shades silenced the visible noise clashing below in the streets of SoHo. Ellie paid no attention, dropping her backpack to glide across the floor plan with the ease of a well-practiced homeowner.

Calling out, "Turn on the lights," only after she passed the living room, Ellie never saw Gusev sitting in the burnt-orange accent chair. She set music to fill the air with smooth R&B before peeling off her polo, its front stained a darker shade of blue. Clothing piled up as Ellie stripped naked, the ponytail braid covering only a thin strip of ebony skin running from her shoulder blades down to her upper thigh. She stood in front of the dresser and stared at her reflection. Two fingers traced along stretches of flesh where they had beaten, bruised, and violated her body, leaving their marks during the months in captivity. But all those wounds had healed and no longer told the tale of those months away from her ivory tower. Minutes passed in silence before she wrapped the braid in a bun and stepped into the shower for a quick rinse of the day's troubling reminders.

With purple sweatpants and her oversized T-shirt on, Ellie grabbed a wedge of protein bread and a glass of water from the kitchen. In the living room, Gusev waited in silence until she froze when they locked eyes.

"Please have a seat" sounded more like a plea than a command. His Russian words did nothing to her. Options to scream, run, collapse, or fight never took form. Average features defined a man Ellie recognized as pure evil, but her body refused to reveal the fear she should have felt.

"Why are you here?" Her words were soft, and the tone never wavered as deep breaths through her flaring nostrils calmed the spiking beat of her heart. Her weight shifted until she was standing even on both feet.

Gusev gestured toward an empty chair and repeated, "Please."

Ellie sat, placing both items on the table that separated her from the intruder.

"I am not here to harm you," Gusev said while lowering his hand to where it rested in his lap.

"Then, why are you hiding?"

"I am a criminal in your country."

"Then, why did you come?"

"I am a criminal in mine."

"What do you want?"

"Salvation."

Ellie stared into the eyes of a monster, but the beast never appeared. Instead, a man suffering from the torment he had inflicted on others described the lasting image she had planted the day Sokolov's Surgut facility burned to the ground. He introduced himself as Leonid Romanovich Gusev.

"My job was to approve the Sensations we created." Without reacting to the horrifying experiences, he said, "Every moment I had to re-create made me hate the world even more than I despised myself." Lifeless eyes searched for more to say about those captures but put nothing into words until a smile broke free from the vacant stare.

"Your thoughts were the only peace I found."

The chair molded to Ellie when her once-frightened body settled into the conversation. Gusev explained the difference between her message of strength from the cries of sorrow that flooded his mind.

"When I described it to my coworker, she told me your message was in her, too." His eyes widened at the glorious revelation. "Everyone we work with had that in them."

Ellie pulled her memory of the event she had captured.

"It was our only peace in the world of shit we continued to create under Alexander Sergeyevich." Gusev's smile faded at the mention of Medvedev's North Korea operation, but the gloom was temporary.

"The wicked memories I had. They began to disappear, one by one...."

Ellie jumped into the story to share in his excitement. "When the release discs failed as well."

Gusev popped from the chair; his ragged blue wool blazer and tan trousers had wear marks in the most unusual places. A messy beard added to the impression that he had traveled the entire way without changing that outfit, the only set of clothing he owned.

"It *was* you."

The confirmation sent Gusev into a frenzy. He stepped behind the chair and began pacing the living room, planning how to "contact my comrades and let them know Eleanor Nickerson will save us." But, the words came as a shock to him.

"You will save us from their nightmares that still remain, will you?"

"There are nightmares born all the time, Leonid Romanovich."

Gusev waved his arms like he was trying to scare away her last comment.

"No, no, no, no," he insisted. Finally, dirty hands pulled his arms out until the elbows locked in front of Ellie.

"We stopped that," he proclaimed. His tired eyes widened as rapid head nods confirmed the statement.

"We killed Alexander Sergeyevich Popov," he boasted. His face framed a tender look that begged for approval. "For you," he pledged.

Harsh strikes against each syllable formed his first English words.

"We got him."

Simple conversation replaced his quest for salvation that night. Ellie's time was not spent saving the oppressed but instead rescuing their oppressor.

"Let me show you something." She invited Gusev to her protein bread and glass of water on the table before leaving the room.

He mouthed the words "Thank you" as his body sprang and grabbed the chunk of food. Every bit was gone when she returned a few moments later. Even the crumbs that fell onto the plate disappeared as he devoured his first meal in days. They stuck to his moistened fingertip one by one, then disappeared in his mouth.

She returned with a white serving tray, carrying the rest of the bread, a pitcher of water, and her tablet. His eyes rolled with delight as a second piece, then a third, filled his belly before he gave in to Ellie's request, "Drink some water, Leonard." The American name made Gusev giggle. Creases on his thin face already seemed to fill. His red, blotchy skin was on a softer pale shade.

With access to the library of Sensations created by Nickerson Enterprises, the two toured a world where there was no place for violence. Instead, exhilaration resulted from pushing their exhausted body across the finish line of her first ultramarathon. They drifted into the wave of joy that followed shock from the roar of "Happy Birthday" and dangling in anticipation to find out who "The winner is." Gusev learned what it was like to deny the once-irresistible temptation that plagued an addict. The blackened heart of losing a loved one did not compare to gratitude for holding their hand in those final moments. Overwhelming struggles for breath when bringing a new life into the world faded when they grasped a tiny finger for the first time. His mind was once again flush with raw stages of awareness, yet he welcomed them all. But knowing the joys others held in life left him angry for the moments Ellie could not absolve him of.

"I have done horrible things," he confessed.

The next day, he found that salvation on his own. Flanked by Ellie and Zach, he walked up First Avenue and surrendered to the International Criminal Court. Sunrise brought unique dazzling rays into Manhattan that morning, splashing every step along the way with fresh memories of the day Leonid Romanovich Gusev began to pay for the atrocities he had committed. Years later, he described that experience as "The greatest gift our God has granted me."

Chapter 42

As news outlets scrambled to unravel the sighting of Eleanor Nickerson walking alone out of the twenty-story, darkened-glass tower next to the United Nations, a small Midwest congregation gathered at their tiny church. Twelve rows of pews made from the finest red maple available at the time were the only original pieces remaining inside the 234-year-old house of worship. Only the old, sick, or mothers holding young children filled them that day. Everyone else packed shoulder to shoulder to witness Adam Lerner's deliverance ceremony. The older men dressed in formal attire, the women in their Sunday-service best. Young children followed suit, with button-down shirts and khakis picked out by their mothers. If anyone wore jeans or some ragged T-shirt, it was a rebellious teenager counting the minutes until they could meet up with friends and gossip about what they did to Adam.

A middle-aged man nudged the mop-haired kid standing next to him.

"Keep it up and you'll be up there next week, mister."

The vague threat worked like a charm. A wide-eyed head nod and sheepish "Yes, sir" were the boy's only unscripted reactions for the rest of the sermon.

Rustling bells in the distance cued the organist to play slow, somber chamber music that poured from brass pipes throughout the small rectangular building where eggshell-white rafters stretched one hundred feet high. Two middle-aged men wearing flowing red robes and a teenager dressed in a similar style, but all white, stepped forward from the crowd and approached the altar. One robed escort stepped to the pulpit and switched on its microphone.

When he spoke his first words, "Let us pray," the entire congregation, even the rebellious adolescents, dipped their heads.

"Lord, we gather here today to save the soul of our beloved Adam Lerner." When he heard his name, the white-robed teenager opened his eyes to peer into the crowd. He focused on three kids around his age, but none of the boys ever looked back at him.

"Adam's unnatural sins were not his willing path."

Several voices shared their disagreement with the preacher, offering grunts of "Uh-uh" and "Nope."

"We gather here today to celebrate his rejection of the homosexual temptations of Satan."

After smatterings of "Amen" from the congregation, the preacher described Adam's unholy encounter at the high school dance and promised the same protective care and guardianship that "saved the other boys."

When the other red robe raised a black disc, up-tempo gospel music electrified the crowd. Adam's eyes grew wide as he watched his friends and neighbors erupt in celebration, their voices drowning the monotonous noises of the pipe organ. One press of that disc cut his awareness off from their celebration. In his world, there was no noise to distract his enlightenment.

I found the Lord today, and He welcomed me back into the flock. I am loved.

Adam smiled as the two red robes grasped him by the shoulders and lowered his body to the floor with care. The congregation sang and danced as he lay in a frozen state of repentance.

He will guide me and protect me. I wait and pray for the day He leads me to a ripe woman, the only one with whom I am meant to share my love and my body, all in His name. Praise be to God.

The congregation welcomed their commitment to Adam through their calling, celebrating, and singing for fifteen minutes of his salvation. Throughout his ceremonial awakening, no one noticed a young man in the back of the church. The blackened, greased fade and acrylic plugs in his stretched earlobes should have stood out among the conservative congregation, but the crowd remained focused on young Adam.

He entered the historic church just as Adam's ceremony began, raised a smartphone high above his head to record the unusual ritual, then left before anyone noticed.

*
**

Unraveling the bizarre chain of events over the last twenty-four hours had to wait until Sandy finished scolding her boss.

"I can't believe you went down there in sweatpants." The baggy purple bottoms clashed with her black hoodie, *NYC* branded across its front in a rainbow-mixed cartoon font. A casual shrug of her shoulders was Ellie's only reaction she could spare. The rest of her focus was on raising an oversized

Gulag Burrito to her mouth. That first bite sent her eyes rolling up to the heavens.

"Mmm, sorry," were the mumbled words she shared between chews of George's re-creation. "You guys really should try this. It's delicious." Bacon grease and butter dripped from one end of the folded pancake, splattering on the plate, table, and her clothing. Looks of disgust on everyone else sitting in the booth told a different story.

Danette spoke for the rest of the group when she said, "That's revolting."

Ellie dismissed the comment with a wave of her pinky, the burrito inching closer to her mouth for another bite. She turned her head across the empty diner.

"George," she yelled into the kitchen, "this dish will go viral when my story breaks." Clashes of metal on metal followed by a hilarious uproar poured from the kitchen when she added, "It'll make you rich."

"I'm already rich, remember?"

Danette jumped back into the conversation they were having. The lawyer wanted to know, "What do you think he's going to tell them?"

"Everything he knows," was Ellie's instant reaction. "He asked me the same question." Another bite interrupted her story. "That's what I told him to say." She stretched her hands across the table to offer Kaylee a taste of her late-night breakfast. Flickers of neon-green nail polish shooed the creation away.

"This trippy little story you're writing is going to turn our market space upside down."

"Kaylee, that's not even the half of it," was Danette's cryptic response. "We need to follow up with Zach once the ICC finishes taking his statement."

"They'll want to talk to El."

"Let me handle that."

While the rest of the table sipped on coffee and espressos, lieutenants debating how they would protect her, Ellie ate the burrito like she didn't have a care in the world.

Private conversations, debates of her calculated next steps, revealed themselves only to Sandy through the silent murmur of her lips.

Chapter 43

Will it always be like this?

"No, my love. Only until we take away all their suffering."

Emptiness blanketed Ellie's senses as she waited for guidance no one should ever want, for answers she should never dare seek.

"Please show me your suffering."

Persistent brutality struck the Mother of Sensations with a force that gave her a glimpse into the depths of human depravity. A collection of souls oppressed for the sake of capturing the instance of their agony continued growing in an open field nourished by her own fears.

"What did you expect was going to happen?" she heard Andy demand the answer again while she absorbed the suffering of one, only to have it replaced by the sorrow of many.

"Sex. Depravity. Violence. More sex."

Each instance joined the screams and rage of terror already inside her. Their pleas to stop became her cries for mercy, yet she continued to beg Owen, "Please show me your suffering."

"You offer people unfettered access to emotions and desires. What the fuck do you think they'll want?"

Tormented visitors filled every crevice of her mind, defiling whatever purity stood in their way, yet she begged for more.

"Please show me your suffering."

Whispers of air circulating high above her bed marked the only disturbance in the room. Lifts and falls of her chest edged a slight crease in her olive-green T-shirt. Like an innocent newborn drunk on their mother's milk, Ellie's body lay motionless in the bed as her mind suffered the siege brought on by that beautiful creation she had unleashed upon the world.

Then the shrieks and tremors erupted.

"Will it always be like this?" Her cries for mercy made noise in both worlds.

Yes, mon chérie.

Ellie faced an infinite array of choices. She wanted nothing more than to welcome the security of Owen's embrace, but there was only one thing she continued to do.

"Please show me your suffering."

Chapter 44

Hints of nutmeg weaved their way into and out of the bundle of savory aromas that wafted across the conference room. Sandy laid out a special selection of treats prepared for Nickerson Enterprises' 2024 first-quarter board meeting. A plate of eggnog cookies, Marcus's favorite, sat in front of his chair as an incentive to rush through the bad news.

Those frosted delights made it difficult to keep focus on the presentation, even as he reported, "Our first quarter numbers are in the red." Bar graphs and line charts on slides one through nine told the story of a financial bloodbath. "In every sector, sales are up, but revenue is down."

With a quick snort, Kaylee added, "It was fun while it lasted," then snuck a bite of the gingerbread fudge George had baked for her.

Leonard's treat was a hearty slice of homemade pumpkin pie.

"We still have some cash to burn through. My team will keep its focus on cost measures, but you two need to figure out our best price points to break even." Both Sales and Finance acknowledged the comment. Marcus gave a head nod while Kaylee snapped a whimsical salute with her purple-fingernail hand.

"Legal," he said with his fork at the ready, "why don't you go next."

Danette's normal put-together appearance was subdued, with her blonde locks pulled back in a ponytail, her eyeliner, lipstick, and mascara washed away by the cold-water scrub she had needed in order to energize for the meeting. Since Gusev's arrest, a nonstop barrage of lawsuits and subpoenas had turned her department into a twenty-four-hour operation that continued to fall behind.

Any conversation with a lawyer that started with, "Well, just when I thought it couldn't get worse," was sure to create anxiety. To make matters worse, Danette never even took a nibble of the banana-nut muffin waiting for her.

Instead, she pushed the plate out to the center of the table and continued.

"I got this sent to me to add to our pile of sh... stuff." She paused for a moment, wringing both hands to collect her emotions. After one sharp exhale, she tapped a button on her keyboard to play the Adam Lerner video. "A friend of mine sent this to me. It's been circulating through some online LGBTQ chat groups. It's kind of hard to see in the picture, but apparently, this church is using Sensations to, and I'm paraphrasing here, 'wash the gay out of this kid.'"

Parishioners singing and dancing obscured most of the ceremony, but the camera caught glimpses of Adam lowered to the floor in a catatonic state. The man behind the camera tried to describe what was happening, but his words faded into the sea of rejoicing. Once outside, he described the ceremony in detail. He was careful not to turn the camera toward himself and spoke with a rag over his mouth.

"This is the second ceremony they have performed today," the disguised voice said. "The first was

Stephen." He pointed the camera toward the historic steeple, made from 150-year-old maple timber with a polished brass spire, and held a photograph out at arm's length.

"This is Adam and Stephen."

Two young teenagers sat together on a green park bench. One had shaggy blond hair curling at the collar of his pale-blue Oxford shirt; the other kept his hair trimmed close to the sides and back with a top filled with bouncing red coils. The blond boy smiled as the redhead planted a kiss against his cheek. "They're going to do this ceremony every day until they wash all the gay out of them."

The phone image began to shake and scramble when someone yelled, "Hey, what's going on?" and sent the man running. It cut out moments later.

Zach broke the stunned silence when he asked if Ellie had seen the video. He had already devoured the southern peach pie on his plate, even before its trail of scented steam had a chance to fill the room.

"No, but it gets worse." Danette lifted a binder of examples she had collected after researching the Adam Lerner case. It documented involuntary uses of Sensations to support church organizations' doctrine and reprogram criminals, the mentally ill, or otherwise "unruly" children.

"I'm confused," Kaylee said. "Wouldn't she know about these things already? With her, you know," she waved her hand with the turquoise fingers high in the air and made spooky ghost howls.

Mimicking her gesture with an added smirk, Danette said, "I don't know how *this* works, but these captures were created voluntarily. They're harmless." Her hand landed back on the table. "They're just used in godless ways."

In unison, "So, where is this going?" rang out from both ends of the conference room. Leonard and Zach exchanged glances before turning their attention back to Danette.

"I'm outta my league, guys," was her knee-jerk response as she reached deep into the table and grabbed her muffin. Crumbs scattered across the laptop as she jammed the brown-and-beige-speckled dessert into her mouth. After three chews and a healthy gulp of coffee, she added, "There is not a person in the world who can predict what's gonna happen next."

*
**

Metallic jingles from beyond the door interrupted the fast-paced clickety-clack of her keyboard. Ellie turned from across the room to watch Zach ease his way into the condo. Under his coat, he wore the same black corporate T-shirt from the meeting they'd had earlier that day.

He whispered, "Sorry," when he saw Ellie at her workstation. "I thought you might be asleep." She just smiled and waved him in, but jumped from her chair and ran to the door when she saw the George's Diner box in his hand. Twenty seconds later, powdered sugar from a jelly donut dusted her full, rusted-pink lips and the front of her long-sleeved crew.

"Oh my God," she chirped, "how did you know?" winking and waving her hand in the dining room's direction. Zach watched as Ellie devoured one, then another, then half of a third donut before waving off the rest. He scurried to the kitchen and returned with the water pitcher and a glass. In between gulps, she thanked him with another erratic wave of her hand before adding, "It's been a while since I've eaten."

Food was fourth in line on her list of priorities, if not worse. Grappling with the devastation caused by her programming consumed more time than ever before. Coding and releasing improvements gave users a more robust experience with Sensations. Drained by the constant focus needed in both areas, Ellie revived her physical and abstract frames on New York City's maze of running trails, where spectators lined the roadways to catch a glimpse of the Mother of Sensations and her entourage whenever their *WheresEllie* tracking app notified them she had left the condo for her daily mini-marathon. Nourishing her chiseled ebony frame happened somewhere between the things she needed to survive.

A wilted smile betrayed Zach's purpose. He slid a chair over to sit close as Ellie placed her glass on the table. She wrapped her arms around him and welcomed the tender squeeze of his embrace. Without warning, tears flowed down both cheeks; he met her soft whimper with a shushing exhale meant to ease the demons. Ellie closed her eyes and leaned her temple into Zach in search for her father's protection.

"Here we are again," she said. "Is this a personal visit?"

It was another question that needed no response. Zach refused to say anything, relying instead on the whispers of his exhale to prolong their bond. When his grasp finally relented, a tear-stained expression forced the unpleasant conversation about the swamp of turmoil.

He vowed they would face it together.

Withering glows of a setting sun, or perhaps vibrant rays from a morning still in its infancy, seeped through drawn shades in the living room when Zach and Ellie finished talking. The beam layered everything on the floor plan until it crossed over Ellie's foot. She leaned back in her chair and inspected the damage left behind after their binge.

"I don't think there's any more food left in the fridge."

Zach rubbed his belly and pushed air through puffed cheeks long enough to agree with her assessment. He grabbed the carafe and refilled both cups with lukewarm coffee before continuing their conversation.

"How confident are you that your plan will work?"

Ellie tapped two fingers on the dining room table before she lifted her cup for a healthy sip. With the bitter dark roast still perched under her nose, the creased skin across her forehead previewed conflicting thoughts.

"My part, I'm certain." Her shrugged shoulders and raised eyebrows answered the rest of Zach's question.

Two chirps on Ellie's phone mixed with the silent rumble inside a small brown leather case on the table. Zach checked his text.

"Danette wants us to check out Global News."

"Good morning, and good day around the world. It's Thursday, April 25, 2024. I'm Michael Yao, and this is Global News." Blue and yellow burst from the news outlet's iconic logo as it faded from digital screens worldwide, leaving Michael in the studio against a pale backdrop. Images filled that canvas as he discussed the broad list of ICC charges against Gusev. His tone compelled viewers to despise the man in an orange jumpsuit filmed walking from the courthouse to an unmarked black SUV with his hands shackled in the front. He described the charges as "crimes against humanity and crimes of aggression." Michael's voice finally cracked when he confessed, "I don't think I can repeat specific examples he confessed to in that Russian factory used to produce horrific recreations for capturing Sensations experiences."

Video of roaring flames from inside the Surgut facility captured the chaos recorded when twenty-two people were killed on what Gusev's statement described as "the day Ellie Nickerson unleashed her vengeance on Dema Zlovich."

"Dema Zlovich Sokolov," Michael explained, "is the man believed to be responsible for the world's largest international ring of criminal Sensations activity. He was killed in what Russian authorities previously believed was an attack by an unidentified rival organization."

The screen went dark until an image of one person began to appear. Michael's voice presented his assessment of otherwise random events.

"Four days later, Eleanor Nickerson returned from her unexplained exile."

Zach's helpless stare focused on Ellie as she watched Michael Yao describe factions of the world divided over their judgments. Opposition to the Mother of Sensations painted her as a criminal, working alongside Sokolov until her desire for unconditional reign led to a power grab. Others saw her as pure evil, driven to control humanity by manipulating their minds with dark magic and indoctrination into her unholy cult.

Michael also presented the loyal flock, who believed Ellie's creation was their only chance for salvation, redemption, or acceptance by the same people trying to dismantle her legacy.

A prominent leader in the Sensations industry insisted, "It's just a computer program. A good one, but just a program." From behind his rustic-stained executive desk, the slick twenty-something charmer pointed to a glass display case filled with his capture-and-release devices. "Now that it's out there," he said, "it's up to companies like SenseMasters to make the experience even better."

Nothing in Michael's news report stirred a visible reaction from Ellie. She remained still until her body

jerked when Zach said, "Your children are all
scattering to their separate corners." His sarcasm
put a smile on her face, but that faded when Olivia
Beacon appeared in the next segment, smiling like it
was her overdue debutante introduction to society.
Six members of Congress stood behind her on the
steps of the US Capitol. Instead of playing the audio
as she fired a blast of accusations and demands in
front of the bustling crowd of reporters covering the
ICC's breaking news, Michael spoke over her muted
tirade.

"Representatives from the FCC and other agencies
are calling for lawmakers to revoke all licenses and
patents granted to Nickerson Enterprises
immediately."

Ellie's smile returned. She licked a finger and
swiped the inside of the donut box to enjoy its
powdered sugar remnants. "That poor woman" went
unexplained. Three more dabs of her finger swiped
the box clean, so she stood to inspect every container
on the table for something to eat. Zach slid a
zucchini casserole dish in her direction, wincing his
face at the sight of the cold, four-day-old leftovers.
She clacked with joy and dug her fork in before her
body settled back in her chair.

"They're going to try to take away your creation,"
Zach said, amazed by the absurdity of the moment.

"Mm-hmm." Her mouth was way too full for words.

"Something you give away for free."

What sounded like the word "Yep" spilled from her
mouth, along with a few speckles of Parmesan
cheese.

Disbelief slumped his shaking head when he admitted, "So they can isolate the technology under the name of national security."

Ellie wiped her mouth and placed the napkin on the table among the casualties from the night of binge eating. Zach watched the silent, heated discussion that overtook her lips and hands. When the dust finally settled, she reached for her smartphone and dialed a number in her favorites list. Muffled ringing broke the quiet. While waiting, she shared her thoughts.

"The enemy has destroyed my enemy, so now they're after me, my friend."

*
**

Beacon took full advantage of her new celebrity status. By the evening, she had fielded enough calls from news outlets and politicians to insist that one of the office interns work after hours at her modest 1,600-square-foot brownstone. It was in one of those run-down neighborhoods overzealous real estate agents pump as "soon to be up-and-coming."

"Have them follow me when I leave in a few," she instructed her secretary while priming her jet-black hair's bangs. It was too late to care for her split ends and silver roots. After a quick peek through the office blinds, she put her phone on speaker to apply a fresh layer of Wild Fusion lipstick. "Make it the cute one, Jan." Her gravelly wheeze joined Jan in a chuckle. "That's right, Mr. Preppy!"

Careful that she didn't lose Mr. Preppy in traffic, she took longer than usual to make it home on that warm spring evening. Blood rushed from the skin underneath her foundation-caked cheeks and jowls when she pulled into her neighborhood. Flashes of blue and white from four police cars behind a street barricade filled the pre-dusk sky.

"Fucking junkies," Beacon growled. She drove past the officer waving for her to turn left and continued to the roadblock less than one hundred feet from her home. Before anyone could lecture her on what to do when a cop tells you to turn the other way, she opened the window, releasing a stale cloud of menthol.

"I need to go there." She pointed past the line of single-plank barriers.

The kid in a pressed Metro Police uniform kept pushing his arms back.

"Road's closed, ma'am. You're going to have to turn around."

The declaration, "I'm Olivia Beacon," for the first time in her career, parted a sea of blue.

"Fucking-A right," she boasted, adding, "Let him through, too."

As the cars approached, her mouth gaped wide. Two officers were walking down her front steps, carrying cardboard boxes, the kind her husband kept in their basement.

"What the...?"

Her self-identification was no longer necessary, but the lieutenant who approached the car still wanted to hear the words.

"Ma'am," he said, "are you Olivia Beacon?" When she nodded, her hands shook ashes and embers across her tie-dyed polyester office dress as the officer introduced himself as Lieutenant Davis.

"Ma'am, this is not because of you. We're here about your husband."

"No, no," she insisted. "Jimmy isn't in town this weekend."

As it turned out, James Beacon was in custody with the Virginia State Police as D.C. cops executed search warrants on his home and a dilapidated cabin buried in the Allegheny Mountains. The collection of Sensations included abuses against fifteen women, one of whom was Olivia. Though several of the captures were blank, wiped clean, the police would discover far more with repulsive evidence. Ellie's programming upgrade that retained release data was pivotal in his prosecution.

"He brought these things across state lines, so your husband's not going anywhere for a while, ma'am." Olivia Beacon and her intern stood in the middle of the closed-off street while Davis fed the panicked wife what little information he knew. News teams had already begun to gather, ready to report on her second moment of fame for the day. The dancing lights faded one by one. Left behind were the bright shine of camera bulbs recording her humiliation. Overwhelmed, she buckled under the weight of it all, falling into the arms of Davis and the intern.

"Is there somewhere you can take her? There is nothing she can do here."

The intern walked Beacon to his car. Her faint voice begged him to hold tight and not let her fall.

Wedged into the passenger seat of his hatchback, Beacon scrambled through her purse while the last news camera cut its beacon.

"Is there somewhere safe I can take you, ma'am?" the angelic intern asked.

"Wherever you kids normally go to get a drink, Rudy. I'm buying."

With a fresh menthol dangling from the corner of her upturned lips, Beacon lowered the window and began flicking her lighter to catch a spark.

Chapter 45

Its hallway reeked of shortcomings that sprouted up in the name of democracy, only to rot under the same roof where hopeful ideals still thrived. Elaborate murals decorated the ceilings and walls, elevating the founders of democracy to positions of deity without acknowledging their hatred of a government built to worship false gods. As descendants of those forefathers huddled behind closed doors, interns scrambled through the halls of Capitol Hill to deliver food, photocopies, and the occasional message that would change the trajectory of America's future.

A vibrant but conservative red spring dress flapped in the breeze created by its wearer's run through those historic halls. She entered the room marked by a polished brass plaque reading, *Committee on Sensations Oversight.* All the seven members seated around the grand oak table were at least three times her age. None appreciated her interruption, but she ignored every icy stare and focused on her task.

Locking eyes with one man who had flanked Olivia Beacon the day prior, she said, "Excuse me, Senator Hargraves. Nickerson Enterprises is on the phone in your office."

Hargraves huffed at the intrusion, sharing his superiority with the rest of the table.

"Tell her I'll call back when my meeting is over."

His predictable response failed to intimidate the petite apprentice, as she had anticipated the obligatory pushback.

"She said to tell you now, or her next call is to Speaker Alameda."

"The hell it will be," were the only words Hargraves shot back. His intern fought to contain the smirk on her face when he bolted from his plush leather executive chair and battled through the maze of bodies roaming those hallowed halls. Six minutes later, he stood over the office desk with the receiver pressed against his sweaty face.

"This is Hargraves."

"Thank you, Senator. Hold for one moment, please."

He did not recognize Sandy's voice on the other end of the line but had no option but to wait as instructed.

"Senator Hargraves, good morning," she said after a short but irritating delay. Her respectful tone seemed to aggravate the politician even more.

"Who's this?" Hargraves barked into the phone when another unknown voice entered a world where his authority was fading.

"Senator, my name is Danette Reddy." The cheerful coos only flicked Hargraves on the edge of his nose with their arrogance. "I am lead counsel for Eleanor Nickerson and Nickerson Enterprises."

Threats to "Get Nickerson on the phone now, or I'll have her testifying under oath tomorrow in front of my goddamn committee" pulled him into their plan deeper than he realized. Throughout his tirade that followed, Danette interjected "Senator" no less than nine times before the Sensations committee chair, with over forty-two years in Congress, surrendered control of the conversation.

Danette reshaped any plan Hargraves may have had when she started with, "Your proposal is strong, but Ms. Nickerson wants more." Burning red with rage, he agreed with Danette's outline and schedule before handing the phone to his intern.

"Get all of her details," he ordered the only person who still seemed to remain under his thumb. On the slow walk back to the committee office, Hargraves swallowed two pills from a pack he pulled from his suit jacket while grumbling about how he was going to "skin that bitch alive in front of the whole fucking country."

Chapter 46

Frightful cries escaped through the thin opening she created. Kaylee hesitated, her speckled, glazed fingertips frozen on the door handle. "Come on in," broke her trance, so she walked to the living room and lifted a bag of George's creations high in the air to present her sacrifice. Danette smiled.

"Yummy. E's going to love those."

The violent wailing from Ellie's bedroom sounded like the blackened past of every tortured soul she saved was tearing to escape through her body, their final act of revenge for her creation.

"Jesus, Dan. Does she do that all the time?"

"It's getting worse."

Kaylee's startled expression settled to match the nauseated frustration her friend wore. She tried to drive the noise out with small talk. "So, how'd your stuff go yesterday?" Each word chimed out in a lovely tone, humming a tune to the same rhythm as her question, but Ellie's pleas for mercy pierced through the pitiful cloak.

"Perfect."

Danette oversimplified her exhausting afternoon on the phone with Senator Hargraves and his staff. "We're set for Sunday at noon."

With a quick thumbs-up, Kaylee pulled her smartphone out and scrolled through a list of unread messages. "Sweet," she said, giving up on any attempt to mask Ellie's suffering. "I've got Global News waiting for a date." She spelled the last word of her reply to a text, "S-A-T-U-R-D-A-Y," before an exaggerated press of the little *send* icon. "Done!" Her phone dinged moments later. "Yao just confirmed."

Someone asked, "Where's this all going?" and someone shook their head and muttered, "I do not know." It didn't matter who said what. The fear was the same with everyone in Ellie's circle. But Danette raised the question that no one ever dared to ask.

"What are you going to do when this is all over?"

Frozen in thought for three extended breaths, Kaylee set aside her happy-go-lucky style for a moment.

"I shit you not when I tell you my resumé is up to date," she said with one finger extended from her left hand. Her second finger came up when she said, "I've picked out an outfit for my perp walk." With the third, she admitted, "I went out this afternoon and selected a coffin, so I'm ready for anything."

Her smile returned, infecting Danette with the same break from morbid thoughts.

"I don't think I have as many options," she chuckled. "My law license leaves me tied to my client's fate."

The lull in their conversation brought Ellie's commotion back to their senses. All they could do was wait. Someone always waited. Someone was always there until the crying stopped. When it did, Ellie always broke from her prison with a focus that narrowed as each day dawned. Silence was their cockcrow. Danette checked her smartphone as she popped out from her chair.

"Four fifteen," she said, already entertained by her wisecrack. "Do you think they have alarm clocks in that seventh circle she sleeps in?"

Kaylee snickered back with, "Something's keeping her on schedule." She followed to the kitchen, finishing her thought. "I mean, she runs a ridiculous amount and then spends all day programming upgrades to the system. That's not a life. How is she doing it?"

From the living room, they heard, "Ooh, donuts!"

Danette handed off one of the three cups of coffee she poured.

"That's how. Lots and lots of food."

When they made their way back, Ellie was parked in front of the George's Diner bag, reaching for her second chocolate glaze.

"...and lots."

Leonard, Marcus, and Sandy kept the lights on at Nickerson Enterprises. Zach coordinated with Abby and her team to monitor the mounting threats against Ellie, inside and outside government agencies. The last two days of her mission were the most uneventful moments her followers experienced.

On April 27, Senator Hargraves took a break from polishing the finishing touches to his vendetta. Instead, he joined the rest of the world as they watched Michael Yao's exclusive interview with Eleanor Nickerson.

Chapter 47

The makeshift studio resembled a library at story time. Aged children gathered around Ellie as she wove a story none of them were prepared to hear. Michael Yao had long since stopped asking questions or trying to steer the course of his interview. She let him know her tale was complete with a slight tip of her head. Michael searched for some way to respond.

"Is there anything left to share tomorrow?"

Ellie's hands stopped talking and dropped to her lap.

"Not about the past, there isn't."

Michael leaned his back into the sectional. He had that *What does the world want to know?* look on his face, the one every polished investigative journalist should have, but he did not rush the question. When it came, he inched his upper body forward.

"You have immense power to call a joint session of Congress, but you just told us your story. So," he begged to know, "why are you testifying?" The world followed Michael's lead and leaned closer to their screens.

Ellie brushed away his comment with her hand and turned to a blank space somewhere off-camera. Her whispered sighs sounded like, "Power. That's simply a one-sided perception at any snapshot of time," but her voice did not share the rest of the comment. She turned back to the camera.

Vitality returned to her expression when she said, "I want to discuss my original desires for Sensations. Freedom of expression, palliative care, medical aid, and treatment." She reminded the world, "Those are not party lines I spew out just to jockey for a reaction during some sales call," before shifting to Michael. "It's the need to care for and protect those who can't protect themselves."

Hypothetical questions spark debate. Michael seized the opportunity and floated a scenario.

"Let's pretend that this is as far as you go." Ellie scoffed at the absurdity, but her dismissal only encouraged him to press the image he was trying to create. He shrugged his shoulders and threw out a well-worn cliché.

"Let's say you die later today." He pointed toward the windowpane blocked by Global News's temporary shrubbery. "You get hit by a bus crossing the street down there." He gestured past the cameras into their corporate office. "Or, you die from a heart attack right over there." The search for another crude example came up empty. "Regardless, you're dead, so now the Sensations phenomenon is over."

"Sensations are not part of me, Michael." She brushed a thumb into the band of her engagement ring. "It won't just wither and die."

Dogged by the need for more, he raised scenarios that already had answers.

"If this was the end, would you change the way everything played out?"

Ellie chuckled at a desperate attempt to revisit the fruitless tree he continued to scavenge.

He said, "What would be different?"

She countered, "What I have to undo?"

"What are you willing to sacrifice?"

"How far back would I go?"

Michael lost his grip on the interview. In truth, he faced the reality that his thirty-plus years of experience as an investigative journalist finally told him it was a segment he never controlled. Ellie exposed that flaw, then stared through his silent plea for help.

"I am not a god."

"What if you were?"

"I will never have a child of my own; Dema Sokolov made sure of that. But just like any parent who gave their children life, I must now teach the world how to use the resources I have provided it."

"Or else?"

She never shared the thought that pushed a quick snort of air.

"Thank you for this opportunity, Michael," cued the production crew.

"Ellie, thank you." Michael offered a handshake. "Hundreds of millions, if not billions, of Sensations users are glad to see you weathered the storm." Ellie met his sweaty grip. She recognized that twitch as the rapid spasms of withdrawal.

"Many more, like myself, are eager to see tomorrow's exciting next steps." He yanked his arm back and turned to face the camera. "Follow us for tomorrow's live coverage of the historic Joint Congressional Session on Sensations. I'm Michael Yao, and this is Global News."

Mumbling something about, "It's been a pleasure, Ms. Nickerson," Michael scurried off to his makeshift dressing room.

Dismantling the mobile studio took much less time than its setup. Heaven opened up and sent rays of sunshine across the office again, forcing the unnatural clutter of network news and entertainment back down the freight elevator. Ellie finally found a use for three potted plants, peeling off her gray suit in favor of black sweatpants and an oversized long-sleeved T-shirt. She braided her hair into a hurried ponytail while watching the plants shed a desperate trail of soil and leaves during their eviction. The last crew member swept it away.

Like it never happened.

"Um, you're welcome," Ellie scoffed, but they were gone.

She watched as her team scrambled to bring order back to Nickerson Enterprises. Scanning eyes and slumped shoulders betrayed her disappointment that they had honored her request to "have some uninterrupted quiet time" when the interview concluded.

"I am not a god?"

His tone mocked the absurdity of her comparison.

"It worked for you," she threw the jab back at Zach, but that didn't stop him from wrapping both arms around her to hide the pool of tears that started to collect.

"Simply beautiful."

The moment extended longer than they expected but ended before either was ready. Wrapping their fingers around the other, father and daughter shared unspoken expressions of pride, thanks, apologies, and forgiveness.

When Kaylee overheard, "Whatever happens tomorrow, today was perfect," she broke up their moment with erratic flickers of ten golden fireflies.

"Shoo shoo, you two. Go find something to do, will you?" Then, choking back her own sobs, she ran off to find a box of tissues.

Marcus delayed that order by pulling Ellie and Zach tight for his uncommon display of non-accounting delight.

"Oh my God. That was amazing. You were great. Wasn't she great? I can't believe it. Did you see his face? He didn't know how to react. What did you think? Never mind, let's talk about that later. Everyone's coming to my house. We're going to watch the news reports and see how many times Hargraves gets bleeped. I bet he's fuming. Tomorrow's going to be off the hook. What time are you leaving? You want me to drive? No, wait, Danette is taking you. Never mind. See you tonight?"

His one-sided conversation lasted about ten seconds. A sharp pat on the back was Zach's friendly way to rattle his favorite number cruncher back to reality.

"Sounds great, Marcus," he said, "but I've got final security checks for tomorrow that I need to run." Marcus did not seem disappointed, if he heard the words at all. There was a temporary downturn in his ear-to-ear grin when Ellie passed on the invitation.

"Tomorrow's another long day." She delivered the news with a tight hug. "I'm going to crash early tonight."

Marcus and Zach read between the lines, nodding their heads in unison.

Marcus's smile returned to its former glory when he backed away from Ellie, finger guns popping in her direction.

"I'll be watching tomorrow." Pop-pop. "Go get 'em." Pop-pop.

She returned his motivation with a wink and one well-aimed pop.

*
**

Drawn shades blocked every trace of sunshine from the sun that had just begun its slow descent into twilight. Darkness cloaked *De Oppresso Liber*, but she traced her finger across the words on her T-shirt the same way she had done a thousand times before. One press of the black disc sent her back to that world where a cool breeze blew through her old bedroom window.

Will it always be like this?

"Never again, my love."

I will always be there, mon chérie.

Ellie felt his warmth, his thrusts, the coils of his hair. Then, when she lost herself in the sum of all his pleasure, her request brought a river of tears to her frozen body.

"Please show me your torment."

Tending to others was his calling in life. Owen's last act in death was to inflict immeasurable suffering on the woman he loved. He did that because it was her command. Ellie sensed that his heartbeat lay over the top of her rhythm.

God, please let her be safe.

He did not struggle or beg for his own life. He pushed the pain from his broken bones to the back of his mind, but every torment gathered in the tiny space of one instant in hers. She felt someone hold his head high, forcing a stare into the harsh lights while they demanded answers. Even then, she was his only worry.

The moment was already part of her dark memories. But, for the first time, she fought to call out, "Owen." That time she knew it was how Sokolov was going to kill Owen. She was no longer naïve.

Ellie, I'm sorry.

Tastes of his blood pooled in her dry mouth. His body released vile traces of vomit and bodily functions when she had no more strength to hold them. Fear spiked before it gave way to the shocking awareness of plastic wrapped over his head and face. Efforts to take a breath only pulled the film tight against his gaping mouth. Her mind cried in vain. She was helpless, forced to endure the pain of his bound arms tearing themselves free from their sockets in a futile attempt to escape. She could only participate in the collapse of his lungs and throat, losing the fight for one more breath. As he lay face down on the cold tile floor of that dark room, she could only lie on the top of her soft comforter and feel life slip away as one last emotion soothed Owen with euphoric bliss—his love for her.

I will always be there, mon chérie.

The moment his heart stopped, hers found a mountain of reasons to beat. She wiped her eyes dry and walked to the dresser, placing the blank release in a hope chest filled with dozens of now-empty memories. With a shoebox pulled from the bottom drawer, Ellie made her way to the open hardwood space in her home office and slipped on her worn pair of Juliet leather split-sole ballet shoes. The tears returned while she danced to her favorite composition from Amilcare Ponchielli. When the last note struck, she broke second position and returned to the bedroom. Wrapped in that olive-green T-shirt, she placed the ballet shoes in their box, returning those physical reminders to cherished storage in her bedroom.

Ellie Nickerson made peace with her demons that night. They would never fade from her memory, but, nevertheless, she settled in with angels protecting her through the long, uninterrupted night.

Chapter 48

Gentle music hums softened Danette's anxious posture when she pushed the door open. Although the outside was still as dark as New York City was going to be, bright lights lured her into the condo. She followed a convention of inviting scents into the dining room where pancakes, bacon, fresh-brewed coffee, and fresh protein bread joined Ellie in welcoming her friend.

"I figured you were hungry since you never cook at your place."

She unbuttoned her suit jacket to rub her belly before sitting across from the host. With an oversized clip, she pulled her tousled blonde hair off the shoulders and dug in, muttering, "If I get grease on my blouse, I will never forgive you." Her first bite of pancake dipped in strawberry-infused maple syrup muffled those last few words.

Ellie smiled and lifted a cup of coffee to her lips. Words would come later, but the next twenty minutes only had room for an overdue reminder of how they would always be by each other's sides.

"You do realize that any of about two dozen people could be driving us down there?" Ellie waited for a response but shifted to the car visor mirror to tuck a stray hair that had peeked out from under her royal-blue headscarf—random wisps of white piping in the fabric coordinated with the corporate branding on her polo. Black slacks and flats completed a casual look that clashed with Danette's formal attire.

A vigorous shake of Danette's head rejected the suggestion.

"Miss this quality time? No way, E." She shot a quick disappointing look across the front seats.

"I'll concede to my attorney."

"Good idea." Danette's pretend sad face melted when she did the one thing Ellie did not want that day. "By the way," she said, "happy birthday."

Ellie smiled and looked around when they popped out of the tunnel, noting cars in front of and behind them. A roving vehicle also pulled alongside their ride every few minutes.

"How many cars are there?" she asked.

"Zach has four, Abby has two."

Ellie nodded; she showed no interest in pressing for details of her security entourage. Before silence set in, her phone chirped with an incoming text. A devilish smile washed across her face just as the red sedan passed for the fourth time.

It prompted the first question, a vague lead-in that unleashed a watershed.

"How was the party at Marcus's pad last night?"

Danette rocked her head back and started the story with their drinking game. "Let's just say Leonard won, hands down." She howled at how he had guessed the exact number of Hargraves' bleeps. The news clip included him yelling how "That <bleep> Nickerson <bleep> is <bleep> lying. When I <bleep> get her under oath tomorrow, I'm not <bleep> done until she leaves in handcuffs to join her <bleep> commie friend <bleep> behind bars."

"He was more than a little irate," was her polite recap.

The second question was more pointed.

"How many people were there?"

She shrugged and guessed, "I don't know, thirty or forty? Our company leads were there, and most of their team members showed up at some point. Plus, they all brought friends. Maybe closer to fifty, now that I think about it."

Everything led up to the third question, which took the remainder of their car ride to answer.

"So, did you take the little redhead home?"

"Fucking Morris," Danette snapped, "she just can't keep her mouth shut." It was like they were back in their college days as Ellie pressed for details that her friend was more than happy to share. By the time she finished re-creating her exploits, the red sedan had passed for the ninth time.

"Are you going to see her again?"

Danette flipped on her blinker and drifted over to the exit.

"Doubt it. She's 551." She curled her lips and pouted for a half second before changing the subject. "Let me know where I'm supposed to park. We don't want to be late for our execution that doesn't start for nine more hours."

Instead of fumbling through her phone for the details, Ellie pointed to the front.

"Follow the red car."

Chapter 49

Reality shattered Danette's established image of the hallowed Chamber, which had once been reserved in her mind for the most consequential pioneers of American politics. A patchwork crowd began to assemble as the afternoon hours lost their grasp of another picturesque day in D.C. Fine-pressed wool twill suits, each tailored to fit when its wearer was much younger, butted up against polysynthetic blends for those trying to look the part. Subdued flair on dresses, pantsuits, and pullover sweaters marked the singularness of those who wanted to stand out. Unfortunately, critics would remember most fashion choices with the question, "What was she thinking?"

Political grandstanding and dealmaking took place among horseplay and complaints about wasting their valuable time. Some used the opportunity to work on their response to an address that had not yet occurred. Others watched baseball games on their smartphones or shot text messages back and forth with their friends on the Hill, placing wagers on who Senator Hargraves would approach next in his recruiting efforts. By that point, Hargraves had verbal commitments from eighteen senators and one hundred twenty-one representatives to pursue formal charges against Ellie and the officers of Nickerson Enterprises.

Fake smiles followed by nasty snipes under their breath from lawmakers passing by the Speaker's seat at her podium in the center of their judgmental semicircle only cemented her distaste for those proceedings.

"All right, everybody, look sharp," Zach squawked through her earpiece. "We're getting ready to escort Ellie into the Chamber."

Moments later, the Speaker of the House called the session to order. Pomp and circumstance ensued, though the stain of so much crude indifference earlier destroyed any respect Danette may have still held.

Speaker of the House Alameda, another member of Olivia Beacon's mob, made the final introduction.

"Members of Congress, I have the high privilege and the distinct honor of presenting to you Eleanor Nickerson, chief executive officer of Nickerson Enterprises."

An introduction reserved for a presidential address, foreign dignitaries, heads of state, and notable leaders in US history now called upon Ellie to become another notation in the Congressional Record. Her steps up to the podium gave no clue to her thoughts on the enormity of what this computer programmer from New York City was about to say on her thirty-second birthday. She scanned the Chamber but never looked at anyone in particular. Once behind the podium, Ellie placed a black leather binder beneath the microphone but never opened it. Her hands dropped to her sides, where she tucked both thumbs into her pockets and began speaking without warning.

"The COVID-19 pandemic gave birth to a desire within our population to achieve intellectual and sensory stimulation without the need for direct physical contact. My model for all forms of the sensory application collectively known as Sensations was first granted an open-source patent in late 2020. I had, and still maintain, a vision of unrestricted access to a safe and socially beneficial outlet for human emotion."

Ellie spoke to her audience, slowly scanning right to left, left to right, without shifting or fumbling.

"In the United States, the Food and Drug Administration currently regulates all versions of the Sensation Capture-and-Release System, collectively known as SCARS, though there is no detectable interaction with the physiology of a body. Through extensive regulatory oversight, product validation and registration costs have grown significantly in less than four years. However, those dollars pale compared to the revenue collected through sales and usage taxes. Government oversight is pushing prices to a point where only wealthy individuals can afford quality SCARS. As a result, illicit Sensations have become a noted factor for violent and white-collar crimes, as well as death or long-term hospitalization."

She turned her head to address Senator Hargraves and his guest, Olivia Beacon.

"Nickerson Enterprises proposes a joint venture with the US government and partner nations to oversee SCARS certification, distribution, and ongoing quality control. We would implement the program on the condition of eliminating all ongoing administrative costs. These costs include but are not limited to certification costs, licensing fees, and usage taxes."

Mumbles and objections did nothing to disrupt her pace, which was energized by Danette's silent affirmation, "Perfect."

"My concern is not whether I lead humanity to a prosperous future with the technology I built or if you imprison me for the sins you think I committed. I still believe we can return to my intended vision of Sensations. However, if this is not possible, or the FDA is unwilling to revise the current program implementation, I have retained one proprietary and unregistered secret to the SCARS."

There was no dramatic pause when she turned back to address the mass of politicians unprepared for her ultimatum.

"I can turn it off."

Stunned onlookers watched Ellie and Danette rise from the podium, exiting as Hargraves kicked off the frenzy with the demand, "Sit your goddamn asses down."

They did not comply.

Zach and Abby coordinated their departure from the House Chamber without incident.

Chapter 50

Vibrant song streams flowed from the Northern Cardinals buried deep in dense shrubbery that marked an outer boundary to the manicured lawn. From the living room, a petite woman curled up from a vantage point that overlooked the backyard. Ellie and a thirteen-year-old girl sat cross-legged in the grass between her and the birds welcoming a new generation. The child did not have pin-straight hair like her mother. Instead, her bouncing curls were as red as the energized male that wisped from stem to stem in fierce defense of its mate's nest. They were as red as her father's locks once were.

The woman smiled as she watched the two meditate under the springtime warmth of a new day breaking over the tree line. Her senses tingled from the crisp breeze flowing across the back deck, passing through the screen door, and pushing subtle hints of Earl Grey tea up from her cup. Her mind split time between that wholesome moment and the sound of Michael Yao's newscast on the flatscreen TV.

"Today is the imposed deadline for Senator Hargraves to respond to the historic demands set by Eleanor Nickerson during last month's Congressional testimony."

*
**

"Now tell me what you see."

There was no hesitation in the young girl's voice. She responded with a serene tone that matched Ellie's instruction.

"I see the bird." The redhead smiled when the cardinal launched from its perch and swooped between the observers. It flew high overhead before darting back to, then beyond, its guarded position.

"I can feel him flying in and out of the clouds." Her head mimicked the rapid scan pattern her mind recognized. When the cardinal pointed its bill, her nose searched in the same direction. Her nostrils flared and tracked the same scents. "It's beautiful," she cooed.

Ellie watched her breathing slow as the girl separated her thoughts from the crimson songbird. Finally, it was time for more. "Now, I want you to close your eyes."

Soft whispers of "ooh" and "aah" soon gave way to full-blown adolescent giggles.

"It's like my muscles pull us into and out of the clouds."

Her body swayed back and forth, like a glider biting into crosswinds as it soared through the air.

"You got it?"

"Yeah." Her struggles forced the word out.

"You sure?" Ellie smiled as the question probed her confidence.

She begged, "Don't make me laugh," but it was too late. It took a moment before she could suppress the charm and focus on his flight.

"Okay, Harper, do you remember the line of code I taught you to change?"

"I remember."

They were together, but Ellie and Harper were in two different worlds. Ellie watched Harper as her mind fought to protect itself while soaring through the air, even though she knew her body was still in the lush perennial ryegrass of her mother's backyard.

"Whenever you're ready, swap the code."

Harper's mother popped from her chair when she heard the scream.

"Daddy!"

An explosion of joy burst from Harper when she opened her eyes, now filled with the world Andy saw. Her arms stretched out as he stabilized his fall through the sky, fully aware of where both sets of limbs should be. When he checked his altimeter watch, she saw his reflection staring back at her.

"I'm going to bring you back now in three, two," Ellie pressed the center of the black disc and watched Harper struggle to form words. "Pretty cool, huh?"

"Yeah."

Siena Hofer smiled as Ellie pulled a tablet from the backpack by her side and began walking Harper through computer code lines. It would bore her to death if she had to sit with them, but her daughter savored every moment of tedious programming. They could have sat in the grass all day, sharing secrets of their bond—first formed by tragic events that had shaped their common childhoods. Siena prolonged the time as long as possible, dragging her bare feet through the dew-covered grass.

"Ellie," she said with her hand extended, "you've got a phone call. It's General Drew."

Instructing Harper to "Hold that thought," Ellie handed her the tablet and took the cell phone.

"Zach, good morning."

With a quick screen swipe, Harper captured the next twenty minutes.

She opened a new root folder and saved the file. *Day 0.*

About the Author

Kevin Byrne was born and raised in the Bronx, New York. A graduate of the United States Military Academy at West Point, he was diagnosed with multiple sclerosis (MS) in 1999 while commanding a US Army Air Cavalry Troop overseas. He is now medically retired and lives in Portland, Oregon, with his daughter, Rogue.

Kevin devotes much of his energy toward overcoming the challenges of his own MS so he can fight for others. His efforts support the Department of Veterans Affairs, the National MS Society, and NEVER STOP NEVER QUIT, a charitable organization he co-formed to expand his fundraising and advocacy in the fight against MS.

"...fantastic stories, where I'm limited only by my imagination, not by the confines of this stupid disease."

NMSS Leadership Conference
Denver, CO, November 2016

Never Stop. Never Quit...

Acknowledgments

In 2021, after 11 years of publishing the constant noise of stories running through my head, I returned to school and learned how to write.

I owe a great deal of gratitude to my instructors and classmates at Southern New Hampshire University (SNHU). Thank you for opening my eyes to a world beyond the mundane where you once told me, "If this were my movie, as soon as this guy says that, the woman next to him pulls out a wet mackerel and slaps him with it." I keep a salmon filet in my freezer as a reminder to stay on track. That would hurt.

Polishing my craft brought me to where I can look at these pages and say, "This is exactly what I see when I close my eyes and imagine Sensations." My editor, longtime proofreader, and a (sometimes literal) army of beta readers helped me bring Eleanor Nickerson to life. Thank you.

And, to Rogue, My Little Love, your support never wavered. I don't know if there is enough frozen yogurt to repay my debt for all the times your dad lost himself in that mystical world of make-believe. I don't know, but I'll try.

Sensations

© 2023 Kevin Byrne

About the Author photograph
© 2020 Kelly Mooney
www.kellymooneyphotography.com

Published 2023 by
NEVER STOP NEVER QUIT
Portland, OR
NeverStopNeverQuit.com

Never Stop... Never Quit...
Registered, U.S. Patent and Trademark Office
ISBN: 978-1-959235-04-0